ROUGHING

MICHAELA GREY

This book is for everyone out there who's struggled with the idea that they have to do everything on their own. Accepting help is not a sign of weakness. Love yourself enough to accept that we're stronger together than we are alone.

1

CARMINE'S NOSE WAS BLEEDING, lips peeled off bloody teeth in a snarl. His huge hand was tangled in the neck of Saint's jersey, threatening to tip him off his skates with every brutal tug. Saint hunched his shoulder to deflect the next blow. He was losing and he knew it. Carmine was too big, too fast, and—a fist glanced off Saint's helmet and he gritted his teeth. *And* too mean.

His ears were ringing. His arms felt too heavy to lift. But he wasn't going to give this motherfucker the *satisfaction* of knowing he'd worn him out. He blocked another blow with a raised elbow. *Mistake.* Carmine dropped Saint's jersey and his fist connected with Saint's ribs quicker than thought.

Pain exploded in his side and Saint reeled backward but Carmine wasn't done.

He caught Saint's jersey again and punched him in the same place. Once, twice, sharp hammering blows that stopped Saint's breath. He flung an arm out, grabbing desperately for anything to hold onto. He found Carmine's jersey and scrabbled for purchase. His legs gave out and Carmine went down with him, landing on top of him.

Their eyes met and held as the officials converged to pull them apart. There was blood in Carmine's beard. His eyes were very brown. He opened his mouth as if to say something, and a referee dragged him backward before he could.

Six months later

Saint reached the practice arena's side door and slipped inside quickly, avoiding eye contact with passersby. In the dimly lit hall, he stopped and took a deep breath. He could hear skate blades and cheerful shouting, smell the ice, the rubber mats, sweat, metal, and leather—it all mingled in his head and ordinarily it would have made the tension drain from his shoulders immediately.

Instead he took a sharp left and went up

the stairs two at a time, fury churning in his belly. His scalp prickled and stomach twisted, the anger mixing with the constant nerves simmering in his guts. He wanted to throw up, or punch something.

He found the coaches standing at the bay window in the second story conference room, talking in low voices as they watched the players in the rink.

Flanahan saw him first. A big man unafraid to use his size to intimidate opponents into agreeing with him, he'd been the first to welcome Saint to Portland and the most vocal in his support when Saint took the captain's letter. Saint didn't like him very much—Flanahan was far too willing to throw his weight around to get his own way —but he trusted him, at least as far as the team went.

"Saint, glad you made it! How was your summer? How was Calgary?"

Rogelio Reyes and Velvet Brennan turned to greet him as well. Reyes was a tall, thin, watery man, pale eyes that blinked too much and hands that constantly twitched as though he was resisting the urge to wring them.

On the other hand, Velvet was vivid colors in bright contrast to each other. Her dark red hair was cut in a messy pixie cut that highlighted her pointed chin and sharp brown eyes, and the shirt under her staid tan jacket glowed a vivid jewel green. She gave Saint a real smile as Reyes nodded.

Saint barely acknowledged them. "I need to talk to you," he said tightly.

Flanahan didn't look worried. "I figured you would."

"What have you been *doing* to my team? And why won't anyone answer my calls?"

Flanahan shrugged. "We've just made some changes to the roster over the summer."

"You made changes without consulting me?"

Flanahan's eyes narrowed. "This isn't your team, son. You may be the captain but that doesn't mean you get to tell us how to fill the lines."

Saint bit back the angry retort. "I've been following the news. What's *happening*?"

Flanahan rubbed his hands together, a beaming smile breaking out over his ruddy face. "Come see your new team."

His new *team*? Unease shivered through Saint as he joined the coaches at the window to look down into the rink. Some thirty skaters were on the ice, warming up individually, some batting pucks back and forth and others taking shots at the empty net.

Saint squinted. There was Roderick

Murphy, off in the corner doing his stretches. And Jason Carlyle on the near side of the arena, skating through a complicated footwork drill. The rush of relief when Saint saw Felix Papillon in net at the far end was almost dizzying. Besides them, most of his third and fourth lines seemed intact. But his first and second lines were almost unrecognizable.

"Coach—"

Flanahan cut him off. "Management's been busy while you were gone. Lot of deals, lot of paperwork back and forth, but I think we've got a real chance this year."

"Coach," Saint tried again, his throat dry. "Where's my team? *My* team?"

"Right there," Flanahan said, pointing.

"No." Saint shook his head. "This is not the team I played with last year. The core I've spent the last *three* years developing. Where's March? Where's Branson? *Where's Flynn?* Why did you—" He cut himself off as Velvet made an aborted motion toward him, taking a deep breath and touching his thumbs to his fingers in a vain effort to calm himself. "Where's my team, Coach? And who are these people?"

"Be honest with yourself," Flanahan said, gripping Saint's shoulder. His grip was heavy, almost painful, thumb pressing hard against Saint's collarbone. "Were those players going to get us to the playoffs this year?"

"We had a shot!" Saint said, fighting to not pull away. "They were gelling, we were close to finding what clicked!"

Flanahan made a rumbling noise in the back of his throat but he let go of Saint's shoulder. "The owner and GM felt differently. So this year, *this* is your team."

Saint's head was spinning, dread and misery a cold, heavy lump in his stomach. "This is why no one would talk to me," he whispered.

Flanahan didn't even look repentant. "We told those we traded not to tell you, and we kept as much out of the news as we could. Not because of you, but because we want to control the narrative when we're ready to tell the hockey world. Besides, all you would've done is fret yourself to death up there in Calgary. The GM wanted you to enjoy your summer."

"Yeah, I really enjoyed it," Saint snapped. "Especially the part where no one but Butterfly and Roddy would even answer my calls but they didn't know what was happening either. You really think I wasn't turning myself inside *out* up there?"

Flanahan barely seemed to notice. "There's one more thing," he said, all but rubbing his hands with glee. "We have a new D-man."

Saint narrowed his eyes.

"Carmine Quinn," Flanahan announced, without even the decency to look abashed.

"You've got to be fucking *kidding me.*"

Flanahan's eyebrows shot up at the expletive. Saint ignored him.

"Carmine Quinn, who went out of his way to board me or slash me or trip me every time we were on the ice together the last time we played the Otters? Who *fought* me during that game? *That* Carmine Quinn? The Carmine Quinn who fractured three ribs and put me out of commission for six *weeks?*"

"You still won," Flanahan pointed out. "The game, if not the fight. What's the big deal?"

"The big deal?" Saint threw his hands up. "The guy's a thug, Coach! All he's good for is throwing his fists. Can he even skate? Does he know what a puck is?"

"It's the black rubber thing, right?" The voice came from the door and Saint spun.

Carmine was standing there, hands in his pockets. He looked unbothered by Saint's diatribe, but closer inspection revealed lines around his mouth, tightness in his shoulders.

His eyes were dark, almost unreadable in the fluorescent lighting, and the dimples Saint had seen in interviews were nowhere to be found. There were shadows under his eyes, and he rocked back on his heels, raising one sardonic eyebrow.

"I could be wrong," he continued. "After all, I barely know one end of a stick from the other."

Saint opened his mouth and closed it again. Something in Carmine's bearing said an apology would be sneered at.

"Glad you made it!" Flanahan said, falsely hearty. "You know Saint, of course."

Carmine inclined his head, mouth tight.

"And my assistant coaches, Rogelio Reyes and Velvet Brennan," Flanahan continued. "We're all excited to see what you bring to the team!"

"Are you?" Carmine murmured. "Well, first time for everything."

Flanahan gestured for Carmine to join them. "Take a look," he said, pointing out the window. "Your new team. Some of them are from the Embers—the next few weeks will determine who stays. What do you think?"

Carmine stepped up to the glass, keeping Velvet and Rogelio between him and Saint. He gazed contemplatively at the players and Saint averted his eyes from

Carmine's profile, perfect except for the broken nose that had healed crooked.

"I think 47 is weak," Carmine said. "He's slow and his reactions are shit. He's not going to be able to keep the puck, let alone score."

Flanahan peered dubiously down at the ice. "He's done well on the Embers."

"You know best, I'm sure," Carmine said. "Can I get on the ice or did you need me for something else?"

"Just wanted to welcome you to the team," Flanahan said, waving him away.

Carmine nodded and left the room without looking at Saint.

Flanahan's eyes gleamed. "It's going to be a good season," he said. "I can feel it in my bones."

"Are we done?" Saint asked.

Flanahan made an impatient gesture, and Saint escaped.

He took the back way to the dressing room, the one with the lowest chance of running into anyone who'd demand conversation. Halfway there, he stopped and pulled out his phone.

What the fuck, he texted Flynn.

Flynn's response was swift. *They threatened to put me on waivers, man. :(*

Saint blew out a breath. Of course Flynn had chosen to save his career. But it still stung. He closed his eyes. Now he'd never get the chance to find out if Flynn's lips were as soft as they looked, or if the heat in his eyes had meant something or if he flirted that way with everyone.

He shoved down and strangled the misery that welled in his throat. *Arizona's lucky to have you*, he sent, and put the phone away before Flynn could reply.

THE DRESSING ROOM was silent and empty, and Saint thanked his lucky stars as he quickly changed and laced up his skates. The big C on his jersey seemed to be mocking him. *What exactly can you captain? Jack shit, that's what.*

No one noticed him as he stepped into the rink and made straight for Butterfly. Felix's eyes lit behind his goalie mask at the sight of him and he pulled Saint into a rough hug.

"Did you know?" Saint managed in rusty French, his voice wobbly.

Felix shook his head. "*Non, cher.* Not until I got here. I'm so sorry."

Saint rolled his shoulders. "It is what it is, right? We'll make the best of it. At least you and Roddy and Jase are still here."

Felix's green eyes were unhappy. "I

would have told you. Had I known—I would have told you."

"I know," Saint said. He clapped Felix on the shoulder. "That's *why* they didn't tell you. You wouldn't do that to me."

Roderick broke away from the group he'd been talking to and made for them. Tall and craggy, he'd long ago adopted the role of put-upon father to the team of rookies led by Saint. He held out his arms and Saint went into them gladly.

"Missed you, kid," Roderick murmured.

Saint let himself have a brief moment of comfort, closing his eyes as Roderick kept the world at bay, and then he gathered himself and moved back, forcing a smile. Around them, some of the new players were pretending not to watch them while others stared, unabashed.

"You're still on my line, right?" Saint asked.

"Like they could take me off," Roderick said. There were dark circles under his eyes, but then, there were always dark circles under his eyes. He'd looked permanently exhausted for as long as Saint had known him, and yet his energy was seemingly boundless.

"Who else is with us?"

"Arkady something." Roderick gestured with his chin toward a lanky man a few years younger than Saint. Sandy blond hair curled against the nape of his neck and he caught sight of Saint staring and smiled radiantly at him, his eyes bright green and cheerful.

"Incoming," Felix said under his breath as Arkady skated toward them.

He skidded to a stop with an elegant spray of ice, careful not to snow any of them, pulled off a glove, and shoved a hand at Saint.

"Arkady Volkov," he said. "They call me Volly but you say Kasha, yes? Is an honor, Sinclair."

"Just Saint is fine," Saint said, shaking his hand. He let go as quickly as he could but Kasha didn't seem bothered, beaming at him. Up close, he was younger than Saint had realized, nineteen or twenty at most. Saint found himself liking Kasha's open expression, the way he shifted on his skates as if hoping Saint would approve of him. "Where did you come from, Kasha?"

"The Direwolves," Kasha said. "But I'm from Russia. Excited to be here!"

Saint eyed him but didn't challenge that. "How long have you been on the ice today?"

"Hour? Maybe two."

Saint nodded. "Tell me what you've seen."

Kasha perked up. "That one—" He

pointed at a big man out of earshot down the ice, the one Carmine had indicated. "Likes to fight, I'm think."

Saint glanced at Roderick.

"David Stahl," Roderick said in a low tone. "And Volly's right—he's itching to throw his weight around."

"What else?" Saint asked Kasha.

Kasha pointed at a slender player on the other side of the rink. Saint couldn't make out details from so far away, but he had dark curly hair peeking out from under his helmet.

"He is good," Kasha said. "Slapshot is *really* good. But footwork nice too."

"Embry Rather," Roderick said. "Second line center, I think."

Embry smacked a puck down the ice, right between the other goalie's knees.

Roderick whistled softly. "You're right, Volly, he's good."

Kasha beamed. He indicated a tall brunet, talking to the equipment manager by the edge of the rink. "Tye. Don't know last name. Good footwork, maybe needs puck time? Seems nice. D-man." He scrunched up his face then and pointed at Carmine, warming up alone in the corner. "Carmine Quinn. He—"

"I know who he is," Saint said, too harshly. He took a deep breath and tried to gentle his voice. "What do you think of him?"

"Good skater," Kasha said, shrugging.

"That's it?"

Kasha looked unhappy. "He is—I'm not know how to say. Bad stories about?"

"Bad reputation?" Felix offered.

"Yes," Kasha confirmed. "He fights. Too much. Is always taking penalties, for stupid shit. He not—*think*."

"Sounds about right," Saint muttered. He rolled his shoulders again. "What else?"

Kasha kept going, naming more players. He had an eye for detail and a dryly funny delivery that had Felix and Roderick laughing as he reenacted a scuffle between two defensemen earlier. Saint forced a laugh, unable to take his eyes off Carmine for long.

Carmine didn't seem bothered by the players milling around him, but he didn't speak to them, either. He stretched and did his warm ups and then began circling the rink in slow, easy laps. Kasha was right—he *was* a good skater, light on the blades and perfectly balanced, avoiding the slower and more clumsy players with ease. Saint couldn't help but wonder what he'd be like with a stick. Were his hands as deft as his skating? He shook himself. Carmine wasn't there for puck handling. He was there to start—and win—fights.

Saint looked away. "Kasha, shooting drills on Butterfly?"

Kasha's eyes lit as Felix groaned theatrically but picked up his blocker and got in his crease.

Saint took the first shot, moving slowly to give his muscles time to warm up. He was aware of the eyes on him, most of the players stopping to watch. Saint didn't bother with anything fancy—Felix would stop it anyway. Instead he skated toward the net at half-speed, watching as Felix dropped his left shoulder invitingly. Saint didn't take the bait.

Almost on top of him, Saint faked left, then scooped the puck up and over Felix's right leg, under his elbow. He couldn't help the grin as he skated back to Kasha while Felix shouted profanities at him.

"Slow is best on him?" Kasha asked, eyes intent.

"Only if you know which way he's going to block," Saint said, leaning on his stick. The other players were gathering, drawn by the action. "He'll try and draw you in, make you shoot a particular way. He's really good at blocking top shelf, go low on him."

Kasha nodded, grabbed a puck, and was off. More players joined Saint, and he nodded at them. A few smiled back, others avoided his eyes. Saint made mental note of

those—he'd have to put in extra work with
them. Down the ice, Kasha made a shot that
Felix easily blocked.

Someone hooted. "Why don't you just
bend over and let him have it?"

Saint stiffened.

Kasha skated back up to them, looking
rueful. "You right," he said. "I'm try top
shelf next time."

But Felix blocked the next shot too. The
same player who'd chirped Kasha before
laughed even louder.

"Maybe if you blow him, he'll let one in,
eh?" he shouted. "Pretty boy like you, you'd
probably like it!"

Saint whirled on him. It was David, the
player Kasha had pointed out earlier, and he
blinked at the fury Saint knew was clear on
his face.

"That's enough," Saint hissed.

David shifted his weight. "It's just chirp-
ing, Cap. Doesn't mean anything."

"While you're on my team—" Saint
straightened and lifted his voice so everyone
gathered could hear him. "On this team,
there will be *no* homophobic slurs, you get
me? None. You go there, you get benched.
No discussion, no debate—I won't put up
with it."

Someone—Tye, Saint thought—raised a
tentative hand. "Can I still call someone a

cocksucker? Because like, I don't *care* if someone sucks cock, but that's kinda my go-to insult, you know?"

"Because you're about as creative as a bag of flour," someone else said—Saint couldn't see who the speaker was.

Tye scowled but didn't argue.

"Look," Saint said, gripping his stick harder. Carmine had drifted over to listen, but he said nothing, eyes intent. "I'm not going to be able to stop you from using *all* derogatory terms on the ice. I know that. But you start calling people 'pretty boys' and inferring they like dick just because of how they look or act, and we're going to have a problem. Get me?" He stared at David, who looked at the ice. Saint lifted his voice. "*Are we clear?*"

"Clear," the team chorused back.

"Then go back to what you were doing," Saint said. The players dispersed, all except for Kasha and Carmine, who was studying Saint intently. "What?" Saint snapped, more sharply than he intended.

Carmine lifted a shoulder. "Just interesting to see the rumors are true." He skated away and Saint looked at Kasha, baffled.

"Rumors?"

Kasha shrugged. "I'm not know. Only thing I hear is Saint great captain, gonna save team, make playoffs, maybe even win Cup."

Saint laughed in spite of himself. "Fuck off."

Kasha grinned back at him. "Is true," he insisted. "Saint is best captain. Even if no playoffs, you best."

Saint ducked his head, cheeks firing. "Thanks," he mumbled. He glanced up. "So tell me more about yourself. I need to know you if I'm going to run effective plays with you."

By the time practice was over, Saint knew almost everything about Kasha, and a lot about the other new members of the team. Kasha missed Russia, but loved American hockey. He had a girlfriend he doted on and was thinking of buying a house in the area if they extended his contract. "Only one year right now," he'd said, making an exaggerated sad face. He loved punk metal, which made Saint tease him about never having the right to choose the music in the dressing room, and Bob Ross, causing Saint to double over with laughter.

"Is good painter!" Kasha insisted over Saint's giggles. "And so nice, yes? Is... calm. Peaceful. Makes me...." He made a frustrated face as if he couldn't find the word.

"Centered?" Saint suggested.

"Yes," Kasha said, nodding. "More

should watch him. Like David, yes?" He grinned, sly, tip of his tongue peeking from the corner of his mouth.

Saint snorted another laugh. "You might be onto something there."

IN THE DRESSING ROOM, it was raucous, packed with players trying to find their spots and arguing over the best ones. Saint ignored them as he got undressed and hung up his skates. He came out of the shower, toweling his hair dry, to find Velvet waiting for him.

Several of the new players were making exaggerated offended noises about a woman in the dressing room. Saint rolled his eyes and lifted his voice.

"First of all, she's seen way better than your shriveled excuses for dicks. Second, I'm pretty sure her wife isn't threatened, so stop acting like children and get back to what you were doing. Which hopefully involves showering, because you fuckers *reek*."

Velvet stepped closer as the dressing room chatter resumed, somewhat muted. "I *can* handle it on my own," she pointed out. "But thanks."

Saint tossed the towel aside. "It's fucked

up, but sometimes they listen better when it comes from a guy. What can I do for you?"

"Coach wants to see you."

Saint groaned. "Again? Can it wait?"

"Unfortunately not." Velvet looked uncomfortable, which made Saint tense.

"What's going on?"

"He made me promise not to say," Velvet said, glancing around the room. "But it involves Carmine."

"*Fuck.*"

HE TOOK the stairs two at a time, eager to get it over with, but Carmine was already in the conference room, drumming his fingers on the table.

Flanahan was sitting opposite him, in the middle of saying something, but he cut off when Saint knocked. "Good to see you, Saint, good to see you!" he said, as if he hadn't talked to him two hours before.

Saint nodded, glancing at Carmine, who wasn't looking at him. "Velvet said you needed to talk to me."

Flanahan looked pleased with himself, which was never a good sign. "Well. The thing is, management feels we've got a real opportunity here. A way to get people through the doors."

Unease crawled over Saint's skin but he said nothing, waiting for Flanahan to get to the point.

"The last time you two were on the ice together, you had a bit of a donnybrook, didn't you?" Flanahan said. He laced his fingers and rested his hands on the table. "And now here you are on the same team."

"No," Saint said flatly.

"You haven't even let me finish!"

"You're setting us up to be rivals," Saint snapped. "You've probably got at least one commercial with the footage from our fight ready to go, don't you?"

Flanahan didn't have the grace to look ashamed. He just shrugged.

"He's my *teammate* now," Saint continued. "Whatever my personal feelings, that all goes away when we step on the ice together. I will not participate in this dog and pony show you're putting on. I won't."

"Good!" Flanahan said, bouncing to his feet, and Saint blinked. "Because Carmine doesn't have a place to live right now, and you're all alone in that huge house with all those guest rooms and it's a perfect solution. You guys can carpool!"

Saint opened and closed his mouth. He'd somehow walked right into the trap Flanahan had set for him. He glanced at Carmine, who hadn't said a word, and back at the coach, who looked far too pleased with himself.

"You're not serious," Saint finally said.

Flanahan's smile showed too many teeth. "You may be the face of the franchise, but you still have to do what I say. And I'm saying Carmine is now your roommate."

"You can't tell me what to do outside this barn!" Saint protested.

"Maybe I can't *force* you," Flanahan said thoughtfully. "But it sure would be unfortunate if a news outlet got hold of the information that Carmine's living in a hostel because you refused to let him bunk with you."

"For how long?" Saint demanded.

"We're thinking three months," Flanahan said, and Saint flinched. "That'll give us time to really build the narrative the way we want."

Saint swung toward Carmine, panic swelling under his ribs. "*You* can't be okay with this."

"Why not?" Carmine said. "Rent-free, nice place—I'm assuming—not too far from the rink? If it's a big house, we don't even have to see each other."

The panic was crawling up Saint's throat. If he opened his mouth, he'd scream. His stomach cramped and twisted. *People*, in his space. Not just people but a person he intensely disliked. *Living with him.*

"Excuse me a minute," he managed. He spun for the door and made it to the bathroom down the hall before his stomach rebelled and he vomited in the toilet, clinging to the porcelain.

Felix found him there. Saint was slumped against the bathroom wall, pale and sweaty. Felix said nothing, just dampened a paper towel and knelt to wipe his face.

"Coach sent me," he said when he was done. There was deep sympathy in his eyes.

"I can't do it," Saint whispered.

Felix sat down beside him, stretching out his legs with a sigh. "Hard practice today. The new guys all want to prove they're good enough. For you."

Saint closed his eyes. "It's too much."

Felix put a hand on Saint's thigh. "For someone on their own, maybe yes. You're not alone, though, are you? You have me. You have Roddy. You even have Velvet—you know you're her favorite. And I think... I think you have Kasha."

Saint rolled his head sideways until he could rest it on Felix's shoulder. "I just want to play hockey."

"And you will," Felix said. "With us."

Saint looked up. "If they traded you, I'd

walk away. I would. I don't even care what they'd do to me."

Felix's eyes creased with affection. "Probably good I just signed a five year contract, eh?"

"You did?" Saint sat up straight and Felix grinned at him. "Five years, Butterfly, that's great!"

Felix shrugged, but he was still smiling. "I don't wanna play unless it's with you either."

Saint leaned back against the wall. "How's your girlfriend?"

"Broke up over the summer, which you'd know if you turned your phone on for anything than to demand news I didn't have." Felix nudged Saint's side. "Met a cute guy a few weeks ago, though. Gonna maybe see where it goes."

"Do you ever wish you could be out?"

"Sometimes." Felix sighed. "I don't wanna do it alone though, you know? Too much... attention." His smile turned sly. "Come out with me, eh? Twice the news, half the attention."

Saint laughed. "You're full of shit." He pushed himself upright. "I should go back." He rinsed his face and mouth with water from the sink before acknowledging that he was delaying. "Butterfly."

Felix, on his feet and smoothing the wrinkles from his pants, glanced up. "Hm?"

"Thanks," Saint said. "I'm—thanks."

Felix smiled at him. "You can do this. Text me whenever you need a break."

2

THERE WAS dead silence after Saint bolted from the room.

"That went well," Carmine finally said. "This was a bad idea, Coach. I'll find somewhere else to stay."

"Absolutely not," Flanahan said, voice harsh. "Saint just needs to get used to the idea. He likes things a certain way, but he'll come around."

"He *ran away*," Carmine said. "And I'm pretty sure he was going to throw up. I know that expression." Guilt and resentment prickled his gut. Was the idea of living with him *that* repulsive?

Flanahan waved that off. "He'll be fine."

Carmine turned away and stared out the window. The players had left the ice, and the arena was quiet. He liked it here, he thought. He hadn't wanted to come, had wanted to retire with the Otters, but he could get used to playing with this team. Some of them were assholes, but that was to be expected anywhere. Carmine liked what he'd seen of Felix and Kasha, and a few others had been welcoming. It could work out. Even if Saint hated him—*if*, he thought scornfully. It was pretty fucking obvious Saint hated him. Still. He could make this work. He *had* to make this work.

They waited in silence until the door opened and Saint stepped through. His face was pale but set. "I have some conditions."

"Let's hear them!" Flanahan said.

Saint shot him a look so filthy, Carmine couldn't help being impressed.

"I'm not talking to you, unless you're planning on moving in with me too. In fact, you don't even need to be here."

Flanahan shrugged, pleased with his victory. "See you boys tomorrow."

The room was quiet after he left. Saint shoved his hands in his pockets and looked everywhere but at Carmine, still sitting at the table.

"I don't know what you've heard about me," Saint began.

Carmine opened his mouth to answer but Saint wasn't waiting for a response.

"I'm neurotic. Prone to throwing fits when I don't get my way or when my routines are fucked with. I don't want a lot of guests. If you want to have a friend or two over, fine, as long as you run it by me first and they're not just random people you picked up in a bar or something. But no parties, no noise complaints from the neighbors, and you check with me before anyone shows up at my front door. Also, you stay in your wing of the house when you have guests."

Carmine tried to say something but Saint was still talking.

"The wing you'll be in has its own living room, den, office, and bedroom. You're welcome to stock the kitchen with whatever you want. Do not fuck with the contents of the fridge, but you can put food in there as long as you don't overstuff it. My wing is off-limits. No one, including you, is welcome back there without express permission. Do what you want in your side of the house, but don't trash it."

"What about—"

"No loud music ever," Saint interrupted. "I don't care about your bedtime routines, obviously, but if you keep me up, there'll be hell to pay."

"Okay, so—"

"Oh, pets," Saint said. "Do you have any? I'm allergic to cats."

Carmine waited pointedly until Saint flushed and gestured for him to proceed.

"I have a dog," Carmine said.

"Is he housetrained? Long haired or short? He's not yappy, is he?"

"He's a pitbull," Carmine said patiently. "Short haired, of course he's housetrained, I'm not a complete asshole. He'll bark if he's left alone too long, but he's crate-trained and I keep him with me when I'm home. It shouldn't be a problem. I'll take him to a kennel for our away games so you don't have another stranger in the house."

Gratitude flashed across Saint's face, there and gone so fast Carmine thought he might have imagined it, but he just nodded.

"Is he here yet?"

"I just got here this morning," Carmine said. "He's with my moms. They'll bring him to me once I'm settled."

"Your... moms?"

"Yeah. Two of them."

"You have two mothers?"

"That tends to happen when they're lesbians," Carmine said, and was treated to Saint flushing again, his cheeks pinking up.

"What was that like?" he asked, and then shook his head as if irritated with himself. "Sorry. Stupid, invasive question. Are you ready to go?"

Carmine stood.

"It was pretty much what I assume any other childhood was like, with a lot more 'go ask your mother'," he said as they headed down the hall.

Saint actually laughed out loud, a giggle-snort that Carmine told himself was absolutely not charming. "Where do they live?"

"Seattle. They're thrilled I'm so close."

They got to the parking lot and Carmine hesitated as Saint kept walking, straight for the exit.

"Where's your car?"

"I don't have one," Saint said over his shoulder.

Carmine gaped at him and scrambled to catch up. "You don't have a car."

Saint didn't look at him, giving the security guard a smile as they passed. "Nope."

"Why *not*?"

"Well, I don't have a license, so why would I?"

Carmine stopped dead at that. "You're shitting me."

Saint sighed, turning. "Look. It's not a big deal, okay? Everyone knows I don't drive. Portland has decent public transportation, and I walk a lot." He scowled. "Can you please stop looking at me like I'm some sort of fucking alien?"

Carmine snapped his mouth shut. "Sorry," he said. "Um. It's just—you're what, twenty-three?"

"Twenty-four," Saint said, turning away to start walking again.

"But you can drive, right? You just... don't?"

Saint didn't answer, picking up the pace.

"You're shitting me," Carmine said, lengthening his stride to keep up. "You really don't know how to drive?"

"We're done with this conversation," Saint said tightly.

"One more question and I promise I'll never bring it up again," Carmine said.

Saint gave him a wary look but didn't say anything, which Carmine took as permission.

"Do you have, like, a thing about being *in* cars? Like they don't freak you out, right? Can you ride in one?"

"Yes, I can ride in them. I just don't know how to drive." Saint spun, jabbing a finger at Carmine's chest. "You tell *any* of the rookies about this and they'll never find your body."

Carmine held up his hands. "Lips are sealed, I promise."

They walked in silence for about ten minutes, Carmine dividing his time between looking at the neighborhood around them and Saint beside him. The houses were pretty; large and set well back from the road that was bordered by wide sidewalks, but Saint was much more interesting.

Carmine had to admit he was ridiculously attractive, with that olive skin and liquid brown eyes. His cheekbones were high and sharp—he needed to put on a little weight, in Carmine's opinion—and his eyebrows said volumes even when his wide, expressive mouth was closed. Carmine wondered vaguely what Saint saw when he looked at him. *Brick shithouse, nose broken too many times, scarred knuckles, mud-colored eyes.* He wasn't in Saint's zip code in a lot of ways, that was for damn sure.

Saint stopped in front of a house with a solid metal gate and punched in a code. "I got people trying to see inside," he explained as the gate rolled back. "Still do, sometimes, but at least now it's more effort."

Carmine shuddered as they walked up the driveway. He would hate that level of exposure. "So are you single?"

Saint sent him an unreadable look. "Everyone in Portland thinks they own a piece of me. If I was dating someone, it would be front page news."

"Ego much?" Carmine mumbled.

"It's not ego when it's true," Saint snapped. "And especially when I fucking *hate it.*"

He unlocked the front door and pushed it open, then paused, taking a deep breath.

Carmine frowned. "You okay?"

"Give me a minute," Saint said, not looking at him. His breathing was rapid and he was touching his thumbs to the tips of his fingers in turn, clearly a calming mechanism.

"Dude," Carmine said, alarmed. "Are you sure you—"

"Shut *up*," Saint hissed, and moved aside, letting Carmine go in first.

Carmine hesitated, eyeing him, but when Saint didn't budge, he stepped over the threshold, looking around him. His first impression was that whatever decorator Saint had hired had clearly not known him very well. The prints on the walls were bright, vivid slashes of color, abstract pieces that were objectively pretty but all wrong for Saint. Carmine said nothing, though, as Saint took another deep breath and pushed past him down the hall. There were no personal pictures on the walls, Carmine noted, following. Well, maybe he kept those in a more private place, like his bedroom or den.

Saint pointed to a huge room off the hall, decorated in cream and muted green. "Main living room. Once a year I'm expected to host either a Halloween,

Thanksgiving, or Christmas party. We mostly stay in here."

"Who hosts the others?"

"Butterfly takes one and Roddy usually does the other," Saint said, taking a right turn. "Kitchen." He flipped a light on.

"The oven range and refrigerator tipped me off," Carmine said dryly. This was a good room, he decided. The countertops were stainless steel, gleaming and polished, and a highly complicated coffee maker stood next to the stove.

Saint ducked his head. "Come on, I'll show you your wing."

Carmine followed him down another short hall and through a door with a lock.

"I'll get you a key," Saint said. "Then you can really have privacy."

Carmine just nodded, inexplicably sad that Saint thought he needed a locked door inside his own house.

"Jesus," he said involuntarily as he stepped into what looked like the living room.

"Yeah," Saint said, rubbing the back of his neck. "I don't... I never come over on this side, I told the designer to just do whatever she wanted."

"It looks like a hotel," Carmine said, glancing around at the bland seascapes on the walls and the neutral-colored furniture.

"There's no personality whatsoever, what the fuck."

Saint shrugged. "The house is too big for me. I mostly took it because of the location—close enough to walk unless the weather's bad—and also the house itself is far enough back from the street that people can't see inside unless they climb the walls. Which happens occasionally, but thankfully not that often." He looked at the art and sighed. "It's terrible, I know. You can redecorate however you want, okay? Go nuts. Anything's better than this."

"If you mean it," Carmine said.

"I mean it," Saint said instantly. He glanced around again and shuddered. "Seriously, please. Do *something* to the place."

"Alright," Carmine said. He already had some ideas on what he could do.

"Want me to show you the rest of the house?"

"Sure."

Saint gave Carmine the extended tour—although he didn't take Carmine into his wing, Carmine noted. Carmine's wing opened onto the backyard from his bedroom, he was pleased to see.

"Steel will love this," he said.

"Steel? Is that your dog?"

It was Carmine's turn to blush. "Um. Yeah. It's because he's gray."

Saint watched him narrowly. "Really? Doesn't have anything to do with you being a Steelers fan?"

Carmine cleared his throat. "Anything else interesting to see in the house?" He paused as a thought struck him. "Hang on, how do *you* know I'm a Steelers fan?"

"Uh." Saint turned away and fiddled with the drapes. "These are a terrible color," he said. "Should definitely get better ones."

"Don't change the subject," Carmine said, suddenly enjoying himself and the way Saint's blush went all the way up to his ears.

"I'm going to make dinner," Saint announced, and escaped.

Carmine followed, grinning. He hopped up on one of the counters as Saint pulled out ingredients for a salad, kicking his feet against the cupboard door. "Sa-aint," he sang. "You still haven't answered my question."

Saint glared at him as he dumped lettuce and baby spinach into the spinner.

"Okay, I'll make you a deal," Carmine said. He leaned forward, thankful for the height and reach that made it possible for him to snag a baby carrot from the island even as Saint swiped at him. "You tell me how come you know I'm a Steelers fan and then you can ask me one question about my personal life, no matter how private or embarrassing."

Saint narrowed his eyes as he put the spinner to work. "Any question?"

"Sure," Carmine said, shrugging.

"Fine. I read up on you after our fight," Saint said in a rush.

Carmine lifted his brows. "That's some pretty in-depth reading. I don't talk about my personal life much."

"*Fine,*" Saint repeated, slamming the spinner down on the counter. "I read up on you *before* our fight, okay? And I maybe asked a few of your teammates about you. Okay, one of them. Well, two. But that's it."

"*Did* you now?" Carmine leaned back on his hands, grinning. "And why would you do a thing like that?"

Saint turned to the refrigerator and pulled out a package of steaks, carefully not meeting Carmine's eyes. "You're an enforcer," he told the countertop. "And I'm a goal-scorer. I needed to know what I was up against."

"Is that the *only* reason?"

Saint's eyes flicked up. "There's no other reason I'd want to know anything about you," he snapped, and stalked out of the kitchen.

Ouch.

CARMINE STAYED where he was for a few minutes, but when it became obvious Saint wasn't coming back, he sighed and hopped off the counter. Putting away the food and cleaning the counters took only a few minutes, and then he pulled out his phone and found a highly rated Indian restaurant not far away.

He went down and waited by the gate for his food, carrying it back up to his wing when it arrived and settling himself in his very boring living room, where he enjoyed chicken tikka masala and thought about why Saint hated him. He had a few theories and he didn't like any of them.

SAINT STAYED in his wing until he was sure Carmine had gone to bed. He'd expected more panic when Carmine had stepped over the threshold, but Carmine was quiet, listening to Saint speak, taking in his surroundings, and somehow not overwhelming Saint with his presence.

His phone buzzed and Saint leaned over to the nightstand to see the screen.

It was from Felix. *Have you murdered him yet? Has he murdered YOU yet?*

Saint huffed to himself, typing out his reply. *Fuck you. He's in his wing. I was only rude to him once, thank you.*

What'd you do?

Saint scowled. *Maybe it's what he did.*

Felix's silence was telling.

He was pestering me, I walked away.

About what?

Saint huddled into his pillows. *Stupid stuff. Forget it. I just… I shouldn't have let him get to me.*

His phone rang a minute later.

"Are you okay, *cher*?" Felix asked gently.

Saint rubbed his face. "I… don't know yet."

"It's big, letting him into your house. Flanny's an idiot, but Rod and I—we know."

"I'm not a baby," Saint snapped. "I can handle another human being in my living space. I host the damn party every year, don't I?"

"And you have panic attacks for days before," Felix said. "But still you do it. For the team."

"They're what matters." Saint fought the urge to roll over and hide his face in the pillow. "Why did you call me? I'm okay, see?"

Felix sighed. "You're not okay, *cher*, but

if that's what you want to tell yourself. See you at practice."

Saint hung up, sure he wouldn't sleep. How could he, with a stranger in his house? *A stranger would be preferable*, he thought, punching his pillow viciously. He still remembered how hard Carmine's fists were, the dazzling starburst of pain in his ribs as Saint took them both to the ice. He also remembered the dimples that flashed in Carmine's cheeks when joking with his teammates before the game, the way his agate eyes gleamed with amusement.

Saint had been fascinated by him, but Carmine hadn't even looked at him. Not until the puck dropped, and then Saint hadn't been able to shake him, like a particularly relentless burr sticking to his skin. He hadn't said anything. Saint might have been able to handle that. Words didn't bother him—he'd heard every slur in the book, and none of it touched him.

Instead, Carmine had foiled every attempt Saint had made on the goal, somehow always there every time Saint had lined up for a shot or caught a pass, knocking the puck away or opting for the simpler expedient of running Saint into the boards and leaving him dazed and gasping like a landed fish, until Saint had lost his temper after the umpteenth covert slash and dropped his gloves.

He'd lost that fight, and left the ice to the jeers of the crowd, laughter and booing following him down the tunnel. Saint hadn't been able to resist looking back as he was escorted away. He'd met Carmine's eyes across the rink. Even from that distance, Saint had been able to see the amusement in them.

He closed his eyes and began counting backward from a thousand.

3

Saint woke up the next morning with a muffled gasp, sitting bolt upright before remembering his surroundings. He'd slept, somehow, and now he had to face Carmine, and apologize for his bad attitude.

He found him in the kitchen, humming along to the music from his phone as he stirred eggs.

"I have Bluetooth speakers," Saint said without thinking. "You can hook your phone up to them."

Carmine turned to look at him, an eyebrow going up. "Good morning."

"I'll give you the password," Saint said. He could feel the flush crawling up his throat. "Um. Good morning." Carmine

43

didn't *look* angry, but then, his face rarely revealed much emotion. Saint swallowed and blundered on. "I'm sorry about last night."

Carmine blinked and said nothing.

"I shouldn't have—" Saint rubbed the back of his neck. "I was rude."

The song on the phone ended and another began.

Carmine abruptly shrugged. "Whatever, man. I look offended?" He turned back to the stove and flipped the eggs.

Saint watched him for a minute but finally decided it was safer just to make coffee and let the matter drop.

"Oh thank God," Carmine said, watching him retrieve the coffee grounds from the cupboard. "I couldn't figure out that rocketship thing you've got going there and I'm dying for caffeine."

"It's preprogrammed," Saint said. He pointed. "Put the grounds in, add water, hit the button. Usually I set it the night before but I forgot."

"Can't imagine why," Carmine said dryly. "Seriously, though, I'm cool if you are. No harm done, right?"

Saint stared down at his coffeemaker, gleaming chrome and black. He could see Carmine's reflection in it, distorted and blurry.

"Cool," he echoed.

"Great! Hope you like eggs. I got this recipe from my mom."

THEY ATE at the table Saint almost never used, tucked into the breakfast nook that looked out over his huge, sloping lawn.

"Steel's gonna love it here," Carmine commented, cutting into his sausage. "It's okay if I let him run in the yard sometimes, right?"

"Yeah, sure." Saint was watching Carmine's hands, deft on his knife and fork. His knuckles were scarred but his fingers were long and graceful.

"I usually get my cardio by running with him," Carmine continued. "Any good trails?"

"One right behind the house, actually," Saint said. He dropped his eyes to his own plate and took another bite. "I go running most mornings."

"Tell me when you're going and I'll make sure we go at a different time," Carmine said easily, and Saint put his fork down.

"You don't have to—look, if we're going to *live* together, you don't have to avoid me all the time."

Carmine frowned. "You don't want me here. I'm not going to force my company on you. In fact, I wanted to talk to you about that. I know Coach wanted us to be roomies for whatever bullshit story he's spinning, but it's obvious how much this bothers you. I'll look for an apartment or something today, okay?"

"No," Saint said immediately. He blinked, surprised with himself at the speed of his response. "It's for the team, right? Team cohesion and all that. They want to see that we can get along, bond or whatever. And it's just a few months."

"Saint, man, you're miserable with me here," Carmine said. He looked genuinely unhappy. "I can't do that to you."

"Yeah but—" Saint swallowed the panic that welled every time he couldn't find words. "It's not... *you*. I just—I have routines and I like things a certain way and as long as you can respect that, you don't have to tiptoe around me or anything. It's not—I know you now. It's not a stranger in my house. It's... you. So I mean—I'll be fine. Okay?"

"Sure, man," Carmine said. He smiled suddenly. "I'm easy to get along with, I promise."

"I'm not," Saint admitted, looking back at his food.

"The great ones are never easy," Carmine said, and startled Saint into looking up.

"I'm *not*—"

"You are, or you will be," Carmine said flatly. The look in his eyes warned Saint not to argue. "You have a sixth sense for where the puck is going to be, and you're there, almost every time. When's the last time you missed a pass from someone? Your hand-eye coordination is incredible, and your foot-work would make Gretzky drool." He grinned. "Not to mention those silky hands of yours. You're allowed to be a little difficult, with all that going on."

"Stop," Saint begged. His ears were burning.

"You just want to play hockey, huh?" Carmine said. His voice was gentle, and Saint took a careful breath.

"Tell me about your moms."

Carmine's eyes lit up. "Lavender and Diana. They're the best."

"Lavender?"

"She's a hippie," Carmine said, grinning again. "Here, I've got pictures."

He was still talking as they walked to the rink, describing the commune his

47

"You are Quinn, yes? I am Arkady. Can call me Volly or Kasha." He offered one big hand and Carmine accepted it.

"You can call me Caz, or Karma," Carmine told him.

Kasha's brows went up. "Why is this?"

"Because Karma will get you eventually," Carmine said, sighing. He'd accepted the inevitability of the nickname back in his rookie year, but that didn't mean he liked it much. He shrugged out of his shirt and bent to pull his pads from his gear bag.

"You're good skater," Kasha said as Carmine got dressed. "But you're fight too much, I think."

"You think, huh?" Carmine said. "Tell the other guys that. I don't go looking for fights but I'm not gonna back down either."

Kasha shrugged. "I'm just say. You're good. Not need fight to show that."

Carmine squinted at him as he settled the chest protector in place. "I'll keep it in mind." His tone was dry but Kasha grinned widely and sat to put on his skates.

THEY HIT the ice and warmed up separately, everyone doing their own familiar routines to stretch out their muscles and get up to speed. Carmine focused on his edgework, looping spirals and figure eights close to the net where Felix was doing his own warm up routine. He wasn't terribly surprised when Felix beckoned him over.

Up close, Felix was sharply handsome, with skin the color of burnt umber, lean features, and a full but unsmiling mouth. He stared at Carmine for a long minute and Carmine let him look, refusing to shift his weight or show unease.

"Be careful with him," Felix finally said. "He is—" His mouth twisted. "He's been hurt."

"And you aren't going to let it happen again?"

"Not if I can help it," Felix said fiercely. His dark eyes were hawk-like, boring into Carmine's, and Carmine was left with no doubt that Felix wouldn't hesitate to drop his gloves and jump him if he needed to.

"He's a big boy," Carmine drawled, resting on his stick, and Felix's mouth tightened. "I'm just saying, he probably wouldn't thank you for babysitting him."

"I am *not*—" Felix broke off and said something that sounded highly unflattering in French. "Watch his back."

"Oh, you want *me* to babysit him?"

Felix bared his teeth. "You know that's why you're here."

"If you say so," Carmine said. He

dropped a wink and skated away. On the other side of the rink, Saint eyed them both suspiciously from where he was talking to Kasha. Flanahan blew his whistle then, and they all gathered at the bench.

Coach was a loud, blustery man who believed volume made up for not knowing his players well enough to properly match them on their lines. Carmine tuned him out, watching Saint where he was standing next to Felix. Saint's eyes were tight, his mouth flat as he listened to Flanahan detailing their various flaws in loud detail. His eyebrows spoke volumes, adding character to his fine-boned features. He liked looking at him, Carmine decided.

"Quinn!" Flanahan shouted, and Carmine jumped.

"Yes, Coach."

"You're on a line with Saint, Roddy, and Kasha," Flanahan ordered. "Carlyle's your other D-man. Second line is Embry, Pasha, and Dylan, with Tye and Zach. Let's go."

They got into position, Carmine shoulder to shoulder with Tye, a young man with sharp blue eyes and pocked skin.

"Big fan," Tye whispered as Coach waited for the centers to set up.

Carmine shot him a startled glance, then grinned. "Thanks, kid."

The puck dropped, Saint won the face-off, and the mock game was on.

Carmine had played against Saint, but never *with* him. Two minutes in, there was nowhere else he ever wanted to play. Saint was never where he expected, but somehow he was always open when Carmine was ready to pass to him, ready and waiting.

Embry—second line center, Carmine reminded himself—stole the puck from Saint and bolted up ice with it, Saint hot on his heels. Carmine was right behind them as Saint chivvied Embry around the net, focused on staying in front of Felix and blocking Embry's view.

Embry made a quick drop pass to Pasha, who wound up and shot. The puck bounced off Felix's pads and Carmine grabbed it.

He charged toward the other end, Pasha and Tye hassling him the entire way. Carmine feinted to one side and dodged past them. Saint shouted and Carmine fired the puck blindly at the sound of his voice.

Kasha's whoop of joy told him it had gone in, and Carmine threw his arms in the air, grinning so widely his face hurt.

Saint was smiling back at him when Carmine arrived at his side.

"Nice moves."

"You're not so bad yourself," Carmine

said, and Saint ducked his head, smile widening.

This could work, Carmine thought.

AFTER PRACTICE, they cooled down, took showers, and had a strategy session. Carmine parked himself off to the side, one knee tucked underneath him, and observed the room.

For the most part, it was a good core, he thought. Roddy and Felix were fiercely protective of Saint, that much was obvious, and the rookies regarded him with a mixture of awe and disbelief, like they weren't entirely sure they were supposed to be in the same room with him yet. The hero worship would fade as they discovered Saint was as human as they were, and the next few weeks would decide the lineup for the first few games—who meshed and who didn't.

47—Carmine couldn't remember his name—was talking to the man next to him, burly forearms folded over his chest and a forbidding scowl on his face. He hadn't made much noise since Saint had torn strips from him for his homophobic chirps, but Carmine didn't like the vibe he was getting.

When the meeting was dismissed, Carmine was slow to stand, still watching the players around him. He wasn't expecting Roderick to stop beside him.

"A word." It wasn't a request.

Carmine followed him out of the room as Felix slipped through the throng to catch up.

"Is this an intervention or a mugging?" Carmine asked as Roderick led them down the hall. "Because I'm not an alcoholic and I don't have my wallet on me but I can go get it—"

"Shut up," Roderick suggested, and opened a door.

Carmine went inside, wary. It was a meeting room, quiet and dark, but his nerves were not improved by the way Roderick shut the door behind Felix and then leaned against it.

"Seriously, what's going on?" Carmine asked.

Felix glanced at Roderick, who nodded.

"It's about Saint," Felix said.

"What about him?" Carmine's voice was sharper than he intended, and he took a deep breath, rolling his shoulders to loosen the tension.

"You're living with him, so there are a few things you should know," Roderick said. He gestured at the chairs. "Have a seat."

Carmine obeyed, still tense. Felix and Roderick settled opposite.

"Saint is not easy to get along with," Roderick said.

Carmine snorted. "You needed to kidnap me to tell me that?"

"I mean it," Roderick snapped. "If you're going to play with him effectively, you're damn well going to understand what makes him tick. So shut the fuck up and listen."

Carmine spread his hands silently.

"He's been groomed for this position since he was two years old," Felix said. "Hockey is all there is, for him. All there ever has been. I have known him since he was fourteen, Karma—we were billeted together. We grew up together. If you want to understand him, you must learn how he plays, and play to his level."

"No one can play to his level," Carmine said immediately, and Felix's eyes softened.

"True. But I have seen you play as well. You can come close, I think. And he is just one man. He can't get us to a Cup on his own—he needs a strong team that under-stands him and accepts him as he is."

Carmine squinted at him. "What are you getting at?"

"I need to know that what I'm about to say will not leave this room. And before you ask, we have Saint's permission to speak to anyone we feel needs to know of this matter."

"Depends what you're about to say," Carmine said. "If you're about to confess to a murder, then I'm not gonna promise confidentiality, but as long as it's nothing criminal, then yeah man, my lips are sealed."

"Saint is gay."

Carmine sat back in his chair.

Felix glanced at Roderick, who said nothing.

Silence gathered as Carmine considered. It made sense, he supposed—the way Saint so fiercely protected his private life, how he never dated, how he dodged all the questions about who he might be seeing.

"Okay," he finally said.

"That's it?" Roderick asked.

"What, is there more?" Carmine said. "Are you going to tell me he fucks barnyard animals or something?"

"You don't have a problem with it?" Felix asked. His eyes were sharp and searching.

It would be easy, Carmine thought. So easy just to open his mouth and say *so am I*. But he didn't know these men. So he shook his head.

"It's all fine by me. Doesn't affect his hockey, does it? Or would he play better if he were straight?"

Felix narrowed his eyes and Carmine grinned at him.

"Exactly. Is that everything?"

"He has personal space issues," Roderick said. "You can hug him on the ice but don't touch him otherwise unless he initiates it. Don't crowd him. You're a big guy—don't use it against him."

"I wouldn't," Carmine objected, faintly offended.

Roderick didn't challenge that, pressing the point. "He really hates being touched if it's not his idea. If you can keep others from pawing at him, it'll help."

Carmine nodded. "Does he date?"

Felix laughed outright at that. "Between trying to get us together for a Cup run and not being out, and having so much attention focused on him, that's a little out of the question. He's out to only the people on the team we trust, no one else. He doesn't want to come out publicly, and he may not until he retires."

Carmine raised his hand and Felix gave him a sour look.

"This is not school. If you want to speak, then speak."

Carmine dropped his hand, hiding his smile. It was easy *and* fun to yank Felix's chain, and he wanted to keep doing it, but he actually did have a question. "You said he's only out to people you trust. What made you decide you could trust me?"

Felix shifted his weight. "Ah… it was what you said to him."

"What'd I say?" Carmine asked, genuinely curious.

"Regarding living with him. Saint told me you tried to leave. That you… understood, somehow, what it meant for him to allow you into his home." Felix's eyes were sincere, and Carmine suppressed the urge to rub his neck. "You are a good man, I think, Karma. Too prone to using your fists, maybe, but where it counts—" He lifted his hands.

Carmine nodded. "Thanks, I guess. Anything else?"

"Don't fuck with his routines, and if I hear you mocking them, I'll put itching powder in your jock for a *month*," Felix said. "Whatever it is he has to do to get in the right headspace to play, you let him do it and you keep the others off his back." He flattened his hands on the table. "He didn't have a childhood, Quinn. Do you understand what I'm saying?"

Carmine thought about it, about what it might have been like to be shoved into the role assigned to him the moment he was old enough to put on skates. He loved hockey, but there was more to life than ice and pucks and sticks. But it was all Saint had ever known, all he'd ever had.

MICHAELA GREY

"Yeah," he said after a minute. "Yeah, I get it. Anything else?"

"That's not enough?" Felix sniped.

Carmine grinned. "I like you," he said, mostly for the startled expression that got him. "You're looking out for your boy. Fine. Thanks for telling me. Can I please go now?"

Roderick flipped a hand in clear dismissal. Carmine dropped a wink at Felix and left, straightening his shirt.

He found Saint not far from the dressing room, his brows pinched together as he hurried down the hall.

"Where were you?" he asked.

"Sorry, didn't realize you needed constant updates on my whereabouts," Carmine said. "I can invest in an ankle monitor or chip implant so you can track me, if you want?"

Saint glared at him. "Are you always this sarcastic?"

"I'm actually restraining myself," Carmine told him, and laughed out loud when Saint shuddered.

"I don't have your phone number," Saint said. "And I don't have an extra key yet. I was going to do that today. You can wait here, or I can take you to the house and let you in, but if you want... you could come with me?"

60

Carmine blinked. "I—uh... sure?"

"I mean, if you don't have anything else you're doing, and you're not too tired, and—"

"Chill," Carmine said gently. "It'll be nice to see some of the city."

Saint's shoulders eased. "Okay," he said, and summoned up a half-smile. "Um. Thanks."

"No big deal," Carmine told him. "You ready now?"

4

THEY LEFT THE RINK TOGETHER, Saint tugging a snapback down over his hair and slipping on a pair of sunglasses.

"Worried about paparazzi or locals?" Carmine teased.

"It's not really the locals," Saint said, shoving his hands in his jacket pockets. "They leave me alone, mostly, just ask for an autograph and selfie, tell me their thoughts about the team. But tourists...." He shook his head. "Anything goes. I just thought... they don't really know you yet, right? So—"

"You're hoping it'll throw them, you being with someone else?"

"Basically. Maybe they won't think it's me." Saint sounded young, and exhausted, and Carmine wanted suddenly to step between him and the world.

"So show me some of your city," Carmine told him, and when the car arrived, they slid into the backseat, Carmine careful not to touch him.

The ride was more comfortable than he'd expected, as Saint pointed out sights and favorite restaurants and the grocery store he went to.

"That reminds me, I need to stock up," Carmine mused as the car rolled by the store.

"Me too," Saint said. "We can go after we get the key, if you want?" He sounded abruptly unsure of himself, as if offering more of his company was the last thing Carmine would be interested in.

Carmine gave him a smile. "That sounds good. Do you like to cook?"

Saint shook his head. "I'm not fussy, but I'm usually too busy. I can make salad and steak but not much else."

"That's something I love to do," Carmine said. "So if you want, I'll take over doing that. Any allergies?"

"No, but I don't like peanuts. Or mushrooms."

"No peanuts, no mushrooms, got it."

"Are you—sure?" Saint was looking at him quizzically, eyes worried behind his sunglasses. "Cooking for me—you don't have to do that."

"I'm doing it for myself anyway," Carmine said. Saint's expression didn't ease, and Carmine resisted the urge to nudge him with his shoulder. "Hey, it's no trouble to make a little extra, really. You're letting me live with you, after all. Speaking of which, you sure you want me around for a couple of months?"

Saint ducked his head again. "Coach said... it's important. He's really pushing this 'former rivals' narrative. And you're a good guest."

"Works for me," Carmine said. "No loud parties, I promise."

Saint's mouth twitched, almost unwillingly. "You can have guests over," he said. "Just... keep them in your wing."

"Did it hurt to say that?" Carmine asked. "You can tell me. Scale of one to ten, how much pain are you in right now?"

Saint ducked his head, but not before Carmine saw the smile curving his lips. "You're a dick."

"Yeah, but it's fun," Carmine said comfortably, lacing his hands across his stomach. "Speaking of, what do you like to do to relax?"

"Never heard of it," Saint said with a straight face, and startled Carmine into a laugh.

"Was that an actual sense of humor?"

"Shut up," Saint told him, but he stopped fighting the smile. "I read. Watch movies."

"Me too, what genre's your favorite?"

"I'll watch nearly anything." Saint shrugged. "I like horror movies, though."

Carmine lifted an eyebrow. "Really?"

"Why do you sound surprised?"

"You just don't seem the type," Carmine said. He leaned across Saint to look out the window. "Vietnamese! I haven't had that in too long." When he sat up, the top of Saint's cheekbones were faintly red. "Sorry," Carmine said. "I forgot about your personal space thing."

"It's fine," Saint said, not looking at him. He hesitated and then glanced at him. "Did Roddy—"

"Kidnap me into a dark room with Felix's help and vaguely threaten me with grievous bodily injury if I did anything to hurt you? Yep."

The blush darkened in Saint's cheeks. "I'm sorry." He sounded as if he meant it.

"Don't be." Carmine leaned back in his seat and laced his fingers again. "They're looking out for you. It's what I would do, in their position."

"Did they... say anything... else?"

"Oh sure, we had a nice, *long* conversation." Carmine took a minute to enjoy the way Saint squirmed in his seat before taking pity on him. "It's all good, man. Really." He lowered his voice. "Maybe we can find you a cute boy."

Saint put his head in his hands. "How is this my life," he moaned.

"Could be worse," Carmine said, and resisted the urge to pat him on the back.

CARMINE WANDERED THE HARDWARE SHOP, inspecting the contents of the shelves, as Saint talked to the man behind the counter, who apparently had opinions about the way the next season should go. The shop was small, and Carmine could hear Saint's quiet voice even from across the room as he made interested noises and agreed with the opinions the shopkeeper was laying out.

Poor guy, Carmine thought. There were benefits to being a little-known goon with no real shot at glory—at least he didn't have to worry about being buttonholed by every Tom, Dick, and Harry who'd watched a hockey game once and had Opinions.

The door jingled but Carmine didn't look up. He pulled out his phone and

falling into step beside him. "Or Jagr, for that matter. Although I could probably rock a mullet. What do you think?"

Saint's lips twitched. "Listen, about back there—thank you."

"Sure thing," Carmine said easily. "Some people don't know what boundaries are."

"It's part of my job." Saint's voice was soft, low enough that Carmine had to strain to hear him. "I just—"

"Yeah, I know." Carmine thought he was beginning to get it, somewhat—why Saint was so neurotic. He'd been able to control so little throughout his life, it made sense he'd cling desperately to what he *could*. If routines and rituals made him more comfortable, brought out those dimples Carmine had only seen a few times, and if keeping fans from overwhelming him helped, then he was a little startled at his own willingness to step up and help. "I'm hungry. Do you want to go to the store or a restaurant? My treat."

Saint snorted a laugh, sidestepping a slower pedestrian. "Pretty sure I make more than you. I can pay."

"It's the thought that counts," Carmine protested. "Besides, you don't know where I was gonna take you." He shot him a grin and headed for the nearest food cart. Behind him, Saint groaned but followed.

HE IGNORED Saint's protests and bought gyros for them both, overtipping with a wink, and they resumed their walk. Carmine unwrapped the top part of his gyro and took a huge bite, moaning happily at the mingled flavors of spiced lamb and tzatziki sauce on his tongue.

"'Kay, the food's not bad," he said through his mouthful.

Beside him, Saint was eating in a much more restrained fashion, eyeing him with amusement.

"You just—go for it, don't you?"

Carmine swallowed and wiped his mouth. "What do you mean?"

Saint lifted a shoulder and tore off a piece of flatbread, rolling it between his fingers. "You want something, you go for it. You see a problem, you say something. You don't care what others think."

"I wouldn't go *that* far," Carmine objected.

"Okay but...." Saint sighed and took a dainty bite, chewing and swallowing before he spoke again. "You still just *do* it. I don't —" There went his shoulders again, up around his ears.

"You try being raised by two lesbians who were at every major political protest in

the country and *not* being outspoken."
Carmine shrugged and took another bite.
"My mouth gets me in trouble," he said,
garbling the words and enjoying Saint's
wince at his manners. "Maybe I should be
more like you."

"No." Saint's voice was sharp and final.
"You don't want that." He lengthened his
stride and Carmine hurried to catch up,
swearing at himself for his blunder.

Saint was tense the rest of the way to the
grocery store, but by the time they were
inside, his posture was easing again. He
grabbed a basket and raised his eyebrows at
Carmine.

"Find you after?"

"Sounds good. No peanuts or mushrooms." Carmine grinned at him, took a
cart, and headed for the produce aisle.

He had some ideas about what he could
cook, and he was pleased to find an excellent selection of fruits and vegetables. He
took his time, browsing them all thoroughly
before selecting the best ones. Then he
moved on to the bakery section.

He saw Saint a few times as they worked
their way around the store, but they didn't
stop to speak, although Carmine didn't miss
the dubious glances Saint threw at his basket
every time they passed each other. Carmine
just grinned and kept going.

They met up at the checkout as promised, and Saint leaned over Carmine's basket to fish out a small bottle.

"Seriously," he said, "what is this?"

"That, you cretin—" Carmine swiped the bottle from his hand, "—is truffle oil, and I can't believe you don't even know what it is."

"Well, what's it *for*?"

Carmine rolled his eyes. "It. Tastes. Good," he said slowly and clearly, and Saint huffed a startled laugh and pushed his shoulder. Carmine barely even swayed, but he couldn't help his smile as Saint turned to unpack the contents of his own basket onto the conveyor belt.

Carmine was dismayed to see that the driver of the car they called to take them home recognized Saint. Sure enough, he launched into questions about the upcoming season before he'd pulled away from the curb, and Carmine watched help-lessly as Saint's shoulders notched higher and higher, even as he smiled and answered every question with gentle grace.

Halfway back to the house, Carmine couldn't take it anymore, and he pulled out his phone. One quick text and two minutes later, Saint's phone rang. He pulled it out of his pocket, murmuring an apology to the driver, and frowned at the display.

put these away in my fridge, but I'll make dinner for us if you want?"

Saint nodded, one side of his mouth tucking up into a smile. "See you then."

5

He spent the rest of the afternoon watching game tape, curled up on the over-stuffed sofa in his bland living room. He could hear Carmine moving around in his wing, doors opening and closing, but he didn't come out. Saint reached for his phone several times, on the verge of asking if he wanted to join him, but stopped himself each time.

He doesn't want to be here any more than you want him here, he told himself. *He sure doesn't want to spend* more *time with you.*

Finally he shoved the phone between the cushions and focused on the television.

He was still there when Carmine emerged from his wing and padded into the living room, pausing to knock on the doorframe with a knuckle.

"I'm gonna start dinner," he said. His

eyes were sleepy and there was a crease in his cheek, like he'd been napping. He looked rumpled and soft, and Saint felt a tug of something he couldn't identify, deep in his gut. "Are you busy or do you want to keep me company? You can help me chop veggies or something."

Saint opened and closed his mouth. Carmine looked friendly and curious, as if he wasn't upending Saint's world by actively seeking out his company for something other than hockey.

"I'm not a very good cook," he finally said.

"Can't really fuck up chopping vegetables, unless you cut off a finger," Carmine said, shrugging. "Come on."

In the kitchen, Carmine pulled out his phone. Saint gave him the password and Carmine made short work of connecting the phone to the speakers. When the first notes sounded, Saint raised an eyebrow.

"Taylor Swift? Really?"

"Be nice," Carmine said, unperturbed. He lifted the chopping board off its hook and set it on the counter beside Saint, then selected a knife from the block next to the sink. "She's got good music and you can't tell me you don't sing along when you hear her on the radio."

Saint glowered but said nothing.

Carmine snickered and retrieved the turnips from the fridge. "Peel these and then chop them into one to two inch chunks for me."

They got to work in silence, Saint stealing glances at Carmine as he peeled. He moved with comfort and ease, at home in the space like he'd always lived there, even though he didn't know where anything was.

"Big pot?" he asked.

Saint pointed with his knife and Carmine grunted thanks, pulling out Saint's biggest stockpot.

"You said you don't cook?" he asked as he filled it with water.

"I just never really understood the point, I guess," Saint admitted. "I inevitably burn something or forget to set the timer or whatever, and I never know when things are done—you know how some people just sort of instinctively know?"

Carmine hummed, busy chopping potatoes.

"Well, I don't have that. So it's either underdone or dried to a husk. I eventually stopped trying because it's not like I can't afford to have food delivered."

"You know what I've always wanted to

try?" Carmine said abruptly. "One of those daily meal prep services. They deliver all the ingredients and all you have to do is put them together. Fresh, delicious, gourmet meals, and you don't even have to go to the store."

"They do that?" Saint peeled the last strip off the turnip and set it on the chopping block.

"Yeah, it's pretty fucking convenient. Say what you want about this world, it's nice to have options like that." Carmine's phone rang, interrupting the music, and he growled, setting down his knife. He hit answer with one knuckle and then speaker, raising a quick eyebrow at Saint, who nodded. "Hello?"

"Hello, my darling," said a familiar voice. Saint knew that voice. She'd given him gardening tips for nearly ten minutes earlier that day. "How is my beautiful boy?"

"Mom," Carmine said, sounding pained. "I'm twenty-nine years old. Can you *please* stop talking to me like I'm nine?"

"Never," Lavender said. "Am I on speaker?"

"Yes, and Saint is here," Carmine said.

"Um, hi," Saint said awkwardly.

"Saint, darling!" Lavender said. "How are you?"

"Not much different from when we

talked two hours ago," Saint said, amused. "Thank you for that, by the way."

"Well, you're certainly welcome, although I don't know *why* it was necessary."

"People think they're all entitled to a piece of him," Carmine interrupted. He was back to chopping potatoes and tossing them in the pot. "You saved him from a stressful conversation."

"Then I'm very glad I could help. Carmine, love, when can we bring Steel to you and see your new city?"

Carmine raised his eyebrows at Saint.

"Oh," Saint said, gathering his wits. "Um. Anytime? Carmine has a key."

"Just a second, Mom." Carmine rounded the counter and leaned in close. "You sure you're okay with them being here?" he whispered, just low enough for Saint to hear.

It took Saint a minute to gather his thoughts.

He nodded, swallowing. "Yeah." He kept his voice low. "I mean, they're your parents. Of course it's okay."

Carmine's eyes crinkled and Saint looked away, clearing his throat.

"This weekend, Mom?" Carmine asked, lifting his voice.

"Sounds good," Lavender said. "Di's got

honey for you and we have housewarming gifts. I can't wait to see you!"

"Tell Ma I love her," Carmine said. A few more rounds of goodbyes and Carmine finally hung up. "Sorry about that."

"For what, having a mother—*two* mothers—who love you?" Saint focused on getting the turnip cut just right. "You should never apologize for that."

"Where are your parents?" Carmine asked.

"They have a farm outside Montreal," Saint said.

"Do you get to see them a lot?"

"They come down for games when they can." *Drop it*, Saint thought, and chopped the next turnip a little too aggressively.

Carmine didn't seem to notice. "They must be proud of you."

"Oh sure," Saint said.

"Supported your hockey?"

"Of course," Saint said, staring at the turnips. His throat was tight. *Five years old, begging to be allowed to go inside where it was warm, his legs so tired they were shaking. His father folding his arms, that familiar forbidding scowl in place. "Run the drill again. Unless you don't* want *to play in the NHL."*

Saint's knife slipped and he swore, dropping it. He watched in slow motion as blood welled from his thumb and dripped onto the turnips.

Then Carmine was there, grabbing his wrist. "What happened?"

Saint didn't answer. His thoughts were slow to form, hard to grasp.

Carmine steered him toward the sink and turned on the water. He held Saint's wrist, keeping his hand under the stream, a worried wrinkle on his brow.

"Saint, can you talk to me?"

Saint didn't say anything, mesmerized by the drips of blood.

Carmine shook him gently. "Saint!"

Saint took a deep breath. "I... got blood on the turnips," he whispered.

"Least of my worries right now," Carmine said gently. "You're kind of freaking me out a bit. What's going on?"

"Nothing," Saint managed. His thumb was beginning to sting, nerve endings waking up and protesting. "Just clumsy."

Carmine's expression said he didn't believe him, but he didn't push. He just turned the water off and raised Saint's hand above his heart.

"Keep it there. Where's your first aid kit?"

"Oh... my bathroom," Saint said.

Carmine swore. "Do you want to go get it or do you trust me to?"

Saint wasn't entirely sure his legs would obey him. Carmine's eyes were dark and kind, no judgment in them.

"You can," he said. "Under the sink."

Carmine patted his arm. "Be right back. Don't move."

SAINT WAITED, hand still obediently above his heart and over the sink. The blood flow had slowed to a trickle, still bleeding sluggishly and dripping in fat, crimson splats into the stainless steel sink. He wondered, distantly, what Carmine thought of his living space. Did he like the art he had on the walls? Did he appreciate the trophy display case filled with Saint's greatest achievements or had he even stopped to look at them?

From the speed with which Carmine returned, Saint suspected the latter. He was clutching the box, which he set on the counter and flipped open.

"How's it feeling?" he asked as he pulled out disinfectant and bandages.

"Starting to hurt," Saint admitted.

"This'll hurt more," Carmine said, and poured antiseptic over the wound. He caught Saint's wrist in an iron grip when he instinctively recoiled, hissing through his teeth at the blistering burn in his hand.

"Hurts," Saint panted, flexing his fingers uselessly.

"I know," Carmine said gently. His thumb was stroking Saint's pulse point in absent, soft sweeps, and Saint breathed through his nose in desperate gulps and focused on Carmine's touch, the nearness of his big body.

It took a few minutes, but slowly the worst of the burn began to fade and Saint's breathing steadied.

"Okay?" Carmine murmured.

Saint nodded.

"Alright, I'm going to bandage you up. The cut's not deep—you should be able to play just fine. Just keep the bandage clean and swap it out as soon as it gets sweaty and gross."

His hands were steady and confident as he wrapped the thumb in layers of gauze and taped them in place.

"Think that'll fit under your glove?" he said after a minute.

Saint inspected it and nodded. "Should be fine."

"Good. Since you so cleverly managed to get out of chopping vegetables, you can just do my scut work instead." Carmine slanted him a grin as he packed away the first aid kit contents and washed his hands.

"I'm sorry," Saint said.

"It was an accident," Carmine said. "I'll leave the kit here so you can put it away yourself, okay?"

Saint swallowed hard. How did this man know him so well already, in just the space of twenty-four hours? "Okay," he whispered.

"So, line a baking sheet with foil for me, then melt some butter in the microwave and get the salt and pepper. Then grab the asparagus from the fridge."

Saint obeyed, following Carmine's instructions on how to arrange the spears on the baking sheet, brushing them with butter and sprinkling the pan with salt and pepper. Carmine was a blur of motion, rinsing the turnips and adding them to the pot, going from the stove to the counter and back again, muttering to himself as he tested the ingredients of various pans with a scowl. Saint was fascinated.

"You're really good at this," he remarked as Carmine set the first salmon steak in the pan.

Carmine lifted a shoulder. "Been doing it all my life, since I was old enough to hold a spatula. Hey, do you have a grill?"

"Uh... I might?"

Carmine tipped his head back and

laughed, deep and full-bodied. Saint watched, bewildered, until Carmine had sobered into hiccuping giggles, wiping his eyes.

"What's so funny?"

"You don't even know if you have a grill," Carmine said, still grinning. "How much more of this house is undiscovered?"

Saint glowered. "I don't cook, let alone grill. Why would I care?"

"Eh, fair. But I'm here now, and grilling is a far superior method to prepare meat, so I really hope you have one." He set the spatula down and winked. "I'll go check right now. When the oven beeps, put the asparagus in and set the timer for eight minutes." With that, he was gone, leaving Saint standing in his kitchen and feeling faintly like he'd been run over by a steamroller.

He followed Carmine's instructions and then wandered in the direction of the back patio, curious to see if he really *did* have a grill.

Carmine was bent over a blackened metal contraption, crowing happily to himself, when Saint stepped outside.

"This baby is *gorgeous*," he told Saint, patting the hood. "We're gonna make so many steaks and burgers, it's gonna be great."

"The asparagus is in," Saint told him.

"Good!" Carmine gave the grill one last proprietary pat and straightened. "How's your hand?"

"It's fine," Saint said. He'd almost forgotten about it, he realized as he followed Carmine back inside. "Anything else you need me to do?"

"You can mash the turnips and potatoes," Carmine decided.

"I… don't know how."

"Do you have a masher?"

"How would I even know?" Saint asked, bewildered, and surprised Carmine into another laugh.

"God, how did you survive?"

"Takeout," Saint said.

Carmine found a weird contraption in one of Saint's utensil drawers and brandished it triumphantly. "Now *that's* what I'm talking about!"

Saint eyed it. "It looks like a torture device."

Carmine waved it in Saint's direction. "We have ways of making you talk, Mr. Levesque. Tell me the secret to that sick backhand of yours."

Saint couldn't help his giggle, and Carmine's grin widened. He handed the masher over, then cast around the cupboards until he came up with a colander. He poured the boiled turnips and potatoes in, waited for them to drain, and then dumped them back in the pot.

"You're up, kid," he said. "Squash the fuck out of 'em. No chunk left alive, got it?"

"Got it," Saint agreed, and went to work.

Beside him, Carmine was busy seasoning the salmon steaks, flipping them again and feeling the surface with one judicious finger.

"Why are you touching them?" Saint asked as he mashed.

"You can tell by feel whether something's cooked all the way through."

"Really?" Saint peered at the pan, fascinated. "How?"

Carmine shrugged. "It's... hard to explain? But like, it feels firmer and... different, somehow, when it's done."

"Huh. Who taught you to cook? Lavender?"

"Oh god no. Lavender couldn't cook her way out of a wet paper bag. No, that was all Diana. She passed on her appreciation of good food to me. Some of my favorite memories are when I was eight and nine years old, standing on a stool at the stove because I was too short to reach, stirring whatever she was making. I burned a lot of crap, but she never lost patience with me, and eventually I got better." He glanced at Saint. "You know—" He broke off and shook his head. "Forget it."

Saint squinted at him, but Carmine ignored it as he added butter and salt to the potatoes and turnips. He tasted it, hummed thoughtfully, and scooped up another small spoonful, offering it to Saint.

"Tell me what you think."

Saint accepted the spoon and tasted it warily. The potatoes and turnips were creamy and rich on his tongue, and he blinked. "Oh. That's… nice."

Carmine made a dissatisfied noise. "Needs more garlic. Well, too late now. I'll add more next time." He turned back to the salmon. "You can set the table, I'm ready to plate."

THEY ATE TOGETHER at Saint's too-big table. The salmon was cooked to perfection, although Carmine grumbled that it would have been better on the grill, and paired perfectly with the asparagus and potatoes.

"It's delicious," Saint said after a few minutes.

Carmine smiled at him across the table. "I'm really not a bad guy, you know."

Saint froze and set down his fork. "I know."

"Do you?" Carmine tilted his head. "Because I know you don't want me here. And I don't really blame you, but for some reason, I don't want you to hate me."

"I—" Saint swallowed. "I don't." He turned the fork in his fingers, staring at the tines.

"That game in Boston," Carmine said, and stopped.

Saint went stiff. "No," he said through numb lips. *Leave it*, he thought desperately.

Carmine seemed to get it. "So I know they hired me to be your muscle." His mouth quirked wryly. "Seems to me you can handle yourself, for the most part. Which means they're probably looking at someone or some team in particular. Am I close?"

Saint picked up his fork again. "Yeah," he said. He dragged the tines through the mashed potatoes, watching the little peaks form.

"A person or a team?"

"The team's not... great," Saint said, still looking at his plate. "But it's more a person. Last time we played each other, he took me out for a month with three broken ribs."

Carmine winced.

"Well, it's not all on him." Saint took a bite of salmon. "I might have tripped him...

once or twice. And I goaded him into taking a penalty, but that was because he boarded my rookie."

"What's his name?"

"Simon Fall."

"Of the Richmond Ravens?" Carmine demanded. "Shit, I know him. Guy's a fucking goon. Gets called for more penalties than me, and that's saying something."

Saint shrugged. "Well anyway, the team hates him, and all of the Ravens. So we end up drawing stupid penalties and getting in fights and it's ugly. And of course management plays it up, makes a big deal of the rivalry so the fans will get hyped. It's... tiring."

"Good to know. So." Carmine set his glass down. "Game-day rituals."

Saint blinked. "Yours or mine?"

"Yours," Carmine said. "I don't have many. But I want to know what to expect from you."

"You sure you want to get *that* close up with my neuroses?" Saint asked, fidgeting.

"Just tell me," Carmine said, and Saint sighed, giving up. Carmine was going to think he needed to be committed, but something about the set of his mouth said he wasn't going to let the question go.

"Left foot on the floor first when I wake up. Piss, shower—left foot out of the shower, shave. Breakfast is oatmeal with pecans and brown sugar. Lunch is pasta, but I'm willing to be flexible on sauces. Grilled cheese sandwich before the game. No one touches my equipment. *No one.*"

"Not even the equipment manager?"

"Pat. He's allowed any other time but not on game-day, not unless I ask him for something. He's a good guy. Very patient."

Carmine nodded. "Anything else?"

"EDM on the way to the rink. Helps get me hyped up. I ride with Butterfly to the rink, since it's farther than the practice barn." He hesitated. "You can come with us if... you want. Unless you want to get your own car?"

Carmine's eyes crinkled with his smile. "I have a car, the moms are bringing her down. But until then, yeah, that'd be nice. Keep going."

"What makes you think that's not all of it?"

Carmine snorted. "Because there's no way that's the extent of your superstitions." He made a beckoning motion. "Keep 'em coming."

Saint fought the desire to hide. "Fine, *fine*. Left foot into my underwear and pants, left sock on first, same with left shoe. My tape goes on counter-clockwise and I have to have fifteen wraps or I'll take it back off and start over. That's enough, right?"

Carmine shrugged, his expression hard to read. "Depends. Is there more?"

"Left skate first on the ice, and after the anthem plays, I push off the line with my left foot for three steps." Saint's face was burning. "Are you satisfied with my level of crazy? Because I'm sure I could think up some more rituals if they'll help."

"Easy," Carmine said, lifting his hands. "Hey, Saint, I didn't ask for all that to make you feel like I was judging you or some shit, okay?"

"Then why did you?"

"So I know what I need to do to help you get your head on straight," Carmine said. "And now I know. Can I make the breakfast for you, or does it have to be you?"

"Has to be me," Saint said immediately. He paused. "I could... make enough for you too, though. It's not bad. Filling."

Carmine smiled at him. "That sounds great. I don't think you're crazy. I've seen way worse, believe me."

"Sure," Saint scoffed.

"Oh no, really," Carmine said, leaning forward. His expression was earnest. "This one guy I knew refused to take a shit at the rink before a game, because once he did and they lost. So he'd go before he got there, but if he had to go again, he'd literally have to run down the street to the damn McDonalds so he could shit in safety."

Saint's laugh startled him. "You're kidding me."

"Swear to God," Carmine said, grinning at him. "And he had a *terrible* backhand. If he'd spent less time worrying about his shitting ritual and more time practicing that backhand, maybe he'd have made it out of the AHL."

"We really are all some variety of insane, aren't we?" Saint said.

Carmine's smile widened. "Normal is boring."

pretty. But she not like Portland much. She wanted me to go for Lions, so she could go for Hollywood, you know? But I had chance to play with Saint—can't pass up."

"Fair enough," Carmine said, bumping shoulders with him gently. He stripped down and got into his compression gear, then followed the others to the workout room.

He spent his time on the bike watching the team interact. Kasha was talking to another rookie in the corner as they waited for turns on the squat rack. Felix was off doing some goalie zen thing in the corner with Ivan, the rookie goalie from the Embers. Jesper was talking to Roderick, who was in the fitness bands as the trainer worked with him, and 47—David, Carmine had finally remembered his name—was over by the weights, talking loudly about how much he could press.

Saint... Carmine couldn't help the way his eyes followed Saint as he went around the room. He seemed to take a random path from one piece of equipment or set of trainers to the next, but he somehow always ended up involved in the conversation of the players around him, and when he drifted on to the next one, he left smiles and relaxed shoulders behind him.

Christ, he's actually good at this, Carmine

thought. The switch from painfully awkward and shy to calm and confident captain was startling to see, and fascinating to watch. Carmine had seen it happen in flashes before, but he still couldn't look away. Saint seemed to know instinctively how to talk to everyone—Carmine was pretty sure he heard him speaking Swedish to Jesper and Oscar, and even David seemed more settled after Saint moved on.

Felix cleared his throat and Carmine nearly fell off the bike.

"Where the *fuck* did you come from?" he demanded.

Felix's eyes glinted. "You were a little preoccupied watching our *capitan*. How are things going?"

Carmine shrugged, slowing his cycling speed. "I'm not sure if he likes me or not, but we went and got a new key and groceries, and I made him dinner last night. He helped me cook, a little bit."

Felix's eyebrows climbed his brow. "He did what now?"

"Well, he chopped some vegetables. Nearly cut his thumb off."

"I noticed the bandage," Felix said. "I thought perhaps you could tell me what happened." There was tension in his slim body now, the way he stood lightly on the balls of his feet as if poised for action.

"If I hurt your boy, they'll never find my body," Carmine said, and stepped off the bike. "Relax, man, he's fine. It was an accident. I bandaged it up for him and it's all good."

Felix hummed thoughtfully, glancing in Saint's direction. "He likes you," he said out of nowhere, and Carmine nearly tripped over his own feet.

"What?"

"He likes you," Felix repeated. "He ate dinner with you. Went *shopping* with you. He even let you clean and wrap his wound. Trust me, Karma, he would not have done those things if he did not like you."

"Huh." Carmine considered Saint, on the far side of the room talking to Ivan. Warmth curled in his gut at the thought that Saint might actually like him, not just endure his company.

Saint glanced over and his eyes narrowed. Felix waved cheerfully and Saint glared at him, then pivoted on his heel and went to speak to Roderick.

"He'll think we're colluding," Carmine said, amused.

"Good," Felix replied. He gave him a conspiratorial grin. "Keep him on his toes."

David laughed at something and Felix's expression soured.

"That one," he muttered.

"Anything in particular, or you just don't like him?" Carmine inquired.

"I've heard… some things," Felix said. "I don't like to tell tales out of school, or believe rumors without basis, but he… bothers me." He rolled his shoulders and refocused on Carmine. "How long do you think you will be with Saint?"

"I don't know, honestly," Carmine admitted. "They're pushing the rivals-to-friends narrative, according to Coach, so he was saying two to three months, maybe, if Saint can stand me that long."

Felix's expression lightened. "I think he can. But I ask because that puts you with him for the holiday parties. You've already noticed he has… problems with people in his space, yes?"

"Yeah, that didn't escape me," Carmine said dryly. "Why'd you ask about the parties?"

"Ah. So Saint usually takes the Christmas party. We have it catered, all he has to do is open the door and let people in, but I just wanted to warn you that for the week or so before, he will be… a mess. So perhaps a little more patience even than usual would be good."

Carmine sighed. Why did people seem to think he was going to snap and unload all his frustrations on Saint? "Am I really that bad-tempered?"

Felix's lips twitched. "You do have a certain… reputation, *non*?"

"Yeah well, I've never been one to judge another for how they deal with their shit, okay? Saint needs extra patience, he'll get it. He'll get whatever he needs. Because—" Carmine faltered.

"Because it's Saint," Felix said softly, eyes still sharp on Carmine's face.

"Yeah," Carmine said. "He's going to be incredible. He already is, but God, when he hits his prime—" He shook his head. "I hope I'm around to see it."

Felix slapped him on the shoulder. "Come to lunch with us."

CARMINE AND FELIX WERE PLOTTING, Saint could *feel* it. He did his best to ignore them, talking to Roderick about assigning rookies and trying not to look anywhere but Roderick's craggy, honest face.

The team was in good spirits, even the rookies getting more comfortable. It would be a week or more before they knew who was staying and who would be sent back down, but in the meantime, Roderick and

Saint both had a good hunch which was which.

"How about Jason for Kasha?" Saint suggested. "I think they'd be a good fit."

Roderick nodded thoughtfully. "Kasha might even be interested in Jason's My Little Pony collection."

"*Hey!*" Jason yelped. "I heard that!"

"Good, you were meant to," Roderick shot back. "What grown man keeps a collection of toy ponies?"

David snickered. "I can think of a few kinds."

Saint threw him a warning look over Carmine's shoulder as he approached and David shut his mouth. Jason was sputtering.

"They're not *toys*, they're *collectibles*. They're worth actual money, Murph, and they're my retirement fund."

"You play professional hockey," Carmine said. "What kind of retirement are you planning?"

Jason glared at them.

"You have My Little Ponies?" Kasha asked, popping up beside Jason. "My little sister, she's play with those all the time when little. Sometimes I play too. Can I see?"

Jason shot Saint and Roderick a vindictive look and turned back to Kasha. "Of course you can," he told him with a slap on the back. "And these assholes aren't invited."

Carmine followed him into the hall, eyebrows lifted. "What's up?"

Saint headed for a conference room without answering. Inside, Carmine stepped to the side and Saint closed the door very quietly.

"Whoa, hey, you okay?" Carmine said. "You don't look—"

"Don't," Saint cut him off. "*Ever*. Do that again."

Carmine's eyebrows rose. "Sorry, what are we talking about?"

"*Protecting* me from my own teammate," Saint spat. He balled his fists, mostly to hide how his hands were shaking. "I am the goddamn captain of this team, and I don't need you shielding me like I'm some helpless infant, do you hear me?"

Carmine's eyebrows were in his hairline. "Is that—you thought that's what I was doing? Jesus Christ, Saint, I wasn't—"

"You were," Saint interrupted. "Whether you realized it or not, that's exactly what you were doing. You ended up being between us every single time we weren't moving. I'm the *captain*, Carmine. I have to be able to handle myself, make them respect *me*, not some... hired thug!" He snapped his mouth shut, horror flashing through him. *Fuck.* "I didn't mean—"

"Yes you did," Carmine said. His jaw

was clenched, eyes tight. "Good to know that's what you think of me, *Captain*. Are we done?"

Saint couldn't think of anything to say. He nodded silently. Carmine wrenched the door open and was gone immediately.

Great going, Saint. You fucked up again.

He sank into one of the chairs and put his head in his hands. *Fuck.*

MOST OF THE team was gone by the time Saint emerged from the conference room, a few players getting the last of their gear packed up. He made short work of changing and escaped out the side door, thinking hard.

He had to fix this. Carmine was living with him now, like it or not, although Saint wouldn't blame him if he came home to Carmine packing his belongings.

The house was silent when he opened the door, though. Carmine was still out, then. Saint wasn't sure if he was relieved or disappointed by that.

He stood in the kitchen, remembering Carmine's sure movements as he cooked and talked to Saint and bandaged his thumb, the way his voice had gone gentle as he'd poured the antiseptic on, how his eyes had crinkled at the corners when he'd made Saint laugh.

"I'm such an asshole," he said aloud. He breathed through his nose, counting to ten as he touched thumbs to fingers, but it wasn't helping. He had *no one* to talk to, to tell him what he should do. Roddy would sigh and be fatherly and disappointed. Felix would probably yell at him—he and Carmine were getting pretty cozy. No one else was in Saint's confidence except for Flynn, all the way down in Arizona, who didn't even know Carmine. He wished, miserably and for the umpteenth time, that he could call his mother.

An idea struck him and he pulled his phone out and dialed before he could think better of it. It rang three times and he was just about to chicken out when it clicked in his ear.

"Hello?"

"Hi, uh, Lavender?" Saint said.

"Saint!" Lavender said. She sounded absolutely delighted to hear from him. "Sweetheart, how are you?"

"Oh, um, I'm fine?" Saint managed. He took a breath. "Do you have a minute? It's okay if you don't, it's not important, I just—"

"Of course I do," Lavender said firmly.

"Let me get out of the sun. My knees were complaining at me anyway."

Saint smiled in spite of everything. "Are you gardening?"

"Every chance I get," Lavender said. "We're bringing you veggies and Carmine will probably make you some of his incredible stew, among other things."

Carmine's name recalled Saint to his unpleasant duty and he hesitated. This was a bad idea. This was the worst idea he'd possibly ever had. What the *hell* had he been thinking, calling Carmine's *mother* for advice? Now *she* was going to hate him too.

He took a shaky breath and reached for the counter as anxiety climbed in mounting waves through his chest, up his throat to strangle him.

"I'm—I shouldn't have—I should go."

"What? Saint, *wait*," Lavender said, and Saint hesitated, struggling to breathe. The room was spinning. "Are you okay, honey?"

"No," Saint whispered, and was faintly proud of his honesty. Of more pressing concern was the fact that his knees were about to let go, though, and he opted for the simplest expedient of sliding down the kitchen cupboard to land on the floor.

"Breathe," Lavender said sharply. "In through your nose, out through your mouth. Listen to the sound of my voice. Are you sitting down?"

"Yes ma'am," Saint husked.

"So polite," Lavender said, sounding amused and affectionate. "You sit there and breathe and listen to me for a minute. Whatever's going on in your head is not reality. You are safe. You are loved. You are *wanted*, okay?"

Tears stung Saint's eyes and he swallowed desperately around the rock in his throat. "I'm not—"

"You are." Lavender's voice held no room for debate. "You are good and kind. I've only talked to you three times and I can already tell that about you. None of the rest of it matters. *None* of it. Keep breathing for me. I'm going to tell you what I'm looking at right now. My garden is on the hill in front of our house, where it gets as much sun as possible. In Seattle, you have to fight for every scrap of sunlight you can. We terraced the beds going up the hill, so we could use every inch of ground available." Clothing rustled and Saint closed his eyes, listening to her voice.

"I'm sitting on the bench Diana bought for me two years ago." A smile dusted Lavender's voice and she sounded far away suddenly, lost in thought. "It was our thirtieth wedding anniversary and she wanted me to have a place I could rest in between weeding the turnips and tying the tomatoes. Steel is in the dirt at my feet, sound asleep. He's spent all morning swimming in the pond and catching Frisbees with Charlie, the little neighbor girl who comes over to help out and do odd chores. So of course now he's muddy and we'll have to give him a bath before we come down. For the life of me, I will never understand why dogs love swimming but hate baths."

The panic was receding, bit by bit, and Saint's next breath was steadier.

"I did something bad," he whispered.

"What did you do, Saint?" Lavender sounded nothing more than gently curious.

"I... hurt Carmine." Shame squirmed through Saint's stomach and he tipped his head back as nausea swirled. "I was—he... there's someone on the team. Carmine doesn't like him very much. *I* don't like him very much. But... he's team. And Carmine kept getting between us today, like he was keeping him from me, like I couldn't—" He closed his mouth abruptly and shook his head. "I told him I didn't need his protection. That—" This was the hardest part. "I... called him a... a hired thug."

"Ah. I imagine he didn't like that very much." There was no hostility in Lavender's voice, no anger or judgment, but guilt still made Saint squeeze his eyes shut.

"I'm sorry," he whispered. "I shouldn't have called."

"I'm glad you did, Saint," Lavender said. She sounded exactly the same as before, just as gentle and affectionate and kind. "What do you need from me?"

"I—I don't... I don't know? How do I fix this? What do I do? I keep *doing* this, I keep putting my foot in my mouth and I don't *mean* to, I don't mean to hurt him, b-but I have to make it right. How do I make it right?"

"Okay, sweetheart, here's what you're going to do."

7

Carmine stayed out a long time—after lunch with Felix and Roderick, during which he'd pushed down the anger and hurt and pretended everything was fine, he'd gone for a long walk, exploring downtown Portland. He liked this city, he was realizing, even with its high hipster ratio—everyone was friendly, welcoming, and he even got the occasional autograph request, but no one invaded his space. He bought a burrito from a street vendor and wandered, thinking.

He still missed Boston's cramped, narrow, twisty streets, the grimy buildings, the fans, the exuberance, even the smell of melting snow and exhaust. He wanted to be back in his tiny apartment, just him and Steel, secure on his team and in his role with them. There, he knew what people had

MICHAELA GREY

wanted of him, and he'd been able to deliver.

He'd been off-balance from day one in Portland. Bumped and jostled and swung this way and that until he didn't know up from down. Saint hated him. Resented him. Maybe didn't hate him. Maybe even liked him? Carmine couldn't keep up, couldn't follow the twists and turns of Saint's brain, but he was pretty certain Felix had been wrong.

Saint didn't like him. He'd made his opinion very clear in that conference room when they first met, and there was no reason for it to *hurt* like this. Carmine stifled a sigh, took the last bite of his burrito, and disposed of the wrapper before calling for a car.

Maybe Saint would kick him out as soon as he got there. Carmine leaned back against the seat as the driver negotiated the streets and thought. Had Saint been right? *Had* Carmine been shielding him from David? He didn't *think* he had, certainly hadn't *meant* to, but.... He went back over the events of the day, worked through every interaction they'd had, reexamined where he'd been standing in relation to Saint and David in every single instance.

"Oh *shit*," he groaned, letting his head fall to the rest with a thump. "Come *on*."

116

On top of everything else, now he had to apologize?

The house was quiet when Carmine let himself in. He prowled through it, poking his head into the main living room and kitchen, but there was no sign of Saint anywhere. Carmine didn't knock on the door to his wing.

He was pretty upset, he told himself as he headed for his bedroom. *Probably better to give him some more time to cool off.*

He was being a coward, he knew, but he didn't think he could face Saint yet, see the disappointed twist of his mouth, as if he'd tasted something bitter, as he stared at Carmine.

Safely in the quiet of his bedroom, he got comfortable with a book about the Steelers that he'd been meaning to read for awhile. He'd bite the bullet in the morning, make Saint see that he understood how he'd misstepped and it wouldn't happen again. Maybe Saint would let him make breakfast.

HE WOKE up early and padded down the hall and into the kitchen, scratching his head, jaw cracking with the force of his yawn. Still half-asleep, he didn't register the smell of burning until he stepped inside.

Carmine looked back sharply. "Say again?"

Saint gulped. "I—oh shit, I shouldn't have said that." He slumped in his chair. "Don't tell him?"

"I wouldn't," Carmine said, leaning forward. "But what did you mean by it?"

"I meant—" Saint was looking anywhere but at Carmine, fidgeting in place. Carmine waited as Saint worked through his internal battle and finally blurted, "I like you, okay?"

Silence fell between them, puddling in soft, velvety folds around their feet.

Carmine leaned back again, draping an arm over the chair. He could feel the smile tugging at his mouth. Saint was bright red to the tips of his ears, still determinedly not looking at him. He was tense in his seat, clearly on the edge of bolting.

"You... like me," Carmine said, testing the words.

"Just more than David," Saint said immediately.

Carmine waved that off. "Yeah, but you like me."

"More than David," Saint repeated. "It's important that that distinction is clear. I like you *more than David*."

Carmine grinned at him. "I knew you wouldn't be able to resist me forever." He leaned forward, pasting mock-solemnity on his face. "Saint, I just want you to know it's okay if you fall in love with me. Everyone does, eventually."

Saint opened and closed his mouth, blinking. "I—oh my God, you're fucking with me."

Carmine laughed out loud. "You're kind of an easy target, can you blame me?"

"I'm sorry," Saint said, and Carmine sobered. Saint's blush was receding, his eyes steady now as he met Carmine's. "I really am."

"So am I," Carmine admitted. "I was going to tell you today. I didn't... realize I was doing it. That's not an excuse, and I'm sorry I tried to defend you when you didn't need it."

They stared at each other. Finally, Saint's lips quirked.

"Okay," he said softly. "That's—okay, that's good. Thanks."

"I was going to make you breakfast," Carmine said. He pointedly sniffed the air. "You know humans aren't supposed to eat charcoal, right?"

Saint scowled at him. "I was trying to cook for *you*," he muttered. "My mom brought a box of pancake mix last time she visited and I thought—how hard could it be? Just add water, right?"

Just like that, they were back on solid ground. Carmine didn't hide his smile.

"How about you leave the cooking to me, and you can handle the coffee? Because let me tell you, this shit is amazing. I'm considering proposing."

"To me?" Saint sounded startled, and Carmine snickered.

"No, to the coffee. Grab the eggs from the fridge for me, let's get this party started."

THEY ATE breakfast in silence that was more comfortable than Carmine had expected. The worst of the shadows in Saint's eyes had eased, and even though he didn't say much, his body language was more relaxed, and he smiled at Carmine when their eyes met.

"Your hand," Carmine said when he was on his third cup of coffee. "Shit, did you change the bandage yourself?"

Saint looked rueful. "I tried to, last night. Turns out it's not that easy one-handed."

"If you want to go get the first-aid kit, I'll change it for you now," Carmine told him. He began gathering dishes as Saint obeyed, back in just a few minutes with the kit clasped to his chest, and they settled back in at the table.

Carmine unwrapped the bulky, clumsily applied bandage and inspected the cut. It was healing nicely, he was relieved to see as he cleaned the edges and put a new strip of gauze over it. "Does it hurt?"

Saint shook his head. "Not really, not anymore."

"Good. You'll be able to play tomorrow no problem."

Saint tensed at that.

"Hey," Carmine said, looking up. "Are you worried?"

"Not... not about my hand," Saint said. "Just... pre-game jitters. Nothing new and different. Happens every season." He shrugged.

Carmine gave him a smile, taped down the bandage, and sat back. "Oatmeal for breakfast and stay out of your way. Don't worry too much, okay? We'll be fine."

Saint nodded again, firming his jaw. "I still wish Coach would let me swap Torry for Kasha. I don't like having him on the first line for his first game with us."

"Not his first game ever, though," Carmine reminded him as he put away the supplies. "He'll be fine. Plus he's *good* on your line."

"He's *young*," Saint said. He tapped a finger on the table. "I just think he needs more experience. But it's not like I can really argue with Coach."

CARMINE KEPT an eye on Kasha during practice that day. The young Russian was in his usual high spirits, joking with Jason and several of the rookies. Now that he was getting comfortable with his teammates, he was revealing a very tactile side, always looking for contact from his favorite people. He didn't, Carmine was glad to see, so much as jostle Saint, although he got as close as he could without touching him.

Honestly, Carmine didn't see what the big deal was. Kasha was fast, talented, and smart. He was one of the few able to anticipate Saint's moves, although he wasn't completely there yet and still missed the occasional pass. Even with that, he showed glimmers of the talent he'd grow into, and his plays on the ice were crisp and precise.

Saint was still in a mood when they walked home that evening, hands in his pockets and eyes on the ground.

"Hey," Carmine said, taking a chance and gently jostling his elbow. Saint blinked and glanced up. "Tell me what you're thinking."

"Just trying to nail down plays for tomorrow," Saint said vaguely.

"Talk to me about the Racers," Carmine said.

Saint scowled. "I don't like them. They rely on strength and hard hits instead of playing a clean game. Keep your head up out there—even with your size, they'll try and take you out."

"I'll be fine," Carmine said, but Saint's concern warmed him. "Anyone in particular I should watch for?"

"Spencer McWhorter is dirty. Even get close to him and he'll embellish all over the place. So watch yourself around him, don't make contact unless you know you can keep it clean and legal."

"Got it."

"Their captain, Jefferson, doesn't have a grip on his team. They're not as cohesive as they should be, because he doesn't mentor the rookies properly. That makes them unpredictable. Sometimes they're really good, other times they're all over the place. I don't know which version we're facing tomorrow."

"We'll find out," Carmine said. He took a step ahead and turned to walk backward, watching Saint. His mouth was tucked downward, eyes on the ground again. "This

Carmine nodded. Having met Jefferson, he was inclined to agree.

"Didn't they lose one of their star players in a trade to Colorado a few years back?" he asked. "There was a whole stink about it."

"Gunner Ryan," Saint said. "Yeah, it was ugly. He's talented, too, but he didn't fit with the team. He was a loose cannon there, but he seems to have settled in well with the Direwolves." He paused the reel and pointed again. "There. That's Henrique, their main enforcer. He's not vicious, but he's without remorse. He'll run over anything in his path."

"Yeah, and he throws a mean punch." Carmine rubbed his jaw.

Saint hit play again. "This asshole, though," he muttered, indicating Spencer. "Fucker tripped one of my rookies last year, sent him headfirst into the boards. He missed eight games with a concussion." His expression was tight, mouth drawn.

Carmine hopped up to turn the meat, then sat back down. "Any particular tricks I need to know about?"

"He likes to go after the forwards on the face-off, when they're focused on the puck." Saint scrubbed his face. "I feel like throwing up."

"You getting sick?" Carmine asked, alarmed.

"First game nerves. I'll be fine tomorrow." Saint dropped his hands and summoned a wan smile. "It smells good."

Carmine was learning Saint's signals, and he followed his lead, chattering away about what he was making while he cooked and Saint watched, leaning back in his chair.

After dinner, which Saint didn't eat enough of, Carmine refused to let him help wash dishes, shooing him away gently.

To his surprise, though, Saint stood his ground, lifting a stubborn chin.

"You cooked, that means I clean. Even *I* know that much. So *you* go sit down and let me do this."

Carmine huffed a laugh and wandered into the main den. After a few minutes of idle poking around, he discovered a very nice gaming system below the huge flatscreen, and promptly sat down on the carpet to go through the games.

Saint found him there when he was done, Fortnite ready and waiting for him as Carmine got comfortable on the couch.

"Perfect timing," Carmine greeted him. "You didn't tell me you gamed!"

"Because I don't," Saint said. "It's for the rookies. Keeps them out of the way when it's my turn to host." But he sat down beside Carmine and accepted the controller, eyeing it warily. "I've never played this before."

"It's easy," Carmine said. "I'll show you."

THEY SPENT the rest of the evening shooting things and occasionally each other, and Carmine hid his satisfaction at the way Saint's shoulders gradually loosened, until he was leaning forward and glaring at the TV, focused on getting it exactly right.

"No, no!" he shouted as he got blown up again. "Goddammit, I hate this game."

"We can try a different one," Carmine suggested.

Saint gave him a real smile. "Thanks, but I think I should probably sleep." He climbed off the couch and Carmine followed suit. Saint shifted his feet, clearly trying to find words. Carmine waited. "This was nice," Saint finally said. "Usually—the day before a game I'm usually too wired to do anything. So... thanks for helping me turn my brain off, I guess."

"Any time," Carmine said, and Saint smiled at him again.

"Goodnight."

8

GAME DAY dawned misty and overcast, the sun too weak to burn off the fog as Carmine ambled out of his bedroom, yawning. Saint was at the stove when he wandered in.

"Coffee's made," he said without looking up from what he was stirring, and Carmine made a pathetically grateful noise.

He flopped down at the table with his mug and Saint set a bowl of oatmeal in front of him. Carmine blinked blearily at it for a minute before his brain finally recalibrated.

"Oh. Um, thanks."

Saint shrugged as he sat down opposite and began to eat in methodical bites.

The oatmeal *was* pretty good, although it could be better, in Carmine's opinion. He cleaned his bowl and went back for seconds, then sat back and watched Saint as he ate.

His entire focus was on the food, unwavering, and Carmine wondered briefly what it was like to have that kind of laser intensity and drive.

Lonely, he thought, and took his bowl to the sink.

HE STAYED out of Saint's way until it was time to head for the rink. When he joined him in the hall, Saint looked sharp in a dark gray suit, cut to fit his lean form and hug his muscled legs. He acknowledged Carmine with a nod and opened the door.

Felix was waiting in the driveway, and Carmine blinked at the car. "Is that an SUV? Butterfly, man, do you seriously drive a soccer mom's car?"

Felix glared at him as Saint strode around to get in the front seat. "It's a fucking Porsche Cayenne, you goddamn heathen, and it's not my fault my sisters have kids, okay?"

Carmine snickered and climbed in the back. He buckled as Felix said something in French to Saint, who replied quietly. Carmine waited until they were done and then leaned forward.

"Hey Mom, can I have some animal crackers?"

Felix whipped around, stare hot enough to melt leather, but it worked—Saint laughed. Shock replaced the outrage on Felix's face, and he glanced at Saint, then back at Carmine, eyes narrow and considering.

"If you behave, you might even get a juice box," he finally said, and Carmine fist-pumped, grinning. Felix returned the grin, real warmth behind it, and put the car in drive.

Saint said nothing on the way to the rink, gazing out the window, but his shoulders were loose.

"Pap stroll time," Felix said cheerfully when he parked.

"One at a time or do you go in groups?" Carmine inquired, straightening his jacket as he stepped out.

"Saint goes first," Felix said. "I'll walk with you."

They followed Saint past the photographers who called out greetings to them and snapped pictures but didn't try to stop them. Carmine kept a pleasant expression on his face but didn't smile—it wouldn't do to look *too* friendly. He had a reputation to maintain, after all.

Saint went straight to the trainers, who put him on a table for a massage. Carmine and Felix changed into their compression gear and then he tailed Felix into the kitchen, where a few of the guys were clustered. Felix hip-bumped Kasha out of the way to dig in the refrigerator for a bottle of Gatorade. Kasha turned, saw Carmine, and his eyes lit up as he slung an arm around his neck.

"Karma!"

"Hey kid," Carmine said, looking for nerves. Kasha seemed as happy as usual, bright and cheerful. "Ready to kick some ass?"

Kasha nodded, bouncing on his toes. "Play two-touch with us?"

"Yeah, sure," Carmine agreed, and followed the group into the hall. Saint joined them about halfway through the game, stepping into the circle beside Felix. They played until their muscles were loose, hooting and teasing Kasha when a bounce went wrong and the ball got stuck in the rafters.

"Who's getting it?" Saint asked, hands on hips. No one would catch his eye, and Saint sighed. "Carmine, I need your height."

Carmine went where Saint pointed, vaguely curious, and crouched when Saint told him to. Saint climbed him like a tree, quick and effortless up to his shoulders, where he balanced as Carmine braced himself.

"Up," he said, reaching out and brushing the ball with his fingertips. "I'm almost—"

Carmine straightened his legs, stepped closer, and went up onto his tiptoes. Saint grunted in triumph as he dislodged the ball and it fell, narrowly missing Carmine's head. He bent his knees and jumped lightly off, landing behind Carmine and smiling at him as he turned.

"Good teamwork," he said, and headed for the kitchen.

Felix was looking at him appraisingly when Carmine turned. "I'm never wrong," he said, and Carmine snorted out loud.

"Whatever, man."

FANS WERE TRICKLING into the building above them as they changed and got into their gear. Music started playing, a deep, thumping bass designed to crank up the energy of the arena. Carmine ignored it, falling into his usual comfortable routine of putting on his pads, settling his chest protector, jumping up and down a few times to get it all solidly in place.

At the stall beside him, Kasha seemed to be having difficulty getting his elbow pads on. Carmine stepped in close and took over as Kasha rotated his arm with a grateful noise. This near, Carmine could see lines of stress in Kasha's face, tightness around his eyes.

"Hey," he said quietly, under the noise of the locker room, and Kasha looked up. "You okay, kid?"

Kasha's smile was slightly lopsided and he bobbed his head, sharp and jerky, before flicking his eyes up and past Carmine. "I'm not want to disappoint him," he said in a low tone, and Carmine glanced over his shoulder to where Saint was taping his stick with single-minded focus.

"You won't," Carmine said, just as quietly. "You're here for a reason, okay? Saint likes you. You're going to be fine. Hey, is your girlfriend here?"

Somehow, that was the wrong thing to say. Kasha's expression clouded but he nodded again. "She's in box."

"Cool, maybe we can meet after the game. We're gonna have to go out for drinks to celebrate, after all."

Kasha's face eased and he almost smiled. "We gonna do this."

"Fuck yeah we are," Carmine told him. "We're gonna do this. Let's go!"

CARMINE LINED up for the anthem, barely hearing it as he watched the other team across the ice. There was the captain, looking solemn and focused as he stood at attention. Down the line was the enforcer Saint had mentioned, Henrique. *Not mean, but no mercy.* Carmine had played him before, and respected the hell out of him. He had no intention of ending up on the wrong side of his fists tonight. And there, that was the D-man—Spencer—Saint disliked so intensely. Carmine didn't remember anything about him—he was new to the NHL and had been called up in the second half of the season to play for the Racers. There was a mean slant to his mouth Carmine didn't like the look of.

When the song's last notes faded away, the lines broke up and Carmine skated off without looking back. Felix was in his crease, warming up, unrecognizable in all his bulky gear.

"Watch 23," Carmine told him as he circled the net and scooped up a puck. He bounced it off the wall and went after it, skated in a wide loop and tried to sink it over Felix's knee.

Felix slapped it down easily. "He a problem?"

Carmine pulled up next to him. "Might

be. Don't know yet." He took off again, enjoying the firm ice under his blades.

SAINT WON the face-off with ease, sending the puck behind him to Carmine, who caught it and raced through the neutral zone toward the offensive zone, three players hassling him the whole way. Almost to the net, Carmine deked sideways and knocked the puck over to Kasha, who wound up and fired. The puck made a loud *ding* as it bounced off the post and the fans groaned.

Carmine was too busy going in pursuit to listen to them. The Racers were tough, and they'd clearly been working on speed in the off-season. He could already tell they were going to make the Seabirds work for this.

First game of the season or not, Carmine was determined not to lose. He cleared knots, took players to the boards, drove hard through opposition, and parked himself in front of the Racers' goalie time and again, waiting for Saint to get him the puck. In this position, he could watch the way Saint danced around the bigger players, seeming to barely touch the ice.

Five minutes into the first period, Roddy scored off a backhand from Saint.

The goal horn went off, the fans roaring their approval, and Carmine collided with Roddy, who was hugging Saint and Jason as Kasha barreled toward them.

"Good hustle, boys!" Saint shouted. He was dripping sweat but not even out of breath. "Keep it up, let's ride this edge!" All the nerves had disappeared, and the captain was clearly in control, confident and strong, the leader everyone looked to. He met Carmine's eyes over Jason's shoulder and his smile widened.

But despite their best efforts, no one else was able to score for the rest of the period, and thirty seconds into the next, a forward for the Racers scored on Felix. Right after that, a winger caught a bouncing puck and slammed it home five-hole and the crowd booed as the Racers celebrated.

SAINT MADE the rounds after Coach gave them the standard pep talk during the second intermission. He stopped and spoke to Kasha, Jason beside him, for a few minutes, then patted his arm and moved on.

"Okay?" he said to Carmine in a low tone. His hair was damp and curled with sweat, clinging to his skull, and he looked young but every inch the captain.

Carmine gave him a wide grin, retaping his stick. "No worries here, Cap. Still got another twenty minutes to turn it around, eh? Focus on the rookies—I'm fine."

Saint nodded and went to the next stall.

BACK ON THE ICE, they lined up for puck drop in the neutral zone. Saint lost it this time, the captain of the Racers just barely managing to squirt it between his skates to a waiting defenseman. They charged across the blue line, straight for Felix. Halfway there, Saint took the puck back, sent it to Roddy, and back they went, toward the other goalie. Carmine set up in position, watching eagle-eyed as Saint fought off two forwards, ducking around and past them, to slap the puck across to Kasha.

Who froze.

Carmine watched, dismayed, as Kasha looked at the goal, at Saint, down at the puck, and didn't move. *Do something, kid,* he mentally screamed, and then it was too late. Spencer hit him from the side, knocking him off his skates and sending him skidding across the ice. Kasha bounced off the boards but he was scrambling back to his feet almost immediately, and then Carmine couldn't spare time to watch him anymore, because Roddy needed him and Jason. He snapped into action, but whatever had happened to Kasha seemed to have infected the team. Their timing was off, the other lines hesitant and unbalanced.

Carmine watched Kasha's profile on the bench as the third line battled it out in front of them. Kasha stared at the ground, mouth downturned in misery, and didn't look up as the Racers scored again.

They lost 3-1, and there was silence as they trooped down the tunnel to the dressing room.

Saint took the brunt of the media, of course, and Carmine kept an eye on him as he got undressed and ready to shower. Saint's media mask was firmly in place, his eyes steady and calm as he answered questions with carefully chosen soundbites that gave away nothing.

Carmine heard Kasha's name and his head snapped up.

"—Volkov, and his obvious inexperience?" the reporter was saying.

Saint's eyes narrowed briefly. "Arkady Volkov is a valued member of this team. We've all made our share of mistakes. I'm pleased to play on a line with him."

Kasha grabbed his towel and escaped into the bathroom. Carmine swore to himself and followed, where he found Kasha hunched under the spray, every line of his body tight.

"Hey," Carmine said gently, under the noise of the spray and other players getting clean.

Kasha didn't look at him.

Carmine sighed. "Come out with me tonight."

Kasha shook his head.

"Come on," Carmine said. "You need to talk to someone about this."

"Nadia," Kasha said, his voice a rusty creak. "Have to get her home. She not like go alone."

"Okay," Carmine said. "But Kash… we didn't lose because of you."

Kasha spun. His eyes were red. "Yes we did," he hissed, and stomped away.

When Carmine went back to the dressing room, the reporters had cleared out and Saint was sitting next to Kasha, talking to him quietly. Carmine moved a few feet away from his stall to give them privacy while he got dressed, watching out of the corner of his eye. Kasha's elbows were on his knees, head down, and he seemed impossibly young and fragile, ready to shatter.

After a few minutes, Saint stood and crossed to Carmine. "I'm ordering a car and getting him and his girlfriend back to their place," he said in a low voice. "I'll be home late."

"I won't wait up." Carmine searched Saint's face. There was disappointment there, but none of the guilt and recrimination he would have expected. "What about you? Are you okay?"

"I will be," Saint said. He mustered a small smile. "Truth be told, it's good to have it out of the way. First game, first loss—it's done and now we can go from here. I'll see you in the morning."

"Take care of him," Carmine said, and Saint nodded.

FELIX TOOK CARMINE HOME. The mood was subdued, and Carmine hated it, hated the misery in Felix's expression, but they didn't say much.

The house was quiet and dark, and Carmine turned on a few lamps so Saint would be able to see when he got home. Then he assembled a sandwich with cold roast beef, ate it over the sink, and finally went to bed.

9

HE WOKE to his phone buzzing. Carmine yawned, slapping at it through the usual sleep-fog, but it kept going. Not his alarm, he realized after a minute of fumbling, and managed to answer.

"H'lo."

"What's your gate code?" Diana asked briskly, and Carmine's eyes snapped wide open. He sat bolt upright in the bed.

"Ma? You—are you *here*?"

"Well obviously," Diana said. "Why else would we need your gate code? What is it?"

"Um, shit. Uh… it's 1408." Carmine swung his legs out of bed and stumbled from his bedroom, trying desperately to pull his brain online. "Ma, you're early. Saint might still be asleep. You're gonna have to be quiet."

"We got an early start," Diana said.

"Don't worry, we won't disturb him. Come on out, we brought you presents."

Carmine swore to himself and scrambled for the front door. He collided with Saint halfway there, coming out of the kitchen, and swore again, steadying him with a hand on his elbow.

"Sorry," he said, "sorry, sorry. I—shit, did they wake you?"

Saint's eyes were wide and his breath was coming short and sharp, and Carmine remembered with a nauseating jolt how much he hated strangers in his space.

"It's my parents," Carmine said urgently. His hand was still on Saint's elbow, but Saint wasn't pulling away. He seemed frozen in place. "Saint, listen to me, it's just my moms. Remember they were coming down this weekend?"

Saint blinked. His mouth worked and he reached out, tangling his fingers in the hem of Carmine's T-shirt like he wasn't even aware he was doing it. "Just—them?" he managed.

"Yeah, I mean I assume," Carmine said. "Look—why don't you go in your bedroom for a bit? I'll let them in, show them around the rest of the place, and get the worst of it out of the way. You can come out later and eat breakfast with us, or you can stay in your wing the entire time."

"But that's rude," Saint objected. He was still holding the hem of Carmine's shirt, and Carmine didn't dare move.

Instead, he blew a gentle raspberry. Saint blinked.

"They don't care about rude or polite," Carmine said. "They'll understand if you'd rather not meet them at all, okay? In fact, I'll take them out to breakfast. Get them out of here so you can adjust."

"No," Saint said. He shook his head and let go of Carmine's shirt. "That's... not right. I'll go—in my room for a bit." He looked up, his eyes soft in the early sun slanting through the window. "Thank you."

The doorbell rang and they both jerked.

"Go," Carmine told him, and Saint went.

SAINT PACED his small living room, listening to the voices. They were too low for him to make out much, and he couldn't help but wonder what they were saying. Was Carmine telling them what a neurotic mess Saint was, and why he wasn't there to welcome them?

He shook his head, immediately dispelling the thought. Carmine wouldn't do that.

The voices faded as Carmine took them into the kitchen and Saint felt suddenly, deeply alone. *Don't be stupid*, he told himself fiercely. *That's how you like it.* But he didn't want to be alone. He wanted to be with Carmine. All he had to do was deal with strangers in his space.

But they're not strangers, not really. You know Lavender, don't you? And Carmine adores them both. You can do this.

Saint squared his shoulders, set his jaw, and opened his door.

THE CLICK of nails on wood was his only warning before a gray pitbull rounded the corner and stopped dead at the sight of him.

"Oh," Saint breathed. "Oh, you're beautiful, aren't you?"

Steel considered him for a long moment and then came to a decision. He bounded forward and Saint bent, putting out his hands. Steel shoved his cold nose into them, wagging his tail so hard his whole body wriggled, and Saint went to his knees, unable to stop the smile.

"You're gonna like it here," he told him, and Steel flung himself onto his back, begging for belly rubs. Saint laughed quietly and obliged.

They were still like that when footsteps sounded. Saint looked up at the woman in the doorway and immediately scrambled to his feet.

"Uh, sorry," he said, knowing he sounded inane.

"It's your house," she said, and Saint *knew* that voice. She'd talked him through a panic attack just a few days before.

"Lavender," he said, and Lavender tilted her head and smiled brilliantly. She was a small white woman in her early fifties, comfortably curved, with pure white hair tucked up in a neat bun. Bright blue eyes twinkled at him.

"Can I hug you?" she asked, and Saint blinked hard several times.

"I—yeah. Please." He stepped forward as she held out her arms. Steel danced around them, shoving his nose against Saint's leg in a blatant plea for pets, but Saint ignored him. Lavender smelled warm and sweet, like flowers and freshly turned dirt and just-baked bread, and she held on like hugging Saint was the only thing she ever wanted to do.

When he finally eased back, Saint's eyes were stinging. "Um. Hi," he said, and Lavender reached up and cupped his face, smiling.

"Hi," she said. "It's so good to finally

meet you! I see you've met Steel, too. Don't believe him when he tells you he's terribly neglected."

Saint laughed quietly and bent to pet Steel, who wriggled all over with transcendent joy at the attention.

"Would you like to come meet Diana?" Lavender asked, and somehow Saint found himself following her into the kitchen.

Carmine was at the stove, his eyebrows going up when Saint came in and a smile tugging at his mouth.

"Ma," he said, not looking away from Saint, "this is my captain, Saint Levesque. Saint, my other mother, Diana."

Diana rose from the table. She was at least fifteen years older than Lavender, Saint realized as he shook her hand. Smile lines fanned out around eyes so dark they were almost black, crinkling soft brown skin like fine crepe paper. Her hair was a riotous black cloud streaked with gray, and when she smiled, Saint returned it instinctively.

"I've been hearing a lot about you from both my son and my wife," Diana said. "Thank you for letting us crash your place like this."

Saint ducked his head. "It's Carmine's place too, at least for now, and you're welcome anytime."

Steel bounced back into the room and Carmine's eyes lit up.

"There he is! How do you like the place, huh buddy?"

Steel wriggled happily and Carmine laughed, bending to pet him.

"Oh, Saint," he said when he straightened. "Coffee maker is busted, I think."

"Yeah," Saint agreed. "It spat black goo at me when I tried to start it earlier. That's what I was doing when—" He waved a hand vaguely.

"Let me see it," Lavender said.

Carmine pointed and she unplugged it and carried it to the table.

"I know how you need your coffee," she said, fingers busy dismantling the coffee maker, "so why don't you take your car and go get some for everyone while I work on this?"

Carmine lit up. "My car! Saint, you have to see my car, come on, come see." He nearly dragged Saint down the hall to the door.

Saint whistled at the gleaming, low slung, jewel blue car parked just outside.

"Fancy."

Carmine feigned outrage. "*Fancy*? My pride and joy, light of my life—don't tell Steel—and that's all you've got?"

"Very fancy?" Saint tried, and laughed

out loud at the look on Carmine's face. "Sorry, man, I don't know jack about cars."

Carmine smoothed a hand over the spotless hood. "1971 Hemi Cuda with the cloth top. This baby's older than us, and I found her in a barn outside Boston eight years ago. Fixed her up myself in my spare time. Get in, I need caffeine."

Saint obeyed, buckling as Carmine inspected the interior.

The engine started sweetly, settling into a steady purr that vibrated through Saint's bones.

Carmine rolled down the driveway and through the gate onto the street. He was a careful, steady driver, hands loose and calm on the wheel. He slanted a look at Saint. "You okay?"

"Yeah," Saint said, faintly surprised to realize it was true. "It caught me off guard but I like your moms. Anyway, I need to get better about stuff like that."

"It would make things easier for you," Carmine agreed, taking a turn smoothly. "But it's what you're comfortable with, you know? Anyway, enough about that—how's Kasha?"

Saint grimaced. "Not great. He's blaming himself pretty hardcore for last night."

Carmine nodded. "I hope you told him it was a team effort."

"Of course. But he's convinced he let me down."

"Was his girlfriend—what's her name—there? Supportive?"

"Nadia." Saint sighed. "She was there."

Carmine pulled into the drive-through and quirked an eyebrow at him. "That doesn't sound encouraging."

"I'm sure she's a very nice person," Saint said, and both Carmine's eyebrows went up.

"That bad?"

"Not *bad*," Saint said hurriedly. "Just sort of... impatient? Like she wanted him to get over it faster because she was tired of hearing about it." He squirmed. "I just made her sound like a total bitch."

Carmine looked disapproving. "It's his first game with this team, and especially playing with you. He froze when he had a chance at a goal. He's allowed to take as much time as he needs to deal with that."

"I told him that," Saint said. "He's gonna need a little more attention from us for a bit, I think."

"Not a problem. What do you want?"

Saint blinked at him. "What do you mean?"

"Coffee," Carmine said, lips twitching. "What do you want?"

"Right!" Saint directed his attention to the menu, keeping his thoughts very firmly away from what he wanted.

THE PROBLEM WAS, he couldn't stop thinking about it. What did he want? The answer to that question was sitting in the seat beside him, currently charming the drive-through employee into extra whipped cream. He caught Saint's eye and grinned, unrepentant.

"I'll work it off at the rink today."

Saint tried to look disapproving but had a feeling he missed the mark, judging by the way Carmine's smile widened.

God, that smile was a lethal weapon. It lit Carmine's agate eyes from within, set them to dancing, and when he tucked his tongue into his cheek and that dimple appeared—

"Incoming!" Carmine said, and shoved a drink holder into Saint's hands. "That one's yours," Carmine added, tapping one of the lids.

Saint made an appreciative noise and balanced the drinks as Carmine left the parking lot and headed for the house.

He was developing a crush on Carmine. This was bad. This was very bad. Fraternizing with a teammate was the worst idea ever, even assuming Carmine was queer, let alone interested.

At the house, Carmine parked and took the tray from Saint. "It's okay if you need to hide in your room for awhile," he said.

"Hmm? Oh." He thought Saint was being quiet because of their guests. Saint mustered a smile. "I'll be fine. Do you want me to help make breakfast?"

"Well, I want it to be edible," Carmine said, dimple flashing. "So that's a no."

They were laughing as they stepped from the car. He could do this, Saint told himself, following him inside. Carmine never had to know about Saint's stupid crush. All he had to do was keep his feelings locked down, which wouldn't be hard—he did that anyway.

Lavender had the coffee maker reassembled and it was gurgling happily on the counter when they came into the kitchen.

"Oh," Saint said, looking down at his cup and then up at Carmine, who laughed out loud.

"Clogged pipe," Lavender said cheerfully. "Which one's mine?" She plucked the cup Carmine indicated from the tray and took a sip, sighing in appreciation.

"I'm on breakfast duty," Carmine said. "Saint and I have to go to the rink this afternoon, though. Game tomorrow. How long are you guys staying?"

"Well, we'll stay for the game at the very least," Diana said. "We've already booked a hotel for tonight."

"Oh, you don't have to—" Saint protested.

"Nonsense," Diana said firmly. "We'll sleep better there anyway. And I want to meet your teammates."

"I'm not introducing either of you to the team," Carmine said. "You'll just corrupt their innocent minds."

Saint laughed at that blatant falsehood and both women snickered.

10

THE MORNING PASSED PEACEFULLY. Lavender and Diana left to find a farmers' market and explore the city, and Saint curled up on the couch, Steel beside him. Carmine made disgusted noises about dogs not being allowed on furniture but Saint gave him pleading eyes and Carmine subsided, muttering.

"You're going to spoil my dog rotten," he said, stretching his legs out.

"Maybe he deserves it," Saint countered. Steel's ears were silky-soft and he made little grunting noises in his sleep. It was possible Saint was a little bit in love.

Saint's phone dinged, the distinctive sound of the NHL app updating, and Carmine's did the same, beside him. They both pulled them out and Saint's eyebrows climbed at the headline.

TORONTO WOLVERINES FORWARD ADAM CARON COMES OUT AS GAY

"What the shit?" Carmine said.

Saint started reading. Adam Caron had called a press conference to announce his return to the Wolverines after an injury at the end of last season.

"He nearly went blind," Saint mumbled.

"There's a video," Carmine said, and held up his phone. Saint scooted over so they could both watch the small screen.

Adam was sitting at a table filled with microphones. He had dark hair swept back off a high forehead and blue eyes full of fear and determination, and Saint couldn't breathe.

"Thank you for coming," Adam said. "I have two things to announce, and then we'll have a few questions." He took a deep breath, squaring his shoulders. Beside him, his coach had his arms crossed, looking formidable but content. "The first thing is that I'm happy to say I've signed a deal with the Wolverines for two years, so I'll be in Toronto a while longer."

Everyone clapped, and Adam ducked his head, smiling. When he looked up, the smile was gone, replaced by determination.

"The second thing is… I'm gay." The words fell into silence. Adam shifted his weight, glancing at his coach, who didn't move.

He did it, Saint thought. He was dizzy, Carmine's shoulder comfortingly solid against his own.

"I'll take questions now," Adam said.

Carmine turned the video off and Saint sat up, recalled to himself.

"We're playing them next month," Carmine said.

"I want to talk to him," Saint said.

Carmine nodded. "Of course."

"Dinner. Maybe? Not here. But, um. We could... go out."

"Sure, whatever you want."

"Will you come?"

Carmine's eyes snapped up to his. "Me? But—"

"Please," Saint said. "I'm not—you know how I am with people. You... you're good with them. You charm them. Adam will like you. I just—I want to talk to him."

"Yeah," Carmine said softly. "Yeah, okay. I can do that."

"Okay." Saint nodded and pushed himself to his feet. "I'm going to get ready for practice."

THEY WALKED to the rink together in comfortable silence, although Saint could feel Carmine sneaking glances at him.

"Spit it out," Saint finally said, sighing.

"Just making sure you're actually okay about my parents being here," Carmine admitted.

Saint stopped, irritation prickling his skin. "I'm not a child," he said flatly.

Carmine blinked. "No, I know, but—"

"But nothing," Saint interrupted. "Listen, I freaked out a bit. It's not a big deal, I got over it. You helped me, and I appreciate it. But you don't have to baby me, and I swear to God if you try to shelter or protect me—"

"Yeah, no," Carmine said, holding up his hands. "We've had *this* conversation. I remember. I didn't mean it that way, okay? I just—they can be a lot, and I'm already imposing on your hospitality."

Saint studied his face. Sincerity shone from it, and Saint chewed his lip.

"You're not imposing," he finally said.

Carmine snorted rudely. "Yes I am."

"No, you'd be imposing if I didn't want you there," Saint said, and immediately regretted it.

Carmine's eyes went wide. "You—wait, what?"

Saint hunched his shoulders and started walking. "Forget it."

"Yeah, that's not happening," Carmine said, grinning. He fell into step beside Saint. "So first I'm more team than David and now you actually want me in your house?" He nudged Saint with an elbow again. "It's okay to admit you're falling for me, man. Really."

"Fuck off," Saint said, ducking his head to hide the smile. "God, you're awful."

"Yeah, and you like me," Carmine said cheerfully.

I really do, Saint thought, and lengthened his stride. This, of course, did not deter Carmine, whose legs were longer than Saint's, and he kept pace effortlessly, still chortling occasionally.

At the rink, the players were gathering in the meeting room. Saint and Carmine were greeted loudly, and Saint's eyes went straight to Kasha, sitting in the corner. He glanced at Carmine, who nodded fractionally, and peeled off to go talk to him as Carmine stopped to speak to Felix.

Kasha looked up and gave Saint a faint approximation of his usual blinding smile as he sat down.

"Hey," Saint said. "How are you doing?"

Kasha lifted a shoulder. "Alright. I'm sorry about—"

"No," Saint interrupted. Kasha's eyes widened. "Don't apologize to me again for last night, understand? It happened, it's over. No one blames you."

"I blame me," Kasha said miserably, folding his lanky frame in on itself.

"I know," Saint said. "But everyone fucks up, okay? Everyone. My first rookie game, I passed to the other team."

Kasha looked up. "You?"

"Me," Saint agreed. He was able to smile at the memory now, but at the time he'd felt flayed alive by the horrified embarrassment. "It wasn't just an intercepted pass; that would have been understandable. No, this was me somehow managing to send the puck to a forward on the other team, and he immediately scored."

Kasha almost smiled. "That's... bad."

"Right?" Saint said. He gave Kasha a conspiratorial smile. "If you ask Carmine, I'll bet he'd have an even worse story about his own fuckups when he was a rookie."

"Worse than you passing the puck to the opposition?" Carmine asked, flinging himself into the seat on the other side of Kasha.

"How do you even know about that?" Saint complained, but Kasha was laughing, tension bleeding from him.

Carmine gave him a cheeky grin. "I do my homework, Saint Hockey."

"Well, go on then," Saint said, fighting the warmth spreading in his chest at the thought of Carmine reading about him, searching out information to know him better. "Tell the rookie a few stories. I *know* you've got some."

Carmine put a pious hand over his heart. "I have never once in my life fucked up," he intoned. "I am a paragon of virtue and purity."

"Where did you even learn a word like paragon?" Saint countered. "Don't you have to be able to read to know words like that?"

Carmine clutched his chest. "Kasha, defend my honor."

"You have no honor," Kasha retorted, and that was a genuine smile on his face.

"From both sides!" Carmine said, sagging in his seat as if mortally wounded, and Saint and Kasha shared a grin.

Flanahan cleared his throat. "Hospital, Saint?"

Saint nodded and stood, turning to face the players.

"We're organizing the usual trip to the hospital next month," he said. "I need at least ten volunteers. If you don't step up, you may find yourself volunteered, so I hope you like kids. Raise your hand if you want to go."

Several hands went up, Felix, Roddy, and Jason among them—his usuals. He was pleasantly surprised to see Carmine's hand, Kasha waving his beside him, but even more surprised to see David holding up his. A few other players raised their hands too, and Saint made note of everyone.

"I'll be in touch with each of you individually," he said. "Be prepared to spend an entire afternoon there."

"Now," Flanahan said. "Let's talk about yesterday."

A collective chorus of groans went up.

"Or we could do bag-skates until someone pukes," Flanahan said, eyes gleaming. "Which do you prefer?"

"Talk!" came the chorus.

Flanahan spent the next hour breaking down every play they'd made the night before. Saint settled in beside Kasha again to listen, watching the team. For all Flanahan's bluster, the man knew hockey inside and out. Maybe he couldn't motivate the team as much as Saint would like, but that's what the captain and alternates were for, and he could definitely teach.

Saint was pleased to see most of the players paying close attention to the diagrammed plays and explanations of what had gone wrong. Flanahan made sure to praise the plays that went right as well, especially singling Kasha out for his passes to Saint and the way he'd protected the puck.

Kasha ducked his head, a blush darkening his fair skin, but Saint could see the hint of another smile pulling on his mouth.

"Let's hit the ice, people!" Flanahan finally said, clapping. "Those drills won't run themselves!"

A loud groan went up as players filtered from the room and headed for the lockers. Saint found himself beside David.

"You like hospitals?" he asked.

"Nah, but kids love me," David said. He was watching several rookies with a gleam in his eye.

"No pranking the babies," Saint said automatically, and David scowled.

"It's a perk of being a vet, Cap, c'mon—"

"Not unless Felix asks for your help," Saint said flatly, leaving no room for argument. "No one on this team pulls the slightest trick without his knowledge. You don't like it, take it up with him."

David made a face. "He doesn't like *me*."

Can't imagine why not.

Saint said nothing, walking a little faster until he was beside Felix. "Don't let David help with any pranks," he said in French, keeping his voice low.

Felix didn't look at him. "I wouldn't dream of it."

TRUE TO HIS DIABOLICAL THREAT, Flanahan bag-skated them until a rookie threw up, and then refused to let them leave the rink until he'd shouted at them a while longer about their miserable defense and how Felix couldn't carry it on his own.

"I try," Felix sighed, somehow able to talk despite being as wrung out as the rest of them. "But I am just one man, no?"

"Shut up," Carmine wheezed, hands on knees. "I'll show you defense, *God.*"

"I wish you would!" Felix shot back, grinning. Carmine shoved weakly at him and Felix shoved back, making Carmine slide sideways on the ice.

"Enough!" Flanahan ordered. "Get showered, get the fuck out of here. Be here in the morning for skate—*not* optional. I'm shuffling the lines and if you're not here, you're not playing tomorrow night."

"Yes Coach," a few players mumbled, and they were free.

THEY HAD dinner with Lavender and Diana, Carmine grilling steaks on the patio with Steel happily roaming the huge yard. Carmine kept an eye on Saint, watching for signs of stress, but Saint's eyes were calm when he came out to check on him and bring him a cold beer.

"Doing okay in there?" Carmine asked, flipping a steak.

Saint nodded. His hair was rumpled, like he'd run his hands through it, and Carmine wondered if it was as soft as it looked. "Lavender's doing most of the talking."

"She'll do that," Carmine said, grinning.

"I like it," Saint said. "She has a lot of opinions and she's *funny*. Plus she doesn't demand interaction, she just... carries the conversation. She asked if she could weed the garden out back."

Carmine nodded. "Give her five minutes in any new location and she'll have located the patch of ground most suitable for growing *something*."

"Well, she asked if I wanted to help her, so I did." Saint looked faintly surprised at himself.

"Did you enjoy it?"

"I didn't expect to," Saint admitted. "I was mostly just doing it to be polite." He returned Carmine's grin. "But... yeah. It was actually really relaxing? It felt good. Like I was accomplishing something. She said she was planting sunflowers and she'd tell me how to take care of them." He gave Carmine another smile. "I should get back in there."

No sooner had he disappeared than Diana stepped outside. She slipped an arm around Carmine's waist and he draped his over her shoulders, pressing a kiss to her temple.

"Hey Ma."

"I like Saint," Diana said.

"Yeah, me too," Carmine said. "Didn't really expect to, honestly."

Diana hummed thoughtfully. "You're careful with him, aren't you?"

"Of course," Carmine said, nettled. "He won't let me do much, but I try, okay?"

"Good." Diana squeezed his waist. "He likes you very much."

Carmine poked the steak, absurdly pleased and trying to hide it. "I'm a likable guy, Ma."

Diana laughed out loud. "You pick fights just to watch the fallout, don't try that shit with me."

"I haven't done that in *years*," Carmine protested. He let go of her and slid a steak onto the plate beside the grill. "Ready to eat?"

11

Morning skate went smoothly, despite Flanahan's dire threats of line shuffling. Carmine was still on Saint's line, Kasha still on Saint's wing. David had been reassigned to Saint's other side, which Carmine wasn't thrilled about. Still, he was fast, and his passes usually connected. They ran drills for an hour until Flanahan called a halt and sent them to the showers. David was in a good mood, laughing and jostling the others under the spray. Carmine met Saint's eyes but kept his mouth shut.

They left the building, squinting in the sun, and Carmine glanced at Saint. "Talk about it over lunch at home?"

"Yeah," Saint agreed.

"Hey bitch!" someone shouted, and Saint's eyes went wide but Carmine was already spinning, looking for the speaker.

He found her immediately, leaning against the wall of the barn, a huge smile splitting her face.

"Biiitch!" Carmine yelled, and Henry threw her arms open so he could scoop her up into them. She laughed as he swung her around, squeezing her tight, her heavy dreads smelling like lavender as they fell in his face. "What the fuck?" Carmine demanded when he set her down. "You stalking me now?"

Henry gave him a dazzling smile. She was as stunning as ever, dressed in camouflage cargo pants and a tight crop top that bared her perfect abs, sleek and rippling under ebony skin. Her dreads were pulled up into a mohawk, the sides of her head shaved, and she'd added a tiny gold ring to her left nostril since the last time he'd seen her.

"I *told* you I was coming, remember?"

"Yeah, but you didn't finalize details with me, I figured you got busy," Carmine protested. He was still holding her hand, he realized as he turned to Saint. "Saint, this is my best friend Henry. Henry, Saint Levesque."

"Aw, I'm your best friend?" Henry said. She fluttered her eyelashes obnoxiously at Carmine and held out her free hand to Saint, who was a fraction slow to take it.

"Don't believe anything he's said about me," she said.

"He actually hasn't mentioned you at all," Saint said, and Carmine burst out laughing at the look on Henry's face.

"My world doesn't revolve around you," he told her, and Henry scowled at him.

"Well, it *should*."

"How long are you here?" Carmine asked.

"Today and tomorrow," Henry said. She elbowed him in the ribs. "Got a ticket for me?"

"For you? Nah. You can pay full price just like everyone else." Carmine dodged the swipe of her fist, laughing. Saint looked politely puzzled. "Henry lives in San Francisco, Saint," Carmine said. "She's a bigshot financial advisor."

"I tell people how to spend their money and they give *me* money for the privilege," Henry said cheerfully.

"Sweet gig if you can get it," Carmine agreed. "Hey, my moms are coming over for lunch, you wanna come see them?" He pulled himself up short, turning to Saint. "Shit. Sorry, um. Is it okay if Henry comes over?"

Henry snorted. "You sound like you're asking permission for a playdate."

Carmine ignored her, focusing on Saint,

who didn't look happy. He didn't look angry either, though—more just… blank.

"That's fine," he said, but the smile he gave Carmine had no real warmth behind it. "I've got game tape to watch before my nap, so I'll be busy anyway."

"See?" Henry said, poking Carmine. "Dad says it's okay if I come over."

Carmine pushed her hand away, searching Saint's face. He couldn't ask what he really wanted, not with Henry standing right there. He couldn't find out why Saint looked unhappy, even though he was hiding it well—a stranger would think he was fine, but Carmine had lived with him for weeks now, spent almost every waking moment in his company, and he could read Saint's tells now. It was there in the tenseness of his shoulders, the tightness around his eyes even as he smiled. But Carmine couldn't push. If he did, Saint would just pull away.

"In fact," Saint continued, "I have some errands to run. I'll see you back at the house."

"Errands on game day?" Carmine said before he could stop himself.

Saint just nodded. "Henry, nice to meet you." He pivoted on his heel and walked briskly away without looking back.

Henry whistled. "Okay, he's hot but he's kind of a dick."

"He's not," Carmine said sharply. "He's got a lot on his mind."

Henry's eyebrows went up. "Oho, I see."

"Shut up, you see nothing."

"Oh yeah, no, Mama Henry sees *all*. You *like* the boy."

"Well sure," Carmine said, rolling his shoulders. He glared at her. "As a friend. He's actually really nice, he's just... stressed."

"Uh huh," Henry said, grin stretching until she looked positively diabolical. "And you like him. You like, *like* like him."

"Can you please stop murdering the English language?" Carmine complained. "I'm hungry. Come have lunch with me and shut the fuck up about my nonexistent crush on someone who's very definitely not interested anyway."

Henry slung an arm over his shoulders. "I know you have to nap, so I'll interrogate you more after the game."

"So kind," Carmine muttered. He wrapped his arm around her waist and squeezed. "It's really fucking good to see you."

"I know," Henry said happily.

LAVENDER AND DIANA weren't there yet when Saint got home. Despite what he'd said to Carmine, he didn't have errands to run or game tape to watch. He went straight to his suite, shut the door, and stared at the wall unseeingly.

Carmine's best friend was the most beautiful woman Saint had ever seen. Saint had never seen Carmine light up the way he had when he'd seen Henry. *I want to make him smile like that*, a tiny traitorous part of him whispered. He took his shoes off, set them by the door, and got undressed for bed. He needed rest for the game.

WHEN HE WOKE UP, he could hear voices in the kitchen. Saint lay still for a minute. He didn't want to go out there, put a smile on and pretend he was happy having people in his house. He wanted it to be just him and Carmine, like the day of their first game together. But he couldn't have that, not right now.

He got up and went through his routine, breathing through his nose and thinking about nothing but the game ahead as he showered, shaved, and dressed. He checked his phone as he stepped into his shoes—Felix was on his way. Carmine would probably ride with his moms, or Henry, and that was fine, he told himself firmly as he left the bedroom.

But the house was quiet, and Carmine was walking down the hall toward him in his best suit, smiling his crooked little half-smile.

"I kicked them out," he said by way of greeting. "Have a good nap?"

Saint stared at him for a minute. "You didn't have to do that."

Carmine just shrugged. "I can drive us to the rink, anyway. Unless you prefer to ride with Felix?"

"No, I—" Saint grabbed his phone and sent a quick text to Felix. *Riding with Carmine, see you there.* When he looked up, Carmine was regarding him curiously. "I'll... ride with you," Saint said belatedly. "If that's okay?"

Carmine's eyes creased with his smile. "Of course."

THEY RODE IN SILENCE, but it wasn't uncomfortable. Saint wanted to ask about Henry—how Carmine knew her, how long they'd been friends, if they were *more* than friends—but that was a rabbit-hole he didn't have time to go down. So he kept his mouth shut and his hands on his thighs, staring out the windshield and focusing on the game ahead.

When they got to the rink, Carmine fussed with the seatbelt, the windshield wipers, putting the visors up, as Saint got out. Finally Saint bent, peering through the window.

"You coming or not?"

"Oh, I—thought you'd want to walk alone." Carmine got out, straightening his jacket. The black fabric made his shoulders look even broader, and he'd gone with a tie in deep, burnished brown. It caught the highlights in his eyes and made them flicker gold.

"Don't make me tell you again how much I like your company," Saint warned. "You know how humiliating that is for me."

Carmine's grin flashed. "Only because you haven't admitted your true feelings yet."

"Oh, shut up," Saint said, fighting a laugh.

They walked past the photographers together, Saint smiling impartially at everyone gathered. Inside the stadium, Saint relaxed a fraction.

"I'm gonna find Kasha," he said.

He discovered him in the hot tub, folded forward with his elbows on his knees and head in his hands. His smile when he saw Saint was genuine, though, and Saint sat on the rim of the tub, studying his face.

"How are you feeling, kid?"

Kasha mock-scowled at him. "You're only two years older of me. Why I'm kid?"

Saint ruffled his hair before he could stop himself, and Kasha yelped in outrage, making him laugh. "We're going to have a good game," he said.

"Because you say so?" Kasha asked, and Saint pushed him, water slopping.

"Because I say so," he agreed, and stood. "Come play two-touch with us."

THE RIPTIDE WAS A FAIRLY young team. What they lacked in speed, they made up for in brute strength. They weren't Saint's favorite team to go up against, but they mostly played clean, even if they were too free with the cross-checks.

Saint kept an eye on Kasha as much as possible. He seemed in good spirits, sharply focused on the play, quick on his skates and avoiding several big hits with speed and agility. He sent the puck to Jason, who took a quick wrist shot off the bar.

A Riptide player in white and dark blue intercepted off the face-off and dumped the puck into their end. Carmine fought through the ensuing scrum to send the puck out between his feet to Saint, waiting behind him at the top of the circle. Saint took the shot and it was gloved down by the Riptide goalie, a young, rangy kid in his first season but showing no sign of nerves.

On the bench, he watched as the second and then third lines went through their shifts, fighting fiercely and refusing to give up ground. But they couldn't gain any, either. The Riptide's defense had clearly been strengthened, and Saint made a mental note to watch more game tape of them. Felix was relaxed and loose in his crease, deep in the zone and stopping everything sent at him.

A Riptide player got tripped by Kasha and Saint dodged around him on the way back to the bench. He looked furious as he pushed himself upright and went for Kasha, who was scrambling onto the bench himself. The player peeled off and Saint leaned over.

"Watch yourself."

Kasha was breathing hard, but his confidence seemed back. "He's in my way."

"Doesn't mean he won't kick your ass if he can manage it," Saint warned, but Kasha just shrugged and took a swig of water.

Saint glanced at Carmine, but they didn't speak.

THEY BATTLED through the second period in much the same manner. Toward the end, Kasha had the puck, forging toward the net, head down and focused.

"Look up!" Saint shouted, but Kasha didn't hear him. The player he'd tripped earlier appeared as if from nowhere, slamming into Kasha's midsection with jarring force. Kasha went sprawling and Carmine threw his gloves off, grabbing the player's jersey.

The fight was over quickly. Carmine landed several heavy hits, teeth bared in a feral snarl, blocking the other player's swings with his forearms and then tripping him to the ice. The refs were on them immediately, dragging them apart, and Carmine shook their hands away and skated for the box. Saint watched, jaw tight.

Kasha was already back on his feet, face pink, only a little slow to skate back to the bench. He shook his head when the trainer tried to pull him aside to look at him, sliding onto the bench instead with a mutinous set to his jaw.

Back on the ice, Saint won the face-off and Roddy got the puck, racing for the net. They were playing well, playing sharp and controlled and not taking any penalties since Carmine had gone to the box. Roddy took the puck around the net, made a sharp angle shot on the goalie, and bounced the puck off his shoulder. No one expected Kasha to swing his stick like a baseball bat and knock it in right out of the air.

The stadium erupted as the goal horn went off. Saint collided with Kasha, who had both arms in the air, an incandescent smile on his face, as the rest of the team piled on, yelling congratulations in Kasha's ear.

The locker room was as loud as Saint imagined a roomful of Stanley Cup winners would sound. Someone was howling like a wolf, several others re-enacting Kasha's goal as he sat at his locker, cherry red and grinning from ear to ear. It was just a game, an early season game, nothing that really mattered yet, but it was still two points, and Kasha deserved his moment in the sun.

Saint waited until the happy shouting and cheering died down a fraction before standing. "I think we all know who this is going to," he said, and pulled out the cape.

HE'D BEEN at home one summer after his first season with the NHL, working on his parents' farm, when his father had sent him into town for cattle feed. Waiting next to the truck for the worker to toss the bags in the bed of the truck, Saint's eye had snagged on a fabric display of the little textile shop next door. It was the exact color of the Seabirds' jerseys, dark teal, gray, and gold swirled across white satin like slung there by a paintbrush. Saint had walked inside, pointed at the bolt, and asked for the whole thing.

Back at the farmhouse, he'd spread it across his bed, wondering why he'd bought it so impulsively and just what he was supposed to do with it now he had it.

His mother had put her head in the room with a quick rap of knuckles to the door. "About to start dinner, did you—oh, what's this?"

"I don't know," Saint had told her honestly. "But the colors…."

"They're perfect," she agreed, touching the satin.

"We need something for the team,"

Saint said. "An emblem, something the first star of the game can put on after we win. Some use hats, there are a few helmets, and at least one team uses a collar. We don't really have anything yet. Any ideas?"

His mother considered. "What about— no, that's silly."

"No, what?"

"Well, a cape?" She smiled up at him. "They could throw it over their shoulders, wear it around the locker room, and it's washable, so getting a little sweat on it won't hurt the fabric. Plus there's enough here to make five or six if you want."

"Mom, you're a *genius*," Saint said. "That's perfect. I just need to find someone who'll make it for me. Maybe Roddy's wife—"

"Or I could do it," his mother interrupted. She shrugged when Saint looked at her. "I haven't sewn in a few years but it's not like you forget how. I'll make it for you."

"Thanks, Mom," Saint said quietly, and kissed her on the cheek, making her smile.

SAINT SHOOK OUT THE CAPE, making the fabric snap, and the players cheered. He pointed at Kasha, whose eyes went big, and they shouted louder. "Come on," Saint said, beckoning. "Get over here."

Kasha jumped to his feet and crossed the room to him. Saint smiled up at him and swung the fabric with a dramatic swirl, letting it drape in shining folds over Kasha's bony shoulders to brush the floor.

"Congratulations, Kasha," he said over the noise of the locker room. "You earned it."

Everyone shouted and cheered and clapped some more as Kasha swept a deep bow to the room and straightened, grinning impossibly wider.

"Good game," he said. "Played hard, Felix, you were great—" Felix bowed from the waist, sitting in his stall. "—Saint, that saucer pass in second, incredible. First win of the season, boys!" They roared for him and Kasha gave them all his huge beaming smile as the rookies converged on him and Saint went back to his locker to finish taking off his gear.

"We're going out, right?" Carmine asked.

"Of course," Saint said. *Team bonding, cohesion, spirits-lifting....* He knew all the reasons they went out and even though he hated being watched so closely, part of him wanted to do it, cram himself into a booth next to Carmine, sit too close so he could hear him yell over the music, and get loudly, ridiculously drunk.

Carmine matched his smile. "Great. Is it okay if I invite Henry?"

Saint blinked. "Oh—yeah, no, that's fine."

"You sure? If you want it to just be team, that's totally cool, she'll understand."

Saint mustered what he hoped was a convincing smile. "She's your friend." *Your best friend.* "You don't get to see her very often, of course you should invite her."

Carmine studied his face for a minute, but whatever he saw seemed to convince him. He nodded. "I'll text her. Thanks, Cap."

Saint rolled his eyes. "Don't call me that," he said. "This isn't a Marvel movie."

Carmine grinned at him. "Thanks, *Saint*," he drawled, and Saint suppressed a shiver at the sound of his name in Carmine's mouth. He liked it a little too much.

He coughed and turned away. "I'm gonna shower," he said, and escaped.

12

HENRY MET the team at the bar, and David wasn't the only one to sit up straight in appreciation as she wound her way through the tables, although he was the only one to wolf whistle. Carmine whipped around but Saint was there first, glaring David down until he threw up his hands in submission and slumped in his seat.

Henry reached them and Carmine was on his feet to greet her, turning to the group crammed into the extra-large booth. He had to raise his voice to be heard over the music when he said, "Guys, this is Henry. Henry, the boys."

"Great game!" Henry said, and the players erupted into happy cheering.

Carmine ushered her to a seat, and she slid onto the bench beside Saint as Carmine followed her on and settled back against the vinyl.

Saint hid his disappointment and smiled at her as Henry got comfortable. She'd traded the camo for a sequined top that bared her perfect shoulders and back, coupled with skintight pants riding low on her hips.

"Hi!" she said. "Seriously, that was a great game. You guys looked so good."

"Oh... thanks," Saint said. "We're still figuring each other out, but I appreciate that."

Carmine leaned around Henry's other side to include Saint in the conversation. "Half his team got traded this season," he told her.

Henry nodded sympathetically. "You told me that when you first got here, remember?"

"Did not," Carmine said, looking startled.

Henry slanted a grin at Saint. "Oh yeah, you did. Couldn't shut up about poor Saint and how he'd worked so hard for this team and it all got yanked out from under him and—"

"Drinks!" Carmine interrupted loudly, sounding faintly desperate, and warmth curled in Saint's chest.

Henry giggled and leaned forward, catching Kasha's eye across the table. He straightened, squaring his shoulders as if unaware he was doing it. "That goal was *sick*," she told him. "Your hands are something else."

Kasha's smile was huge, eyes dancing even as a blush rose on his fair skin. "You are Henry? I thought... is boy's name?"

"Usually," Henry said cheerfully. "But it's also mine."

David set his beer mug down. "Are you and Carmine dating?"

Henry's radiant smile didn't dim when she answered. "We're just friends. You're... number forty-seven?"

"David Stahl." He grinned at her, and Saint was reminded that he was a handsome man. It wasn't a pleasant realization, not as Henry smiled back at him across the table. He should be happy Henry was flirting with someone other than Carmine, but he couldn't stop the worry in his gut. He caught Carmine's eye, and Carmine shook his head very slightly. David was still leaning forward, saying something to Henry in a lowered voice, and Carmine cleared his throat and stood.

"Getting another round," he announced. He set off toward the bar and David looked up.

"Be right back," he told Henry, and went after Carmine.

"He's hot," Henry said to no one in particular, and Saint made a noncommittal noise. He wasn't about to slander a teammate, especially not to someone he didn't know, and he wasn't sure how to casually drop a hint for her to be careful, so he kept his mouth shut and watched the team.

Felix and Embry were on the dance floor, a small knot of admirers around them as they danced, and a few of the rookies had joined them in hopes of picking up. Jesper, Elias, and Oskar were tucked off in the corner, heads together. Jesper's wife was pregnant and Oskar had small children, so Saint didn't expect them to stay long.

Carmine reappeared with a tray of glasses, his face like thunder, and Saint straightened, alarmed. Carmine set the tray down and doled out drinks as David slung himself carelessly back in his seat and flashed a grin at Henry.

"So, Henry," he drawled, "what do you do for fun?"

"Bike, paintball, eat men's hearts." Henry shrugged. "The usual."

David pretended to shiver. "Fierce." There was no mistaking the intent in his eyes, and Saint clenched his fists, hating the feeling of helplessness.

His phone went off in his pocket and he pulled it out. It was Carmine.

Henry's a big girl.

Saint glanced up, but Carmine wasn't looking at him, seemingly involved in a conversation with Roddy about backchecking, from the fragments Saint caught. Still, Saint typed out a reply. *He's also hot and charming and I don't trust him.*

Carmine glanced at his phone as Saint took a drink of beer. Henry and David were still talking, their elbows on the table and voices pitched under the thudding music.

I already told her that, Carmine sent. *She can make up her own mind.* But he didn't look any happier than Saint felt.

Sighing, Saint settled in to drink and watch his team. The rookies had struck out and were heading dejectedly back to the table. Embry had a girl in his arms, and Felix was—Saint squinted. Felix appeared to be dancing with a couple, a delighted grin on his face as the girl leaned up to whisper in his ear and the man with her pressed close along Felix's other side, the packed dance floor making the proximity plausible.

Get it, Felix, Saint thought, faintly amused, and raised his glass when Felix glanced over and caught his eye.

"So, Saint," Henry said abruptly, making him jump. David was nowhere to be seen, and Henry was watching him with disconcertingly sharp eyes. "How do you like playing with my boy?"

"Carmine's very good," Saint said. "His footwork is impeccable and his hands are silky as anything. It's a pleasure to play with him." That was his media voice, he knew, but he also meant every word. Henry considered him.

"You don't think he's... what's the word I'm looking for... a hired thug?"

Saint stiffened. Henry's gaze had him pinned to the vinyl seat, stripping him open and probing his core for secrets. Of course Carmine had told her about that. She didn't look angry, but she also didn't look *happy*, eyebrow raised as she waited for him to respond.

"I—" He groped for words. "Look, I didn't—"

Henry waited.

Saint swallowed frustration and tried again. "He was—" *No, don't blame Carmine.* "I said some things in the heat of anger that I—regret. I never intended to—" He hesitated again. Henry's eyes were boring a hole in him.

"Time to dance!" Carmine said, turning from his conversation with Roddy. He grabbed Henry's wrist and dragged her from the booth before turning back to look at

Saint, a question in the quirk of his eyebrow. Saint nodded, not quite trusting himself to speak, and Felix flopped onto the bench beside him as Carmine and Henry hit the floor.

"Is that Caz's girlfriend?" Felix asked.

Saint twitched. "They're just friends," he said, hating the edge in his voice. He forced a smile. "What about you? You were getting pretty cozy out there."

Felix grinned. "Got their numbers. Night's young."

"ARE YOU? JUST FRIENDS?"

Carmine straightened from turning on the stove to look curiously at Saint, slumped at the kitchen table. His elbows were on his knees and he was fondling Steel's ears, determinedly not looking at Carmine, but the tips of his own ears were red.

"Henry, I mean," Saint said, eyes on the dog. "Are you—"

The question mattered, Carmine thought, and he took a careful breath and turned the stove off again to go sit opposite at the table.

Saint still didn't look at him, murmuring nonsense under his breath to Steel, who was in raptures, and Carmine just watched him for a minute, appreciating the curve of his cheek, the line of his jaw.

"Yeah," he finally said. "We're just friends. Henry doesn't discriminate based on genitalia, but—" He waited until Saint looked up. "She's not my type."

Saint got his meaning immediately. "Oh. *Oh*. You're—"

"Yeah," Carmine said, holding his eyes.

Saint sat back in the chair, staring at him. "You're… gay."

"Last I checked," Carmine said, aiming for lighthearted. He wasn't sure how to interpret the expression on Saint's face. Was he angry at Carmine for not confiding in him sooner? Did he think Carmine was lying?

But Saint just nodded. "How long have you known?"

"Since juniors," Carmine said. "You?"

"I was twelve." Saint bent to pet Steel again. "There was a kid in my league. He— that's when I knew."

"Do your parents know?"

"I think Mom knows." Saint kept his head down. "I don't think Dad suspects. I haven't said anything. It… he wouldn't be happy."

Carmine fought the wash of rage. "Why not?"

Saint lifted a shoulder, eyes on Steel's head. "Hockey players aren't gay."

Carmine's snort was loud and rude, but Saint didn't look up.

"I just mean—I've come so far and done so much, and it would just... tear it all down. Everything I've worked for."

"Everything?" Carmine breathed through his nose but it wasn't working—he still wanted to punch something. "All those trophies, all those records, all those goals you set for yourself and then *exceed*, everything you've done and it would just be... nothing? All because you like boys?"

"Hockey players aren't gay," Saint repeated, and this time he looked up. His jaw was set, eyes suspiciously bright.

"Tell that to Adam Caron," Carmine snapped.

"That's different."

"My ass it's different," Carmine growled. "He's a hockey player. So are you. He's gay. So are you. So am I. And you're still one of the best goddamn players in the league. Caron's pretty damn good too, from what I've heard. Doesn't matter if you suck a dozen dicks a day, no one's taking that from you."

Saint ducked his head, blush darkening his cheekbones. "I... have a reputation to maintain," he said, looking at his hands.

Carmine sighed. "Nothing about you has changed, Saint. You're still *you*. You're weird and loyal and awkward and shy and funny and *good*, and your orientation doesn't change any of that."

"I know," Saint said. "Anyway, no. My dad doesn't know. What about your moms?"

"Of course they know," Carmine said, snorting again. "They knew before I did, but they let me get there in my own time."

"That's good," Saint said. "So you and Henry really are just friends?"

"Yeah, and she hooked up with David last night."

Dismay flashed across Saint's face. "Shit."

"She'll be fine. Henry can take care of herself better than anyone I know."

"Yeah, but... David."

"I know." Carmine blew out a breath and stood. "Hash and ham steaks okay for breakfast?"

13

HENRY WENT HOME the next day, hugging Carmine and putting out a hand for Saint to shake. "About what I said at the bar," she said. "Hurt him again and they'll never find the body."

"For fuck's sake!" Carmine complained, but Saint held Henry's eyes, both of them ignoring his spluttering.

"I can't guarantee it," he said quietly. "But I'll do my best."

Henry nodded. "Good enough. Caz, my love, walk me to my car."

THEY WENT on their first road trip the same day, a short four day hop with three cities on the itinerary. Saint found his seat on the plane up near the front, next to Roderick,

Felix across the aisle from them. He got settled as the veterans boarded and then the rookies came bounding in, pushing and shoving in puppyish excitement.

Carmine flopped into the seat beside Felix and stretched his long legs out with a satisfied sigh. "Private jets are the way to go."

Saint was already queuing up game tape on his iPad. He and Roderick spent the flight discussing strategy and logistics, as Felix and Carmine played video games and bickered amiably.

THE GAME WAS rough and brutal, but they eked out a win off a trickle-in goal by Roderick late in the third. They left the building exhausted but elated and rode the high to the next city. The Atlanta Spirit were a young team, fast and agile but with only a few veterans on the team. The main problem would be defending the puck and getting past their defense, especially Saul Garrison.

Saint had played Garrison multiple times over the years as he was traded from team to team, never really seeming to find the right fit. Probably because he was most likely the goon Saint had accused Carmine of being, Saint thought as he laced his skates. Still, Garrison seemed to be meshing well with the Spirit's defensive core. He'd have to be watched.

THE HIT KNOCKED him off his skates, sending him into the boards at an angle. Saint managed to get a hand up to absorb some of the impact, but the collision rattled his bones, teeth jarring together painfully as he hit the ice.

He was vaguely aware of a teal and white jersey grappling with Garrison a few feet away, but he was too dazed to see who it was. He got to hands and knees, head ringing, just as Garrison landed on the ice, Carmine on top of him and still throwing punches.

Shit, Saint thought, and dragged himself up, but the linesmen were there already, grabbing Carmine's arms and hauling him up and off.

Carmine shook their hands away with a snarl and skated away without looking at Garrison, still on his back.

Seething with fury at both Garrison *and* Carmine, Saint headed for the ref. The captain of the Spirit, Sanders, was already there, arguing passionately for Carmine to get a five minute major for excessive force.

"Like the excessive force Garrison used on me?" Saint interjected, and the ref, Bullock, raised an eyebrow at Sanders.

"He's got a point," he said. "Matching five minute majors sound fair, plus the two minutes for that very illegal crosscheck?"

Sanders scowled thunderously. "We'll take the four minutes," he muttered.

"Yeah you will," Bullock said cheerfully, and skated for center ice.

Saint headed for the bench, still angry. Carmine was sitting in the box, a trickle of blood sliding down his forehead as he studiously ignored Garrison in the box beside him. Saint yanked a glove off and took a drink of water as Roddy slid onto the bench.

"I'm gonna kick his ass myself," Saint growled, clutching his stick.

Roddy slanted a look at him but said nothing.

CARMINE STEPPED out of the box, caught the puck as it whizzed by him, and raced down the ice with it to sink it neatly over the Spirit goalie's knee. He was grinning as he circled the net, arms wide in celebration, and Saint almost forgave him for the fighting when Carmine caught his eye, his smile wide and dazzling.

Still. He couldn't let this behavior continue. He was going to have to talk to him.

BUT WHEN THE game was over and they'd won, to the loud booing of the Atlanta crowd, Roddy caught Saint's arm after his shower.

"A word?"

"Can it wait?" Saint asked, eyeing Carmine where he was pulling his shoes on and shaking damp hair out of his eyes as Kasha bounced around him, talking excitedly about the bars he wanted to hit.

Roddy hesitated. "I guess so. Back at the hotel?"

"Sure," Saint said. He smiled at him and crossed the room to Carmine, who'd apparently had enough of Kasha's incessant energy and put him in a headlock. "Got a minute?" Saint asked, raising his voice over Kasha's squawking.

Carmine leaned away from the flailing limbs. "Wanna share a ride to the bar?"

"Can I come too?" Kasha demanded,

voice muffled from being squashed in Carmine's armpit.

Carmine let him go and put a hand on his face, pushing him backward. "Grown ups only this time."

Kasha glared at him and spun to find Jason.

Even frustrated with Carmine, Saint couldn't help the smile. He followed Carmine down the hall and out into the parking lot, where a white sedan was waiting for them. It took Carmine a few minutes to squeeze himself into the back, and Saint waited patiently for him to get situated.

"Okay," Carmine said once the car was rolling. "Shoot."

Saint shot a look at the driver.

"Hey, can you turn the music up?" Carmine asked.

"Sure thing," the driver said easily, and cranked it.

Carmine cocked a brow at Saint, who took a deep breath.

"This has to stop," he said.

"What does?" Carmine asked. "Sharing a car to a dive bar?"

"*Protecting* me," Saint spat, and Carmine's face shuttered. Saint forged on despite the warning signs. "You have to *stop*. I can take care of myself. If word gets around that I'm relying on you to fight my battles for me, no one will ever respect me again. Why can't you see that?"

"So I'm supposed to let you get run into the boards and not lift a pinky to help?" Carmine's voice was low and dangerous.

"*Yes*," Saint said. "If it's an illegal hit, the refs will take care of it. If it's legal, then I can handle it. What I *don't* need is you white knighting me, okay?"

"Saint," Carmine said, and stopped. His mouth was tight, lines carved deep in his brow. "I'm not—you've got it all wrong."

"Do I?" Saint shot back. "Because every time I turn around, it seems like I'm having to tell you to stop getting between me and whatever obstacle I'm facing, and let me tell *you* something, it is getting *old*."

Carmine scrubbed his hands through his still-damp hair, fury and frustration in the set line of his jaw. "I can't do anything right with you, can I?"

Saint blinked. "I don't—what? Of course you can. You do a lot right."

"Sure," Carmine scoffed. "Which is why every five minutes you yank me aside to yell at me *again* about however I've fucked up this time."

Saint hesitated, groping for words, but Carmine just shook his head.

"Forget it. I won't defend you anymore, will that make you happy? In fact, I'll make you even happier and move out, as soon as we get back to Portland." He leaned forward without waiting for an answer and addressed the driver. "Can you just drop me here please? You can take my *friend* to the bar."

The driver pulled the car over and Carmine was out before Saint could figure out what to say.

"See you back at the hotel, Captain," Carmine said, and shut the door.

14

———

SAINT SAT in silence all the way to the bar. The last thing he wanted was to pretend to be enjoying himself, but the team would expect an appearance from him. So he dredged up a smile from somewhere, tipped the driver generously, and headed inside.

It was dark, lit with strobing lights that made Saint wince as he peered through the gloom, looking for familiar faces. Music thumped through the speakers overhead, so loud it made his teeth ache. Saint slid through the crowd, shouting apologies over the din, and finally saw Felix in a corner booth, surrounded by the rest of the team.

He was greeted with cries of delight and everyone squeezed over to give him room to slide onto the bench.

"Where's Caz?" Felix shouted.

"I think he went back to the hotel,"

Saint said. "Said he had a headache or something."

Felix shoved a beer at him. "His loss. Time to get wasted, *cher*."

THREE BEERS LATER, the alcohol had blunted the worst of Saint's frustration. He leaned against Felix's shoulder, nibbling a pretzel and watching the rookies on the dance floor. Roddy tapped the table to get his attention and Saint blinked, focusing on him.

"I'm heading back to the hotel and you should come with me," Roddy said.

"But… team," Saint protested.

"I've got it," Felix interjected. "I'll make sure everyone gets back to the hotel with no public indecency charges."

"That's why you're the best," Saint told him earnestly.

Felix snickered and patted Saint's head. "Go. Hydrate, you don't want a hangover on the plane."

"'Kay," Saint agreed, and followed Roddy out of the bar.

"HOW DRUNK ARE YOU?" Roddy asked once they were in the car.

"Not *that* much." Saint stopped to evaluate. "Buzzed. Kinda warm and tingly, but I'm not wasted or anything."

"Good, then you can listen and not talk for a few minutes," Roddy said.

Saint blinked. That sounded serious.

"You need to ease up on Carmine," Roddy said.

Saint scowled. "No."

"I mean it," Roddy snapped. "You're too goddamn hard on him."

"*He* needs to back off of my business," Saint shot back. "I'm the *captain*, and no one is going to—"

"No one's going to respect you if you can't take care of yourself, yeah, I've heard it a million times," Roddy said. "What you're forgetting is that Caz was literally hired to do exactly what he's doing. Yeah, his defense is solid, he's faster than anyone his size should be, and his hands are gorgeous, but he's also not afraid to use that size against opponents who think running a smaller guy into the boards is a fun pastime."

"He can't—"

"How much do you weigh?" Roddy interrupted.

Saint had to stop and think about it. "190, I think."

"Caz is 240 at least. He's got height, muscle, and bone on you. When's the last time you successfully intimidated someone into backing down when they were trying to get up in your face?"

"That's—irrelevant."

"It's *very* relevant," Roddy snapped. "You *know* how hockey players are. Sure, they respect your speed, your hand-eye coordination, your puck sense. But if they can knock you off your skates and get away with it, they're gonna fucking do it. So you need to *stop* being so goddamn hard on Carmine for doing his *goddamn job*."

He fell silent and Saint stared at him.

"Rod…." He swallowed hard.

"I know," Roddy said gently. "I know how hard you've fought for this position. How hard you still fight, every day. I'm not belittling any of that, Saint, I swear to you. But Caz is here for a reason. And you're not the only hockey genius to have an enforcer. Look at Gretzky, for Christ's sake, and don't you dare say that's different."

"It *is*," Saint protested. "Gretzky is… *Gretzky*."

"And you're Saint Levesque. You're gonna be in the Hockey Hall of Fame one of these days. You're already a legend. We're going to lift the Cup because of you—"

"*Don't*," Saint said sharply.

"I'm not jinxing anything," Roddy said. He squeezed Saint's knee. "You're that good, kid. But you can't do it alone. And you need to back off of Carmine."

Saint buried his face in his hands. "He's mad at me," he said into his palms.

"Because you yelled at him again?"

Saint dropped his hands. "At least I didn't call him a hired thug this time?"

Roddy grinned. "Baby steps. You know what you need to do."

"Yeah." Saint slumped against the door and stared sightlessly out the window. "I'm getting sick of apologizing to him."

"Then stop opening your big mouth," Roddy suggested, and laughed at the glare that got him. "You'll be fine. Carmine adores you."

"What?" Saint straightened. "He what? No he doesn't."

Roddy made a rude noise. "Of course he does. If he didn't, do you think he'd take it so hard when you unload on him? He gets upset because he wants you to think well of him."

"I *do*," Saint protested. "I—he's amazing. And not just on the ice. He's so smart, even though I don't think he even realizes just *how* smart. And he knows what I need, sometimes before I do. He's—" He closed his mouth but it was too late.

Roddy was gazing at him with a knowing expression.

"You could do worse," he said, keeping his voice low so the driver couldn't hear him.

"No." Saint shook his head hard. "It's a bad idea on so, *so* many levels. Just—no. I can't, Rod, it would screw everything up."

Roddy patted his knee. "Think about it."

I have. Saint hadn't thought of much else since he'd realized the extent of his crush. "It's not... reciprocated, anyway. So it's a moot point."

Roddy laughed out loud at that. "Oh buddy. You are so dumb sometimes."

"I am not!" Saint protested, stung. "I've *seen* the way he acts around me. He treats me exactly the same as he does everyone else. He's just—that's just how he *is*."

Roddy rolled his eyes. "Sure, kid. You keep right on thinking that."

The car pulled up at the hotel before Saint could muster a retort, and Saint glowered and followed Roddy out of the car.

Carmine was sharing a room with Felix, but no one answered when Saint knocked on the door. Saint waited a minute, then knocked again. Still nothing. Either Carmine was asleep or he hadn't made it back yet.

Luckily, Saint's room was right across the hall. He'd be able to hear when either occupant got back. He went inside, took his shoes off, and perched on the end of the bed to rehearse his apology.

It felt like forever but was probably only about thirty minutes before he heard footsteps coming down the hall. Peering out the peephole, Saint could see the back of Carmine's head and his broad shoulders as he fumbled with the key.

Perfect. Saint waited until his door was open and then stepped into the hall.

"Hey," he said quietly.

Carmine spun, catching the door before it could close. His hair was disheveled, and there was something odd about his appearance, but Saint didn't bother trying to figure out what it was. He was on a mission.

"Can we talk?" he asked, and lifted his hands before Carmine could speak. "No yelling, I promise. Just talking."

Carmine eyed him for a minute. Finally he shrugged and opened the door wider. "Why the fuck not."

Saint stepped inside his room and rolled his eyes at Felix's usual tornado mess—clothes and shoes strewn across his half of the room, bed rumpled and unmade. By contrast, Carmine's side was almost spotless, only his suitcase open by the bed.

"You want something to drink?" Carmine asked, indicating the minibar.

"You know how much they charge for those things?" Saint said automatically. He settled himself gingerly on the edge of Felix's bed as Carmine snorted.

"We play in the NHL. I think we can afford a seven dollar can of Coke."

"It's the *principle* of the thing," Saint shot back, and shook his head. "Not what I'm here about."

Carmine took his shoes off and sat down facing him, their knees almost close enough to touch. "What *are* you here about then, if it's not to complain about minibar prices or yell at me some more?"

"Please don't move out," Saint blurted.

Carmine's eyebrows went up. Saint squirmed, fighting the urge to run.

"I'm—I like having you there. I *do*. I didn't think I would but you… fit. And… you're a good cook and I love Steel and… please just. Don't go."

Carmine assessed him thoughtfully.

"Don't make me beg," Saint warned.

A smile tucked into the corner of Carmine's mouth, there and gone again. "Is that all you wanted to say?"

"No." Saint squared his shoulders. "I have to apologize. Again."

Carmine eyed him and said nothing.

When the silence stretched on too long, Saint shifted his weight.

"You usually have to speak to apologize," Carmine said unhelpfully. "Like actual words."

"Shut up," Saint snapped.

"Here, let me help," Carmine said, undeterred. He pitched his voice high. "'I'm very sorry for jumping down your throat, Carmine. I should have given you the benefit of the doubt and realized you'd do the same for anyone on the team and it's not just me you're protecting. Also you're very handsome and anyone would be lucky to date you."

Saint glared. "I hate you."

"No you don't." Carmine cocked his head, grinning at him. "Go ahead. 'I'm very sorry'...."

Saint sighed, defeated. "I'm very sorry for jumping down your throat, Carmine," he said softly, holding Carmine's eyes and putting all the sincerity he felt into the words. "I should have given you the benefit of the doubt and—what was the rest?"

"I'd do the same for anyone on the team and it's not just you I'm protecting," Carmine said. All trace of humor was gone and he was watching Saint's face intensely.

"I know you'd do the same for anyone on the team," Saint said. The words felt weighted, a power behind them like that of a gathering storm on the horizon. "And it's not… it's not just me you're protecting." He swallowed hard. "Also you're very hand-some," he whispered. "And… and…."

Carmine's eyes were hot on his, and Saint felt dizzy, like he was standing on the edge of a precipice, teetering before freefall.

"Saint," Carmine said quietly. "Saint, can I—"

There was a hickey on Carmine's collar-bone, Saint realized with a rush of sick horror. Deep and livid purple, he could see *tooth marks* around the edges.

"I have to go," he said, and bolted for the door, leaving Carmine staring after him with his mouth open.

HE PACED HIS HOTEL ROOM, sickness and disgust at himself warring in his chest. *Stupid, stupid, naive*—of course Carmine had picked up. They were in a strange city, where they were much less likely to be recognized, and as far as Saint knew, Carmine hadn't been with anyone since he moved in, which meant it had been over a month. Of *course* he wasn't interested in Saint. Of course he'd gone out to find a willing partner the minute he was able.

Someone knocked lightly on the door. "Saint?" Carmine called, and Saint froze, holding his breath. "Saint, can I just—please can I talk to you for a minute?"

Saint stood utterly still, not daring to move. With luck, Carmine would think he'd stepped out for ice or something and give up.

There was a moment of silence, and then Carmine sighed.

"Okay," he said. He sounded defeated, and it made Saint's stomach hurt. "Okay Saint, I'll see you on the plane." He hesitated. "Sleep well."

Saint wrapped both arms around himself to hold in the pain. His eyes stung. He stumbled to the bed and crawled onto it, still wearing his shoes. Grabbing a pillow, he pulled it to his chest.

You could do worse. Roddy's words echoed in his head.

And Carmine can do better. Saint squeezed his eyes shut.

It was a long time before he fell asleep.

BUT WHEN HE got on the plane the next day, Carmine greeted him with an easy smile. Taken off guard, Saint smiled back briefly and ducked his head, looking away.

When he glanced back, Carmine was deep in discussion with Felix about something—the rules of a card game Felix wanted to play, it sounded like.

So that was that. Saint sat down and pulled out his e-reader.

15

THE HOSPITAL VISIT was the day after they got back from Atlanta. Saint had had his outfit delivered the week before their latest road trip, and he pulled it out with a sinking sense of doom. He was going to look like an idiot, but that was part of the job description. The kids loved it, and that was all that really mattered.

Carmine took one look at him and started laughing.

"Shut up!" Saint complained, tugging at the spandex.

Carmine laughed harder, clutching his ribs.

"The kids love it," Saint grumbled. The pants were riding up and he wasn't sure how he was even breathing, considering how tight the spandex was. "Besides, you look dumb too."

Carmine tossed his hair and looked down at his black cargo pants, black vest, and silver full-length glove covering his left arm. "Excuse you, I'm the best Bucky you've ever seen."

The worst part was, it was true. Saint didn't tell him that, though—no point inflating his ego. But the pants accentuated Carmine's muscled thighs, and the tight shirt under the tactical vest showed off his arm muscles in a frankly unfair manner.

"You look hot, Captain America," Carmine said, grinning at him.

"I really, really hate you," Saint mumbled, and yanked the door open.

HE WAS glad Carmine hadn't let things get awkward between them, he told himself as Carmine drove them to the hospital to meet the others. Neither of them had mentioned the conversation in the hotel. Carmine hadn't offered to move out again. He was cheerful and friendly, the same as ever when he spoke to Saint.

And still Saint couldn't get past the feeling that the other shoe was poised to drop. *You're being ridiculous*, he thought, following Carmine from the car and tugging fruitlessly at the spandex again.

His thoughts were cut short by the sight of Felix dressed as Black Panther, bodysuit hugging his lean body. Carmine wolf-whistled and Felix's grin was blinding as he struck the classic Wakandan pose and then swept a bow.

"You sure you're Black enough to be T'Challa?" David remarked as he strolled up. He was dressed as Peter Quill, but Saint barely noticed, whirling and grabbing him by the arm.

"A word," he said through his teeth before Felix could speak. He started walking, giving David the choice of following or being dragged. When they were out of earshot, Saint let go. "What the *fuck* gives you the right to say something like that?" he demanded.

David ostentatiously rubbed his arm, looking wounded. "Come on, Cap. He's only what, half-Black? And he's light-skinned! Isn't that—what's the word— cultural appropriation or some shit?"

Saint stared at him, momentarily speechless. "You cannot possibly be this stupid," he finally said. He clamped his mouth shut on the words he wanted desperately to say. "*You* don't get to decide for him what parts of his heritage he chooses to embrace, so here's an idea—why don't you apologize to Felix and then keep your mouth shut the rest of the day, except to talk to kids."

David looked sulky. "I didn't mean anything by it," he muttered.

"The sad part is, you probably think that makes it okay," Saint snapped. "Let's go."

They headed back and David mumbled something vaguely apologetic to Felix, who caught Saint's eye. Saint shrugged, a what-can-you-do gesture, and Felix nodded at David.

"We're not here to fight," he said. "Let's go make some children happy, eh?"

Roddy had shown up while they were talking, dressed as some inexplicable character that he explained was from something called manga.

"I don't know either," he admitted, looking down at his costume and trying to keep his spiky wig from falling off. "But my kids are all into it and they begged me, so…." He shrugged.

Jason snickered. "It suits you, man. 'Specially the hair."

"Is it hair?" Saint asked, inspecting the wig from far enough away to keep from losing an eye. "I thought it was like… hedgehog spikes."

Roddy sighed. "Jason, it's not like you have room to talk. My Little Pony, dude? Seriously?"

Jason tossed his blue wig. "I'm Slugger, you heathen. From the original series?" He glowered when he got blank stares from the rest of the group. "Kasha will back me up." He folded his arms just as the door opened and a purple Teletubby waddled through.

Saint blinked and stared. Kasha's face was bright pink, whether with effort or embarrassment, Saint wasn't sure, and he maneuvered the giant foam costume down the hall with small careful steps as the group watched him approach in horrified fascination.

Carmine found his voice first. "You've never looked better, Kash."

Kasha beamed at him. "I'm Tinky-Winky!"

"The gay one?" David said loudly.

Saint shot him a warning glare. "The kids will love it," he told Kasha, who'd deflated slightly. "What do you think of Jason's costume?"

Kasha brightened. "You're Slugger, yes?"

Jason crowed in triumph and slung an arm around Kasha's foam-and-latex covered shoulders. "I knew you wouldn't let me down."

"I only know because you make me

watch cartoons," Kasha continued, as if admitting a secret, and Saint had to turn away quickly to stifle the laughter.

The rest of the players didn't bother trying, and the nurse who approached had to wait for the laughter to die down for several minutes before she could get a word in.

"The ward is ready for you," she said.

THE DAY PASSED QUICKLY as they went from ward to ward, visiting each child. Saint loved and hated this—hated seeing children like this, but loved knowing he could bring a smile to their faces, brighten their day and leave them with gifts of signed shirts, hats, and assorted memorabilia for them to treasure.

He was especially taken by a little girl in the third wing they visited. Her mother introduced her as Lacy.

"Sickle cell leukemia," she said quietly, and tried to smile through the exhaustion clearly dragging her down.

Saint squeezed her hand once. "Why don't you go get some coffee? Maybe a pastry or something. I'll sit with Lacy a little while."

She obeyed, casting a hesitant glance at

Lacy in the bed before slipping out the door.

Saint took his time sitting down and getting comfortable. Lacy was tiny, dark-skinned with jet-black eyes, her bald scalp gleaming under the room lights. She watched him silently but didn't speak.

"Hi," Saint said, smiling at her. "I'm Saint Levesque."

Lacy rolled her eyes.

"Oh, hockey fan, huh?" Saint said, settling in. "You know who I am?"

Lacy nodded. "Seabirds," she said in a soft, husky voice. "You're captain."

"How long have you been a hockey fan?" Saint asked.

"All my life."

"How old are you?"

"Twelve," Lacy said. "You're a good player."

"You think so? Anywhere I need to get better?"

"Your edgework's pretty good but your faceoffs get sloppy when you're stressed," Lacy said immediately, and Saint's eyebrows shot up.

"Is that so? Tell me more."

They talked for nearly an hour, trading hockey tips and Saint listening intently to the stories Lacy told him of being enrolled in the midget league before she got too sick to skate. When her mother finally put her head back inside, Saint twitched, startled.

"I lost track of time." He stood, holding out a hand to Lacy. "Listen, do you think you can come to a game this season?"

Lacy flicked her gaze to her mother, who pressed her mouth together as if to hide emotion but nodded.

"I'll leave tickets for you if you can tell me what dates work best," Saint told her. "Velvet will get the details to you. If you'll let me know you're coming, I'll come by and say hello to Lacy after the game."

Lacy's mother nodded again, lips wobbling briefly. "Thank you," she whispered.

Saint smiled at her. "Your daughter knows more about hockey than I do, I think. It was a pleasure talking to her."

He emerged into the hallway to find most of the group still going through the ward, talking to various children. Saint did a quick head-count, frowning when he realized David was missing.

Felix gave him a shrug when Saint

caught his eye but Roddy motioned toward the door leading to the stairs.

David was standing in the hall, his back to the door and tension running through his bulky frame. "No," he said, sounding frustrated. "I didn't mean—" He stopped and sighed. "No, look, I just—"

Saint cleared his throat before he overheard anything incriminating, and David whirled. He frowned at the sight of him, and Saint raised a brow.

Kids? He mouthed the word, pointing back at the ward, and David scowled.

"I'll call you back," he said into the phone, and the other person spoke. David's scowl grew thunderous. "Yes I fucking *will*," he snapped, and hung up with a vicious stab of his finger.

"Uh," Saint said. "Everything okay?"

"How much longer do we have to do this?" David said, pushing past him into the ward.

"Until we've visited every ward expecting us," Saint replied, right behind him. "If there's anything you need—"

David curled his lip. "Yeah, I don't think so. Let's just get this over with."

"Hey, you volunteered," Saint pointed out. "This wasn't mandatory."

"My agent said I need to improve my image," David said flatly. He tugged on his

MICHAELA GREY

leather jacket. "He said I've got a reputation for being an asshole, and things like this will help."

Saint stared at him. "You're—you seriously came here for a PR bump, not because of the kids?"

"God, I hate kids," David sighed. He jerked on the jacket's lapel. "Something's always leaking from somewhere, they're loud and obnoxious and never shut up, always asking question after question, yada yada yada—"

"Go home," Saint interrupted through lips tight with fury. "I allowed you to come because I thought you *wanted* this, but you're only here for your image, so just. Go."

David rolled his eyes. "Whatever, *Captain*." He was already dialing a number as he sauntered away, whistling to himself. Saint stood still until the urge to chase after him and punch him had faded somewhat, and then he rejoined the others.

"Where's Stahlsy?" Jason asked, perched next to a little girl's bed. She had plastic ponies parading across the table over the bed, and they seemed to be reenacting a scene from the show.

"Had something to do," Saint said shortly, and turned to find the next child to talk to.

It was late afternoon before they were done. They stopped to pose with the reporter who'd come out to cover the story, and Saint stayed to talk to her, discussing their odds in the upcoming game against Vancouver. When he was finally free, Carmine was waiting for him by his car, hands in his pockets.

"Sorry," Saint said, and Carmine's smile flashed in the gathering gloom.

"Part of the captain's job," he said easily. "Doesn't bother me."

Saint folded himself into the car and leaned his head back. Fuck, he was tired. Tired of dealing with David, tired of not knowing how to confront his feelings about Carmine, tired in general.

"So do you have a costume ready for the team's Halloween party?" Carmine inquired, merging onto the highway.

"I'll just wear this one again," Saint said. He smoothed a palm over the blue spandex.

"You *wouldn't*," Carmine said. He sounded genuinely horrified, and Saint lifted his head to peer at him.

"Why not?"

"That's... that's like... wearing white after Labor Day," Carmine sputtered. "It's like socks with sandals. Or crocs in general.

It's a fashion faux pas, Saint, you can't wear the same outfit twice!"

Saint frowned. "Seems wasteful."

"So donate that one somewhere," Carmine said, changing lanes. "You can't wear it again, it's *tacky*."

Saint let his head fall back as the laughter bubbled up, bright and cleansing. Carmine looked briefly startled, but then his lips twitched.

"Fine, mock me. I'm still right."

"I can't believe *you* are advising me on fashion," Saint gasped finally. "You never wear anything but ripped jeans and Henleys unless forced!"

"Just because I choose to embrace a signature look doesn't mean I'm blind to other options," Carmine said. The chill in his voice was belied by the dimple that appeared in his cheek, getting deeper with every word. "Anyway that's not the point. The point is—"

"I got it, I got it. No repeat costumes." Saint stretched languidly, wishing they were home already. "I'll have to think about it. I still have a couple of weeks." When he glanced over again, Carmine's eyes were fixed firmly on the road, hands tight on the steering wheel. "We could, um, match?" Saint offered before he thought better of the idea.

Carmine whipped his head around to stare at him. "You... want to wear matching Halloween costumes?"

"We kinda already did today," Saint pointed out. "And the kids seemed to love it. Hey, we could be minions!"

Carmine's shudder was violent. "Don't you *ever* suggest such a cursed thing again."

"But... they're cute?"

"If you're *demented*, maybe." Carmine exited the freeway as Saint watched his profile.

"I don't get you," he finally admitted.

Carmine sent him a smile. "Welcome to the club. You're still doing better than most."

"So you're okay with matching costumes, as long as it's not minions?"

"Or anything from Elsa. Frozen? If I hear that goddamn snowman song one more time I'm going to McFreaking lose it."

Laughter fizzed in Saint's chest again. He liked this weird, unpredictable, funny man so much more than he'd ever expected. "Deal," he said.

16

SAINT SHOWED Carmine his phone when he stumbled into the kitchen, bleary and yawning. Carmine stopped, blinking, and struggled to focus on the screen.

"Jase got your good side," Saint said dryly.

Carmine squinted until the picture came into view. He was grinning at the camera, his baseball cap askew and jean jacket hanging off one shoulder. He had his arm slung around Saint's waist, cheeks flushed with alcohol as he grinned at the camera. Saint was nearly drowned in his Pikachu onesie, but he was laughing, leaning into Carmine's side, eyes sparkling.

"Every side is my good side," Carmine said through a yawn and handed the phone back. "That on Instagram?"

"Yeah. How's your hangover?"

"Nonexistent," Carmine said. He shuffled to the coffee pot and filled a mug. "That was a good party—Felix knows how to host a banger."

"You suck," Saint muttered.

Carmine squinted at him. "You're looking a little green around the gills, bud. Everything okay there?"

"Shut up," Saint mumbled. "God, this is why I don't drink."

"Aw, poor baby." Carmine sat down and stretched his legs out under the table, nudging Saint's foot companionably. "Need some Advil?"

Saint put his face down on his arms. "Stop existing," he said, voice muffled.

"No can do, buddy," Carmine said. He was feeling much more cheerful as the caffeine filtered through his system. "Afraid you're stuck with me."

"Ugh," Saint told his bicep.

Carmine snickered and bumped his foot again. "I'll make us some greasy food, will that help?"

"Game day. I left you some oatmeal, but you can make yourself something."

"Oh that's right," Carmine said. He got up and turned on the stove to make some bacon. "We're playing the Wolverines tonight."

"Yep." Saint smothered a yawn. "I got Adam's number. We're meeting after the game."

"Nice!" Carmine retrieved the bacon from the refrigerator. "That'll be good."

"Will you—do you still want to come with me?"

Carmine turned to watch him. Saint's head was down, silky hair falling in his face as he fiddled with the hem of his shirt.

"If you want me to," Carmine said.

"Yeah." Saint looked up. There was fear in his eyes but also determination. "I think... it would help."

Carmine resisted the urge to tease him again and just turned back to the stove. "You know where we're going yet?"

"Andina," Saint said. "Peruvian food. I've already made the reservation."

THEY FELL TO THE WOLVERINES, a bloody, exhausting battle that went to overtime. Adam and Saint had faced off for the first puck drop, and Adam had given Saint a wide grin. He was one of the most handsome men Saint had ever seen, dark hair curling out from under his helmet and bright blue eyes that sparkled with eagerness at the fight ahead.

He was also a damn good hockey player, which Saint realized quickly after Adam won the puck drop.

It was a hard-fought game, everyone throwing their weight into it, but the puck bounces favored the Wolverines. One slipped past Felix, then another, and despite the Seabirds' best efforts, the Wolverines eked out a 4-3 win off Adam's between the legs shot, slotted neatly in under Felix's elbow.

AFTER PRESS, Saint did his usual captainly duties, circulating the room and assessing everyone's spirits, giving encouragement where it was needed and praise where it was due. Finally he was able to shower and change.

Carmine was waiting at his locker when he emerged, reading something on his phone. He stood and arched an eyebrow at Saint.

"He's meeting us there," Saint said, adjusting his jacket.

"No being seen fraternizing with the enemy," Carmine said, nodding and following him out. "Smart."

"I just figured it would be... sensible,"

Saint said. He slid into the car and buckled,
trying and failing to stop fidgeting. He
jumped when Carmine laid a big hand on
his knee.

"It's gonna be fine," Carmine said
gently. His palm was warm and solid, eyes
soft in the dark car.

Saint chewed his lip. "What if it's not?
What if he figures out why I'm so interested
and outs me? What if someone sees us and
starts talking? What if—"

Carmine caught his chin and pulled his
head around. "You're spiraling," he said
sharply. "Stop."

Saint took a ragged breath, forcing
himself not to lean into Carmine's touch.
"Maybe this was a bad idea," he managed
after a minute.

"Nope," Carmine said. He started the
car and put it in gear. "This was a great idea
and we're doing it."

Saint sat beside him, hands folded in his
lap. Every once in a while, Carmine would
glance at him, eyes measuring but kind, but
he said nothing, humming along to the
music.

"Have you had a boyfriend?" Saint
asked abruptly. He shook himself. "Stupid
question, you don't have to answer." His
eyes went wide as a thought occurred to

him. "Do you have a boyfriend now? Oh my god, why didn't I ask you before? Were you afraid to tell me about him? Is he back in Boston?"

"Saint!" Carmine was laughing, Saint realized. Surely he wouldn't be laughing if he was offended. "No boyfriend right now, relax. But yeah, I've had them before. Of course I have."

"Why of course?" Saint asked, bristling in spite of himself. "There's no of course, just because you know what you want and you don't care what people think—"

This time Carmine's hand covered his mouth, making Saint splutter.

"I care," he said, dropping his hand and turning into the parking lot. "I care a lot, Saint."

"But you just—" Saint waved a hand vaguely.

"Go charging in like a fucking idiot?" Carmine finished. "That's not a positive character trait, you know."

"You're brave," Saint said quietly, and Carmine went still. Saint looked up at him, wishing he could find the words. "You're— you fight for what you want. You don't care —no, okay, you *do* care but you don't let that stop you. I don't know how to do that. I don't know how to tell the world to go fuck itself just because I—" He drew in on himself. "It doesn't matter."

Carmine touched his knee as the engine cooled, metal pinging and ticking in the soft Oregon night. "It does matter. What you want matters."

"I have hockey. That has to be enough."

"Saint." Carmine waited until Saint looked at him. "You can want more than one thing. You can *have* more than one thing."

Saint shook his head. "Not right now. I —it can wait. It has to."

Carmine sighed and unbuckled. "I don't have time to argue with that right now, Adam's waiting for us."

ADAM WAS INDEED WAITING for them, sitting at a table in the back. He popped from his seat when he saw them approaching, hand out to be shaken. Saint accepted it and then took a seat. Carmine sat down next to him, close enough that Saint could feel his body heat, but not quite touching him, and smiled at Adam.

"That was a good game."

Adam's grin widened. "You guys didn't make it easy."

The server came by and took their drink orders, and Saint perused the menu as Adam and Carmine chatted about the weather and the game and their upcoming schedules.

"Thanks for doing this," he said when a lull fell. "It's probably not how you wanted to spend your night."

Adam shrugged. "You kidding? Good food, good company—at least I've heard good things about you. Not like I'm gonna turn down a chance to talk hockey with you, or anything else you want to discuss."

Saint ducked his head, feeling the flush crawl up his cheeks.

"Tenny wanted to be here," Adam said after they'd placed their orders. "He's at home dealing with a sprained shoulder but we're hoping he'll get called up again soon."

"Tenny?" Saint asked.

Adam's dimple deepened. "My boyfriend. Etienne Brideau. He's playing for the Thunder but he's filled a spot for us a few times, he meshes well with the team."

"So... everyone knows about you guys?"

"Anyone with a working pair of eyes, yeah." Adam's smile turned fond. "Tenny is more private than me—I'd like to take out a billboard or something, but he prefers we play it a little quieter than that."

"How did you meet?"

Adam muffled a laugh with his fist. "I—uh… I was out celebrating with the team after I got signed to the Wolverines. Tenny and his team was at the bar we went to. I might have… propositioned him." His grin turned wicked. "Worked, too."

Saint glanced at Carmine, who wasn't even trying to hide his amusement, and back to Adam. "Have you had a lot of blowback?"

"Some, sure," Adam said. "Most of my team was supportive, but there were a couple of idiots who tried the whole 'I don't feel comfortable in a locker room with him' routine."

"What happened?"

Adam lifted a shoulder. "You'd have to talk to my captain. All I know is, they were taken aside and spoken to individually, and when they came back, they said they were fine with it after all. There was only one nasty piece of work who just wouldn't let it go, and he ended up getting traded in February. Can't *prove* it had to do with me —the official line was that he just wasn't gelling with the team—but it's sure been better with him gone."

"Has anyone—" Saint broke off as their food arrived, and waited until the waitress was gone before speaking again. "Has anyone else in the league come out to you?"

Adam nodded, his mouth full. "Couple of guys, yeah. Made me promise to keep it quiet, which of course I will. But they said it helped, knowing they weren't alone." He grinned again. "I'm thinking of starting a group chat for us."

"Hey, if you do, add me to it," Carmine said, and Saint whipped his head around to stare at him. Carmine gave him a lopsided smile. "Strength in numbers, man."

"And you, Saint?" Adam's voice was quiet, eyebrows raised. "Want me to add you too?"

Saint swallowed hard. His ears were ringing. "I—no. No, I don't—I'm not—" He clamped his mouth shut before he ended up lying outright, but Adam just nodded, no censure in his eyes, and took a bite of his food. Saint stared at his own plate, unwilling to look up and see the disappointment Carmine was surely feeling with him. He wanted to be sick.

Under the tablecloth, a hand found his. Carmine tangled their fingers together and squeezed, eating left-handed without looking at him.

"What about from other players, different teams?" Carmine asked. "Do you get any shit from them?"

"Not officially," Adam said, cutting his steak. "No one's stupid enough to say anything with the officials around. I've gotten a few off the cuff comments when no one's in earshot, but like—" He shrugged. "I've heard it all, you know? It hurt at first, but now I just… it's whatever. I'm better than most of them anyway and they know it. The media, though—" His face clouded. "They're a little different story. I'm under a microscope. If I'm not playing to potential, they speculate that I've had a fight with Tenny or I need a 'self-care day'."

Carmine snorted loudly.

"Pretty much," Adam said, smiling ruefully. "No one's quite gotten to the point of suggesting it's that time of the month when I play for shit, but it's been hinted at."

"Assholes," Saint blurted.

"Yeah," Adam agreed. "But I knew what I was getting into. And it's worth it every single time a young queer fan comes up to me and tells me I'm the reason they want to play pro hockey, that I've shown them they have a place."

Saint's heart constricted and Carmine's hand tightened on his but neither said anything for a minute.

"You don't—" Saint swallowed. "You don't regret it?"

"No," Adam said simply. "It's difficult, sure, but I have to live my truth, you know? Cheesy as that sounds. Besides, I have a great support network. My parents are behind me a hundred percent, and they and my closest friends make all the difference, you know?"

The conversation turned to hockey after that, Carmine and Adam carrying most of it as Saint thought about Adam's words. What would it be like, coming out when all eyes were already on him? Adam's experiences were encouraging, but it was different for Saint, with a father who already deeply disapproved of his orientation and the focus of the entire hockey world on him, expecting him to perform better, do better, *be* better than everyone else. If Adam felt like he was under a microscope, it would be a hundred times worse for Saint.

Ego, his father's voice said in his head. Saint winced. *But it's true*, he wanted to argue. He was the face of the team. He was captain, role model, older brother, mentor, on and off the ice. He'd been chosen for the All Star Game, for Worlds, for the Olympics —Adam was barely starting out, in only his second year of being in the NHL. He had no real idea what it was like, living with so many expectations on his shoulders.

"Saint," Adam said, breaking into his thoughts and making him jump. "Carmine here tells me you wanted to go as *minions* for Halloween?"

"I think they're cute!" Saint said defensively, and Carmine gave Adam an I-told-you-so look.

Adam groaned. "I'm gonna have to reeducate you, clearly. Favorite action movie, go."

"Uh." Saint shot Carmine a look. Carmine raised an eyebrow unhelpfully. "Die Hard?" Saint hazarded.

Adam made a rude noise. "Are you just saying that because everyone says that, or do you really like the movie?"

Saint hesitated. "I've never actually seen it," he finally admitted, and Adam and Carmine burst into laughter.

"You've got your work cut out for you with this one," Adam said when he sobered, and Carmine bumped Saint's shoulder gently.

"I can handle it."

THEY STAYED at the restaurant for another hour before Adam checked the time and ruefully admitted he was close to curfew. Saint paid for the table over the others' objections, and they followed him outside still trying to argue.

"Do you need a ride back to your

hotel?" Carmine asked Adam as Saint shrugged his jacket on.

"I'm the opposite direction, I'll just call a car," Adam said. "Saint, it was a real pleasure playing against you and getting to know you a little better. When you guys come to Toronto, plan on coming over for dinner with Tenny and me, yeah?"

"I'd like that," Saint said, smiling at him. "Carmine too?"

"Obviously!" Adam replied. "You guys are kind of a matched set, aren't you?"

Carmine slung an arm around Saint's shoulders. "Peanut butter and jelly, that's us," he said cheerfully, and Saint couldn't help relaxing into the solid warmth of his frame.

"I THINK THAT WENT PRETTY WELL," Carmine said as he drove them home.

Saint, warm and flushed with the wine he'd had at dinner, made a quiet noise of agreement. "Thanks for coming," he murmured. Carmine's profile was lit by the streetlights, shadows flickering across his face.

"Did it help you decide anything?"

Saint lifted a shoulder. "Maybe. I don't know. Have to think about it."

He dozed off still watching Carmine as he drove, big hands loose and easy on the wheel, and was woken by the rumble of the gate rolling back. Saint kept still as Carmine drove slowly up to the house and eased to a stop.

"Hey, we're here," he murmured. He leaned over and put a gentle hand on Saint's shoulder. "Saint," he said, voice low and soft. "Wake up, we're home."

He was so close. Saint could lean up and kiss him, press their mouths together, finally find out what Carmine tasted like. He could feel Carmine's breath, warm on his cheek, and he opened his eyes to find him only a few inches away.

"Hey," Carmine said. His eyes creased with his smile. "Nice nap?" He was already drawing away, reaching for his door handle, and Saint reluctantly followed suit.

Inside the house, Carmine called for Steel. Toenails clicked on hardwood as he came running, and Carmine bent to greet him, murmuring to him.

"I have to take him out," he said as he straightened.

Saint nodded. "See you in the morning."

He headed for his room without looking back. Teeth brushed, changed into sleeping clothes, he crawled into bed and stared at the ceiling. He'd almost kissed Carmine.

He'd almost ruined everything. And yet he couldn't stop the burn in his gut, the shiver that rolled over him at the drag of the sheet against his skin. He *wanted*.

There was no harm in fantasy, right? Not when he would never—*could* never—act on it. Somehow Saint thought that even though Carmine may not reciprocate, he still wouldn't have any problem with Saint thinking about him.

He slipped a hand under his waistband and grasped himself, stifling a moan. He was only half-hard but rapidly getting harder. He pushed his pants down to his thighs and leaned over to grab the lube from his nightstand drawer.

There—oh, that was good. The lube slicked the slide of his hand, making everything wet and slippery and perfect. Saint closed his eyes, biting his lip.

Carmine leaned over him, a smile mixed with the lust in his eyes. "You want this?" he murmured. "Me?"

Saint nodded, words failing him. Please, he tried to say, but he couldn't make his mouth cooperate, overwhelmed by the nearness of Carmine's big body, hot and solid and smelling so enticing.

"Alright," Carmine said gently. "I've got you."

He pushed his pants down and Saint

folded to his knees in one quick movement. Above him, Carmine made a quiet noise, but he didn't protest when Saint leaned forward and took him into his mouth.

He tasted incredible—salt musk and clean skin, the faintly bitter taste of his pre-come bursting on Saint's tongue. Saint closed his eyes and sank down, swallowing him to the hilt.

"Ah fuck," Carmine hissed. His hips jerked and he brought his hands up to rest on Saint's head, not demanding but simply tangling his fingers in Saint's hair. "Your mouth," Carmine managed. "Fuck, you feel so good. You know how often I've thought about this? Wanted you for so long, Saint, God—"

His fingers scratched restlessly across Saint's scalp, more filthy nonsense falling from his lips, and Saint sped up, fist around the base of Carmine's cock, jacking him rhythmically as he sucked until Carmine's hips were stuttering, hands tight in Saint's hair.

He spilled in Saint's mouth on a punched out noise and Saint swallowed almost all of it, a few drops dribbling down his chin. When he looked up, Carmine was staring down at him, awe in his eyes.

"Come here," he said, hauled him upright, and kissed him.

Saint's back arched as he came, shuddering silently through the bliss with a fist jammed against his mouth to stifle any noise. After, he lay quietly, panting for air as come cooled on his stomach. He felt sticky and vaguely gross but his bones had turned to liquid and he couldn't muster the will to move. He fell asleep thinking about Carmine's mouth.

17

NOVEMBER PASSED IN A BLUR. They were rising in the standings, winning more than they lost, but it was still early days, no matter how much the newscasters liked to pontificate.

Thanksgiving was at Roddy's house. As a Canadian, Saint didn't really care much about the American holiday, but it was a day off and a chance to eat some delicious food. Plus he found himself delighted by the way Carmine threw himself into making dishes to bring.

"I'm doing a bourbon pecan pie," Carmine announced the night before. "And some roasted candied yams, and I started some dough for dinner rolls, if you want to help me make them. They're ready for their second rise."

"I have no idea what to do," Saint warned him, but Carmine just grinned.

"I'll show you."

They spent the evening rolling bread dough into silky balls that Carmine put in a pan and then set aside to rise again. Saint relaxed and allowed himself to enjoy it, the way Carmine hummed along with the music, occasionally stopping what he was doing to dance when a particularly catchy bit came on. He was a terrible dancer, no rhythm at all, and Saint was hopelessly charmed by the way his eyes lit up and he tossed his hair back as he shook his hips.

"Next game we win, I'm getting you on the dance floor," Carmine told him, but Saint just laughed and shook his head.

"All I can do is play hockey," he said, tossing a piece of dough across the counter to Carmine, who caught it easily. "Dancing and I don't mix."

"You've got to have *some* kind of hobby outside hockey, man," Carmine said. "What are you going to do after hockey? What if you get injured and have to retire early?"

Saint knocked reflexively on the wooden countertop and then flinched, waiting for the teasing. But when he glanced up, Carmine wasn't laughing.

"Sorry," he said. "I shouldn't have said

that. But you really should pick up a hobby or something."

"I'm fine," Saint said.

"You told me about gardening with Mom," Carmine said. "Did you like that?"

"Yeah," Saint admitted. It had been relaxing, working to loosen the dirt, pull up the weeds, on his knees in the grass with the sun beating down on his shoulders.

Carmine made a noncommittal noise and covered the last pan with cling wrap. He set it in the fridge and straightened. "There, they can rise overnight and I'll bake 'em in the morning."

"You're really into this," Saint commented as Carmine began gathering dishes to wash.

"Thanksgiving is great," Carmine said over his shoulder, running water in the sink. "Good food, hanging out with friends, a day off—what's not to like? The only thing better is Christmas." He flashed a grin at Saint. "Expect me to go nuts with the cooking for that, since we're hosting."

Saint tensed. He'd forgotten, somehow, that they were hosting. He was going to have people in his space, all over his house. Digging through his bookshelves, eating his food, his life laid bare before them.

Carmine turned the water off and Saint blinked.

"I have to—goodnight."

He escaped before Carmine could say anything.

THEY HAD a road trip after Thanksgiving, all the way across the country to face New York and then Toronto.

Adam sent Saint a text the morning of their game. *Tenny's been called up, we're gonna kick your asses :)*

Saint laughed and showed it to Carmine, beside him on the bus to the hotel. Carmine snorted quietly.

"That's what he thinks."

Losers buy dinner, Saint texted back

THE GAME WAS fast and brutal. Adam had clearly been studying Saint's moves, but Saint had been doing the same, watching endless game tape of the Wolverines until he could recognize Adam by his skating. There weren't as many games with Etienne, but Saint had watched those too. Etienne was fast, his stick-handling slick and graceful. With him on Adam's wing, the Wolverines played hard and ruthless, keeping the score tied for most of the game and pushing the Seabirds to their limits.

Near the end of the third period, Kasha caught a pass from Saint and slammed it home with the toe of his stick. Two minutes later, David found a hole and slipped through to score the game-winning goal thirty seconds before the buzzer. Then it was a game of keepaway from the increasingly desperate Wolverines until the clock ran out.

In the dressing room, Saint gave David the cape and slapped him on the shoulder. David grinned, sweaty and pink, and the others crowded around to congratulate him as Saint went to his locker to handle the media.

His phone had a message waiting when he was finally done with interviews.

It was from Adam, an address not far from the rink.

Saint glanced up and caught Carmine's eye, raising an eyebrow in silent inquiry. Carmine nodded, a faint smile playing on his mouth, and Saint found himself smiling back before heading for the showers.

"That was a good game," Carmine said on the ride to Adam's apartment. His head was back against the seat, baring his throat, and Saint looked away, swallowing hard.

"Yeah," he agreed. "Team's really coming together."

Carmine made a quiet noise of agreement. His eyes were closed, big hands loose in his lap, and Saint looked back out the window before he did something stupid, like let Carmine see just how much he wanted him.

"David's been acting weird, though," Carmine continued after a minute. "You know if he's okay?"

"Weird how?"

Carmine lifted a shoulder. "Crabby. Crabbier than usual," he amended. "Talking on his phone a lot. Seems distracted."

"Yeah," Saint said. "He was talking to someone at the hospital, he seemed upset. Fuck, I have to talk to him, don't I?"

Carmine grinned. "Well, you *are* the captain."

The cab pulled up to the curb before Saint could answer, and he followed Carmine out and into the building.

Adam and Etienne lived on the third floor, down a hall with thick carpet that swallowed the sound of their feet.

Saint knocked, and the door was opened almost immediately by Etienne.

"Hi," Saint said, smiling tentatively.

Etienne regarded him a minute. He was a tall man, an inch or so taller than Carmine but much lankier, with piercing slate blue eyes, a beaky nose, and dark hair swept back off his forehead. Finally he stepped aside, just as Adam came into the hall.

"Hey!" Adam said. "So you've met Tenny?"

"Well, not formally," Saint said, and held out his hand. "Saint Levesque. Hi. You're a badass on the ice, has anyone told you that?"

Adam slipped an arm around Etienne's waist as Etienne accepted Saint's hand.

"I tell him all the time," Adam said, sounding smug. "Tens, this is Carmine Quinn."

"Everyone knows Karma Quinn," Etienne said. His voice was deep and steady, and there was faint amusement in his eyes. "Just like we all know Saint Hockey. Please come in."

Saint and Carmine trailed behind them into the living room, which was huge and spacious, dotted with throw rugs on the hardwood floors and overstuffed couches lining the walls.

Adam disappeared into the kitchen as Etienne let them get comfortable, reappearing with several beers.

"Our old place was *my* old place," he said, handing out bottles. "And I had a golf course in my living room."

Saint blinked, unsure if he was kidding.

"How—" Carmine said tentatively.

Adam beamed and flopped onto the sofa beside Etienne. "Miniature golf. It wasn't very big, but it was fun. But then I met Tenny and we started having people over and it's kinda hard to socialize over a nine hole, you know? So we moved. Only been here a few months but it's starting to come together."

"If you'll just stop leaving your shoes in doorways," Etienne said, poking Adam in the side and making him squawk.

Saint watched them, his heart aching. Their affection was so easy, so intimate, the way Adam curled up against Etienne's lanky frame, the arm Etienne draped over Adam's shoulders and the careless kiss he pressed to his hair. Saint wanted that, the ease of familiarity and comfort with another person.

With Carmine. He was self-aware enough to acknowledge that. He wanted Carmine to touch him, kiss him absently, stroke small circles over his pulse-point with his free hand while he read.

Carmine was speaking, and Saint made an effort to focus.

"—AHL?"

Etienne nodded. "I've got a two-way contract. We're hoping for a more permanent contract with the Wolverines soon, but right now I'm getting a decent amount of callups, so it's good."

"And the guys on the Thunder?" Saint asked, trying to stay casual. "Are they, uh, chill?"

Etienne just nodded. "I didn't hide Adam, but I also didn't advertise it. Not really their business, right? But Adam pointed out that they needed to be able to trust me, so I told my line and a few others. They didn't care. Told me it was my point production that mattered, or something like that. The whole team knows now, and it's...." He shrugged. "It's common knowledge, and not newsworthy. I'm lucky, I know."

"He's modest," Adam told them. "He's worked his ass off to get here and the whole team loves him. He's the reason they won the Calder last year."

"Stop," Etienne protested, laughing as dull red crawled up his neck.

Saint smiled, watching them, and caught Carmine's eye briefly. Carmine smiled back at him as Adam hopped up and headed for the kitchen to check on dinner.

18

It wasn't until they were back in Portland that Saint had a chance to talk to David. He finally found his opportunity after practice between games, a week into December. David was leaving the rink when Saint caught up to him.

"A word?"

David glanced at him. "Busy."

"I wasn't asking," Saint said, keeping the edge from his tone with an effort.

David rolled his eyes. "Fine, whatever, let's make it fast."

Saint showed him into a conference room and they settled at the table. "How have you been?" he asked.

David wrinkled his brow. "You see me every day."

"And I'm asking you how you are," Saint said.

"I'm fine."

"Are you?" Saint watched David's face closely, looking for tells. "You've been distracted. Moody. I know you're a hothead in general, but you've had a shorter fuse than usual lately. You want to tell me what's going on?"

"Nope." David put both hands on the table, clearly ready to stand and leave.

"We're not done," Saint said sharply, and David scowled but subsided. Saint blew out a breath, praying for patience. "I know you don't like me. That's okay—you don't have to. But like me or not, I'm still your captain, and I need to make sure everything's alright with you."

David fidgeted but said nothing.

Saint waited.

It was several minutes before David cracked.

"I'm working through some stuff," he muttered, not meeting Saint's eyes.

"Okay," Saint said.

David shifted his weight. "It's—look, it's personal, okay? I don't want to talk about it."

"Alright," Saint said. "But David— you're part of my team. Whatever your personal feelings for me, I still care about your emotional *and* physical health. You can talk to me anytime you want, or I can set you up with the team psychiatrist."

"No," David said immediately, shaking his head. "No, I don't need that. I just—are we done yet?"

Saint sighed. "Yeah," he said, and David scrambled from his chair and bolted.

"You can't help if he won't let you help," Carmine said that evening as he slid a plate in front of Saint.

"Doesn't mean I don't *want* to," Saint muttered. He snuck a piece of asparagus to Steel under the table, feeling it lifted delicately from his fingers. When he glanced up, Carmine was watching him, an amused smile playing on his mouth. "Uh, sorry," Saint said.

"You're spoiling him rotten," Carmine said, and turned to fill his own plate.

The meal was peaceful, Steel half-asleep on the floor between them, sprawled across Saint's foot. The curtains were pulled back to show the setting sun over the west wall of the back garden. Fireflies winked in the gathering twilight.

It was cozy. Domestic. Saint watched the light casting shadows on Carmine's face and wondered what it would be like to kiss him, slide his fingers into that silky hair to hold his head still and really *taste* him, memorize his feel and smell and the heat of his body.

He cleared his throat. "Why aren't you dating?"

Carmine's eyebrows shot up. "Sorry?"

"You've been here since September," Saint forged on. "You said you're single. Are you not dating because—" He floundered. *Because of me*, he wanted to say, but that felt too arrogant. "Because of our living arrangement?"

Carmine's eyebrows somehow notched higher.

"Because if you want to bring someone home, you can," Saint said desperately. "Like, preferably not a one night stand or anything, but if you *know* them and you trust them and you want to—"

"Saint," Carmine said, and Saint shut up gratefully. "I'm too busy to date right now. A lot on my mind. It's nothing to do with living here, okay? The season's not really a good time to get into the dating scene, in any case."

Saint nodded silently and applied himself to his steak.

"So I've been thinking," Carmine said a few minutes later. "Felix and Roddy said you guys usually cater the Christmas dinner, but I'd like to do the cooking for it. Would that be okay?"

Saint tensed at the reminder but nodded again. "Um, yeah, that's fine. If you're sure—there are a lot of hungry rookies."

"I can handle it," Carmine said, smiling. "The question is, can you?"

Saint stared at his plate. "Sure."

"Really?" Carmine pressed. "Because every time I've mentioned it, you freeze like a deer in headlights."

Saint sighed. "What do you want me to say? I hate this, okay? I hate having people here, I hate my stuff being touched, I hate the mess they leave behind. But I can handle it, I always do. Just... give me some time."

Carmine watched him, dark eyes unreadable. "How can I make it easier?" he finally asked softly.

"You *can't*," Saint snapped. Hunching his shoulders, he tucked his chin to his chest. "Sorry. Sorry, I—there's nothing anyone can do, okay? It's something I just have to get over."

Carmine just nodded. "If you think of something I can help with, all you have to do is ask."

19

THE DAY of the Christmas party, Carmine was up early, in the kitchen making cardamom bread when Saint stumbled in.

"Morning," Carmine said, pulling the first pan out of the oven and putting the next in. "Give me a few minutes and I'll have breakfast ready for you."

Saint slumped at the table, cradling his coffee to his chest as Steel rested his chin on his thigh. Carmine set the plate of sausage on the table and pretended not to notice when Saint broke off a piece and slipped it to Steel.

The cardamom bread followed, wrapped in a towel to keep the heat in. Then spinach and leek quiche and cranberry orange mimosas. Saint's eyes got bigger and bigger as Carmine brought dishes to the table.

"Do you always go this all out?" he

asked, tearing off a piece of cardamom bread and popping it in his mouth.

"When I can," Carmine said. "I didn't get to do it in Boston very much—kitchen was too small. But when I go home, Ma and I like to spend days at a time just cooking anything and everything." He sat down opposite Saint and began putting food on his plate.

Saint looked more alert as he followed suit, nibbling the quiche suspiciously and then humming with surprised approval and taking a bigger bite. His shoulders were tight but he wasn't too jumpy yet, Carmine thought. Although that would probably change when the first guest knocked on the door.

"How many are on the list?" Saint asked, not meeting his eyes.

"Most of the team," Carmine said. "Coach might show up for a few minutes. Velvet's bringing her wife. The others all have the option to bring a plus one but they've been briefed on where they can go in the house, that kind of thing. And Roddy's bringing his kids, is that okay?"

Saint nodded, grip tight on his fork. "They're good kids."

He insisted on helping clean up but Carmine could tell his heart wasn't in it. He jumped at every sound until Carmine finally rescued the glass he was clutching a little too tight and set it aside.

"Saint. Hey." He waited, but Saint wouldn't meet his eyes, shoulders notched up around his ears. Carmine chewed his lip, not sure what to do. "What is it really?" he asked softly.

Saint shot a look at him through his lashes.

"This thing about your house," Carmine said. "What is it that bothers you so much? Wait, don't answer yet." He circled Saint's wrist with loose fingers and pulled him gently into the living room. Saint tucked his feet underneath him on the big couch and Carmine settled near him but not close enough to touch. "Okay," he said when he was comfortable. "Can you tell me?"

Saint heaved a sigh. "It's stupid." He scraped a thumbnail over the warp of the upholstery.

"I'm still here, aren't I?" Carmine asked. "Try me."

"I don't like things being out of my control," Saint said. "My house—it's *mine*. It's my safe space, you know? I know where everything is. No surprises. No changes to my routine. It's a—a controlled environment, I guess. When there are other people here, it—I can't predict what will happen. It's… I told you it's stupid."

"I'll probably just read for a bit," Saint said, pulling the nearest book toward him.

HE SPENT several hours in the living room, curled up in the corner of the sofa as Carmine bustled around the kitchen. Saint surfaced once to find a mug of apple cider beside him, next to a plate of sugar cookies —he hadn't even heard Carmine come in.

When it was time for the guests to start arriving, the panic tried to rear its head, but Saint took a deep breath and shoved it down, locking it away. *Carmine's here. He's going to take care of it. Of you.* The doorbell rang and footsteps came from the kitchen. Carmine put his head in, looking at Saint.

Saint met his eyes and somehow found a smile. The answering smile he got was worth it as Carmine withdrew and went to answer the door. Saint picked up his books and set them on the mantel, turning in time to greet Roddy and Naomi, their children trailing behind them. Naomi was a lovely, statuesque white woman with tumbling brunette hair and sharp brown eyes. She was holding Annika, six months old and still mostly bald. Naomi took Saint's hand and went up on her toes to kiss his cheek, soft and dry.

"Hi, honey," she said, smiling up at him.

"Hey Naomi," Saint said. The butterflies calmed further and his smile was real when he turned to greet Roddy.

"Don't look now, Roddy," Carmine said, appearing behind Naomi in the doorway, "but your kid has no hair. What's up with that?"

"She's a baby, you idiot," Roddy said without heat.

"Where's your bathroom, Saint?" Naomi asked. Saint pointed, and Naomi pushed Annika into Saint's arms. They regarded each other dubiously.

"Hi," Saint finally said. "Remember me?"

Annika pushed a fist into her mouth and said something unintelligible around it as the doorbell rang again.

Guests trickled in in ones and twos over the next hour, until the living room was filled with large hockey players and their partners. Kasha had brought Nadia, a leggy blonde with unhappy eyes and a sour set to her mouth. David was there with a girl Saint had never met. She'd made a beeline for Saint, arms open to hug him, baby and all, and been smoothly headed off by Carmine, who shook her hand and introduced himself and steered her toward the wet bar.

Saint shifted Annika's weight and

headed for the kitchen. Naomi was on the couch, talking to several other wives, but she didn't seem in a hurry to have her baby back, and truth be told, Saint kind of liked the solid feel of her in his arms. She babbled to him happily as he carried her through to find food laid out on all the counters.

"*Look* at all this," he told Annika. "Can you eat solid food yet? I'd maybe better not give you anything yet, I don't want your mom to kill me. Can you believe how much Carmine cooked?" He found an open bottle of wine on the counter and poured himself a glass as Annika smacked his sweater with slobbery hands and bounced up and down. Saint rebalanced her and took a sip, then another. "Wait until you're old enough to drink wine," he said, resting his hips against the counter.

Annika made a lunge for the glass and Saint laughed, holding it out of reach. "Not yet!" He looked up to see Carmine in the doorway, watching them with dark eyes. "Hey," Saint said, smile widening. The wine curled warm in his belly and loosened the knot in his chest as Carmine took a step forward.

"Doing okay?" he asked quietly.

"Yeah," Saint said, faintly surprised to realize it was true.

The doorbell rang again.

"That's probably Felix," Carmine said. "He texted me he was running late."

"We'll get it," Saint said. He drained his glass and they headed for the front door.

Felix was wearing a dove-gray sweater and black pants that suited his rangy form well, standing alone on the front porch.

"No date?" Saint asked.

"Not this time," Felix said. His smile was almost genuine, but there were shadows in his eyes.

Saint frowned. "Come on, get in here." He met Naomi coming down the hall and handed Annika off to her, waving goodbye before grabbing Felix's arm and steering him toward his suite.

"The others—" Felix protested half-heartedly.

"Can wait," Saint said. "What's going on with you?"

Felix rubbed the back of his neck. "You have to be so perceptive, *cher*?"

"Fee," Saint said softly. "Are you okay?"

Felix shook his head. "I'm—Saint…."

Saint pulled him to the bed and sat him down, settling beside him. "Talk to me." It wasn't a suggestion.

"I met someone, few months ago," Felix said. "Start of the season, yes? He didn't want to be serious, so I tried—I tried not to —but—"

"You fell for him," Saint said quietly.

Felix ducked his head, hair falling in his face. "I didn't mean to," he whispered.

Saint touched his arm. "That's not something we can really stop, is it?"

Felix shook his head and tilted sideways, pressing his face to Saint's shoulder. "He's perfect," he said in a muffled voice. "And he doesn't want me."

"Obviously he's not perfect," Saint pointed out, rubbing Felix's bony back. "Or he'd want you back. Only an idiot wouldn't want you."

Felix laughed, the sound a little wet, and sat up, swiping at his eyes. "Sorry, *cher*. I didn't mean to—how are you? You don't seem so panicky. I thought you'd be a wreck."

"I'm… okay," Saint said. "Carmine—he helps."

Felix studied his face. "Ah."

"Don't you dare start," Saint warned, standing. "I've already got Roddy being an idiot about this, and there *is* no this, okay? So just… let it go."

A smile flickered over Felix's mouth. "Okay, *cher*. For now. Is there wine?"

"Of course there's wine," Saint said. "How dare you impugn my honor by asking that?"

They headed for the kitchen, bickering

amiably, to find Carmine pulling rolls from the oven. Felix elbowed Saint, who punched him. They scuffled briefly as Carmine glanced up.

"Hey Butterfly," he said. "Glad you could make it." His face was pink with the heat from the oven, hair curling damply around his temples and over his ears.

"I'm only here because Saint promised me alcohol," Felix said, poking Saint in the ribs and dodging his swipe.

Carmine poured him a glass and refilled Saint's before turning to fill his own. "Everyone's in the living room. Shall we?"

Saint followed them in, perching on the arm of the sofa beside Kasha, who was telling a story in a mangled mix of Russian and English, hands waving. In Naomi's lap, Annika caught sight of him and bounced up and down, pudgy arms out as she made imploring noises.

"You've got a fan," Roddy said, grinning. He scooped Annika up and deposited her in Saint's arms again, where she settled in happily, clutching handfuls of his sweater as she talked to him in incomprehensible babyspeak.

Saint nodded along, watching his guests. They were sprawled over his furniture, talking animatedly to each other. The fire Carmine had lit earlier snapped and popped as the logs settled. Outside, it was dark, the cold gathering as the sun went down. Jason was talking to Ty. Beside them, the Swedes were sitting on the long couch along the far wall, each with a pretty blonde girl beside him. Saint wasn't entirely sure he could tell them apart—were they triplets, he wondered. Hockey players had a type, that was sure.

A timer went off and Carmine hopped to his feet. "That's me. Food'll be ready in about ten, guys."

"You wanna help him?" Saint asked Annika in a low tone. She said something and Saint nodded sagely. "You're right. Let's go."

In the kitchen, Carmine was bent over the oven again, inspecting the turkey. Saint paused in the doorway to appreciate the view, then stepped around the counter.

"Need a hand?"

Carmine straightened. "Nope, just making sure the turkey's basted." He closed the oven door and Saint set his wine glass down.

Two glasses of wine on an empty stomach was probably not the smartest idea, but at that moment, Saint really didn't care. Warmth suffused his bones, buoying him up as he took another step nearer, shifting Annika's weight absently. His eyes were trained on Carmine's mouth, so he didn't miss the way his tongue flickered out to wet his lips.

Just once, Saint thought. *Just so I know what it's like.* He closed the distance between them, Carmine frozen in place, watching him get nearer. Toe-to-toe, Saint looked up, into his face.

"Thank you," he said quietly. "For— making it work. For helping me." *For being with me. For not telling me I'm crazy and walking away.*

Carmine licked his lips again. "Any-time," he said, and Saint didn't think he was imagining the hoarseness in his voice. "I— yeah. Anytime." He was bent forward, his body curved toward Saint open and recep-tive, and it was as natural as breathing for Saint to reach up, hook his free hand around the back of Carmine's neck and draw him down into a kiss.

Carmine's lips were wet and soft. He tasted like wine and cranberry sauce, and Saint made a pleased noise. He pressed forward and Carmine opened his mouth, letting Saint's tongue slip inside.

The kitchen was silent except for the sound of their mingled breath. Saint took his time exploring, tracing the shape of Carmine's lips and memorizing the feel of him. Carmine groaned, the noise reverberating through his chest, and Saint shuddered.

"Ow, *ow*," Carmine said suddenly, breaking the kiss, and Saint blinked, struggling to focus. Carmine was bent awkwardly sideways, head at an angle, and it took a minute for Saint to realize Annika had a handful of his hair and was yanking on it, cooing happily. "*Help*," Carmine said, still tilted sideways, and Saint couldn't stop the laugh that bubbled up.

"You sure know how to kill the moment," he told Annika, and set to work untangling her chubby fingers from Carmine's hair. She resisted, reaching with her other hand and protesting loudly, but Saint got her free and took a step back, struggling to stifle the giggles still trying to escape.

Carmine's eyes were dark, hooded in the dimly lit kitchen, and he watched Saint like a leopard eyeing his next meal.

Saint's laughter cut off like a switch and he swallowed hard, brought back to earth with a thump. "Oh God," he said. "Oh God, I shouldn't have done that."

"What?" Carmine looked confused, brows knitting together at the abrupt left turn.

"I *kissed* you," Saint said.

"Yeah, I was there," Carmine said, lips twitching.

"No, but—" Saint could feel the panic swelling under his ribs, pressing against his lungs and making it hard to breathe. "I—"

Carmine took Annika out of his arms. "Don't move," he ordered.

Like he could. Saint stayed put, gulping for air, as Carmine left the room. He was back almost immediately, wrapping his big hands around Saint's biceps and holding him steady.

"I'm sorry," Saint managed.

"For *what*?" Carmine sounded baffled.

"I shouldn't have—I didn't—I didn't ask if you were into me, I just—and you—" Saint snapped his mouth shut as Carmine's hands tightened.

"Oh, Saint." Carmine's voice was gentle and so, so affectionate. "You think you could make me do something I didn't *want* to do?"

"Still—"

Carmine shook him gently. "I've wanted to kiss you for months, you idiot."

Saint looked up at that. "You—what? But... what about Atlanta?"

Carmine blinked. "Atlanta? Oh."

"That was a hickey," Saint said. He pulled until Carmine let him go, and took a careful step back. "I'm not... judging, or like—it's just—"

Carmine rubbed his face and leaned back against the counter. "That was... a moment of weakness," he said. He sounded as if he was choosing his words carefully. "I was—well, I was mad at you. And it'd been a long time since anyone touched me, Saint. I was lonely. So I went out. But I didn't—I couldn't go through with it. I made out with this guy in the back of a bar but every time I closed my eyes, I was kissing you. I told him to stop, and I left."

Saint clutched the island. "I'm sorry," he said again.

Carmine shook his head and took two quick steps forward to loom over him. "You can be so stupid," he muttered, cupped his face, and kissed him.

It was better without a baby in his arms, Saint decided. He was free to melt against Carmine's solid frame, let his arms go around his neck as Carmine pulled him in, his mouth hot and demanding this time.

Carmine was the one to break it again, tearing away and spinning to open the oven just as Kasha turned the corner.

"Is so dark in here!" He felt along the wall for the light switch and Saint fumbled for the wine, pouring with unsteady hands as light flooded the room. How had

Carmine heard Kasha's footsteps? All Saint could process—still, even with four feet of distance between them—was the searing heat of Carmine's mouth and body. His lips tingled. Surely Kasha would take one look at him and know what they'd been up to.

But Kasha was beaming at him from across the counter, no suspicion on his sunny face, and Saint smiled back reflexively.

"Is food ready?" Kasha asked Carmine, who was busy pulling a massive turkey from the oven.

Carmine set it on the stovetop and nodded. "You can call the others."

20

THE REST of the evening passed in a blur. Saint was hyper-aware of Carmine, sitting to his left as they ate, but he didn't look at him and Carmine didn't touch him. At some point, Annika ended up back in Saint's lap and Naomi instructed him on what foods she could safely eat, so he divided his time between feeding her and watching the guests.

Jason was arguing with Jesper and Elias about something as Oskar looked on, clearly amused. Tye and Embry were discussing forechecking, with Embry using cranberries on his plate to illustrate his point. Velvet was talking to Felix, and next to her, her wife Lisa was chatting with Oscar's date about something Saint couldn't hear.

This was his team. His family. It wasn't perfect—*they* weren't perfect. But no one

holding up a hand. "You can't stop thinking about me?"

Saint rolled his eyes. "Not the takeaway I wanted you to get from that."

"Yeah, but—" Carmine took a step closer, grinning at him. "You can't stop thinking about me."

"Focus," Saint ordered.

"I can't stop thinking about you either."

Saint's mouth fell open.

"Did you think it was one-sided?" Carmine murmured. He stepped into Saint's space, running a hand down his arm. "You're all I've thought about for *months*, Saint. Besides, we're professionals. Are you going to stop passing to me if we have a fight?"

"Haven't yet," Saint muttered, and Carmine laughed.

"Exactly. Even when we're mad at each other, we still *work* on the ice. I think we're both grownup enough to handle it if things do go south."

"But—"

Carmine put a finger over his mouth, effectively silencing him. "You think too much."

"Maybe you don't think enough," Saint retorted, and then winced. "Sorry, I—"

"No, don't apologize," Carmine said. He couldn't help the smile. "I love that you tell me how you feel. Don't ever stop doing that, okay?"

"Not sure I could," Saint admitted, and Carmine couldn't wait any longer. He pressed their mouths together, savoring the soft gasp, the warmth of Saint's skin under his hands, the way he crowded forward, plastering himself against Carmine's body.

This was what he'd been waiting for, and it was worth every single aching moment, the longing and lonely nights. Saint was solid and real in his arms, kissing him back with every bit as much hunger as Carmine was feeling. Carmine tightened his grip and deepened the kiss, sweeping his tongue inside Saint's mouth in quick, gentle passes. The moan he got went straight to his groin.

"Fuck," he gasped when the need to breathe reasserted itself. "You're killing me."

Saint's lips were kiss-swollen, shiny and pink. His hair was in his eyes, his breathing rapid. Carmine brushed his hair out of his face.

"Talk to me," he ordered gently. "How are you feeling?"

Saint scowled and ducked his head. He pressed his face to Carmine's chest briefly and then stepped away. "Everyone's got you wrong, don't they?"

Carmine blinked. "Come again?"

"The whole—" Saint gestured. "Goon thing. It's an act. All brawn, no brain."

"I wouldn't call it an *act*," Carmine hedged.

"Okay, then it's a front." Saint leaned a hip against the counter and looked him over. "People don't take you seriously because you're built like a Greek god-slash-body builder, when actually you're ridiculously smart and more emotionally intelligent than anyone else on the team."

Carmine sputtered a laugh. "Greek god? Seriously?"

Saint lifted a shoulder, lips twitching. "Everyone thinks you're just big dumb muscle. But you're not. I mean, I've known that for awhile, but like... you're *really* not. Why do you let people think it?"

Carmine sighed. "Can we get comfortable for this conversation?"

Saint led the way into the living room and they settled on the couch, Saint crossing his legs on the cushion facing him.

It took Carmine a minute to figure out the words. "I had a boyfriend," he finally said. "Dylan. I was in major juniors, he lived next door to my billet family. I... thought I loved him." He *had* loved him. That was the true kick in the balls. Dylan had been sunny summer days, freckled nose and sunkissed hair, bright laughing blue eyes and hands that knew how to draw the perfect responses from Carmine's body.

He glanced up. Saint was watching him carefully, hands folded in his lap.

"I loved him," Carmine said softly. "I wanted him to be proud of me."

"What happened?"

"I was pretty nerdy as a kid," Carmine said. "Nose in a book anytime I wasn't on the ice. When I turned sixteen, I hit a growth spurt and grew into my body, but I still loved to read. I wanted to go to college, get a degree in English lit. Dylan—he said it was too much."

Saint's eyebrows shot up but he said nothing.

"He said that my height and muscle were intimidating enough as it was, that when I tried to show off my brains too, people didn't like it."

"And you believed him?" Saint's voice was faint, as if he was still figuring out what to feel.

Carmine shrugged. "I loved him," he repeated. "I think *he* was intimidated, honestly. But I wanted to be with him. I couldn't do anything about my height, and I need the muscle to do my job properly, but... I could hide my brains. Make myself less threatening intellectually."

Saint covered his face.

"I know it's fucked up," Carmine said. "I *do*. But I guess… it became a habit. People look at me, they see a big guy who knows how to throw his weight around. They don't expect anything else from me. It's easier that way sometimes."

Saint dropped his hands and reached out, cupping Carmine's face. "Don't hide from me," he said fiercely. "Don't ever hide any part of yourself from me."

Carmine wrapped his hands around Saint's wrists, warmth surging through him. "I won't," he promised.

"You—you're so incredible," Saint continued. "How can anyone not see that? This guy, *Dylan*—" He spat the name. "He's a fucking idiot. An insecure, tiny-dicked asshole who was too threatened by you to realize how amazing you are."

Laughter bubbled up and Carmine squeezed Saint's wrists. "To be fair, he didn't actually have a tiny—"

Saint wrenched a hand free and covered his mouth. "Tiny-dicked," he repeated. "And we're not talking about him anymore, got it?"

Carmine resisted temptation manfully for all of three seconds and then licked his palm. Saint jerked away, nose wrinkling, and Carmine grinned at him.

"You never answered *my* question," he said.

Saint frowned. "Which one?"

"I asked you how you were feeling. About… this. Us."

Saint sat back. "Ah."

"The truth," Carmine added.

Saint met his eyes. "I'm scared," he said quietly. "I'm scared of fucking it up. Chasing you away."

"As I'm fond of pointing out, I'm still here, aren't I?" Carmine picked up one of Saint's hands and pressed a kiss to his knuckles. "I've seen you dealing with a lot of shit. None of it's been a deal-breaker."

"You haven't seen me melt down when my routine gets fucked up," Saint said. He sounded slightly breathless, eyes fixed on Carmine's lips, still close to his fingers.

"We'll deal with that if and when it happens," Carmine said, and kissed his hand again. Saint swallowed hard. "Saint," Carmine whispered.

"Yeah," Saint said, sounding mesmerized.

"Can I take you to bed, Saint?"

Saint's throat bobbed when he swallowed again. "Y-yeah," he managed.

21

CARMINE WASN'T sure how they made it to his suite, after. He couldn't take his hands off Saint, and Saint seemed to feel the same way, judging by how he kept crowding up against Carmine, sliding his palms flat under his shirt and running them over the planes of his back.

They stumbled through the door and Steel yipped plaintively from his crate. Carmine twitched and straightened.

"Fuck, I have to—" Saint looked so debauched already, hair rumpled and cheeks flushed, that Carmine couldn't help leaning in to steal another kiss. "I have to—God, you taste so good—I have to let him out. Can you—"

"Can I what?" Saint asked, hooking a finger through Carmine's belt loop and pulling him closer.

"Stop being so goddamn *sexy* for a minute," Carmine gasped. He was so turned on he could barely breathe, his erection pressing painfully against his zipper.

Saint laughed and released him. "Take care of your dog so you can take care of me."

Carmine snorted, turning to open the crate. "Corny, Saint Hockey, very corny. Is that your best line?"

Steel danced around them, delighted to be free and in the presence of his two favorite people, and Carmine bent to rub his ears briefly before opening the sliding glass door that looked out on the overgrown garden. Steel dashed outside and Carmine turned back to Saint.

"That should buy us at least thirty minutes. Where were we?"

"You were mocking my moves," Saint said. He was smiling but there were nerves in his eyes as he rubbed his forearm.

Carmine crossed the room and backed him up against the bed. He gave him a gentle push and Saint sat abruptly. Carmine crawled onto the mattress, straddling his thighs, and pressed on his shoulder until Saint was lying flat on his back staring up at him.

He was so beautiful, Carmine just had to bend and kiss him again. Then he pulled him up until they were both fully on the bed before lying down on his side next to him.

Saint turned his head to look at him. He was still tense, worry competing with the want in his eyes, and Carmine leaned in for another kiss.

"What do you like?" he asked. He let his hand wander, up Saint's ribs and down, ghosting over his hipbone.

"Um." Saint's eyes were squeezed shut.

Carmine kept exploring, tracing the ridges of Saint's abdomen with a finger and dipping just below his waistband before retreating.

"Gotta tell me, lover," he murmured.

"I don't know," Saint said in a rush. "Fuck, I don't—I don't *know*, I've never—"

Carmine stilled his hand. "Ever?"

"Not... no, I mean, not never, but—" Saint pulled away, trying to roll off the bed, and Carmine lunged, getting an arm around his waist just in time.

"You're not running from this," he said in Saint's ear, and Saint shuddered violently and went limp against him. "That's better," Carmine crooned. "What did you mean?"

Saint licked his lips and turned his head into Carmine's, asking wordlessly for a kiss. Carmine was delighted to oblige, and they spent several long moments exploring each other's mouths before Carmine somewhat reluctantly drew away.

"We're not doing anything else until you tell me," he said, pecking Saint's nose lightly.

Saint sighed. "I gave a guy a handjob in major juniors," he said, staring at the ceiling. "He didn't—it doesn't matter. And then year before last, I went to Europe by myself during the summer. Amsterdam. I was—" He swallowed. "I wanted to find a bar where they didn't know me. Where I wouldn't be recognized."

"And did you?" Carmine asked, keeping his voice gentle.

"Yeah." Saint's lashes swept down. "I met someone—he, um. Blew me?"

"Was it good?"

"I guess," Saint said. He wriggled in Carmine's arms, getting comfortable. "It was kind of messy. I wasn't very good at returning the favor but he was nice about it. That's... it." He met Carmine's eyes. "Is that a problem?"

"Why would it be?"

"I don't know, I just—I'm not experienced."

"It's not about experience," Carmine said. "It's about being *with* someone. Fully present in the moment. You think you can do that?"

"There's nowhere else I want to be," Saint said, and the raw honesty in his voice silenced Carmine briefly.

"*God*," he managed, and rolled on top of him. "You're going to be the death of me," he said, propping himself on his elbows.

Saint smiled up at him. "Can we get this show on the road?"

Carmine hummed. "Excellent idea." He pulled Saint's sweater and shirt up to his armpits and lowered his head. The shiver he got when his lips met skin was delicious, and he smiled as he kissed his way slowly down Saint's chest. His skin was satin-soft, dotted with the occasional mole, and Carmine took his time, inspecting every exposed inch until Saint was squirming, wordless pleas catching in his throat.

"Off," Carmine said, tugging at the sweater, and Saint got the idea and curled forward far enough for Carmine to yank it off over his head. Then Carmine scooted down the bed, until he was straddling Saint's thighs. He could see the erection straining the fabric of Saint's slacks, a damp patch spreading slowly, and he licked his lips. "So you weren't impressed with the blowjob, huh?"

Saint gulped. "I mean. It was... fine? I came, so I guess—"

"I think I can do a lot better than 'fine',"

Carmine purred. He flicked Saint's pants open and dragged the zipper down inch by tortuous inch, watching the way Saint twitched and struggled to be still.

"How come I'm naked but you're not?" Saint said breathlessly.

Carmine obligingly pulled his sweater off and Saint sat up, one tentative hand out. Carmine took it and guided it to his chest, and Saint ran his fingers through the soft curls there, eyes wondering and lips parted.

Still, Carmine was on a mission, so after a minute he rolled off the bed and took his pants off before getting back in position. Anticipation was half the fun, and Carmine prided himself on his ability to drive his partner out of his mind with soft, barely there touches, always skirting the prize as he worked Saint's pants down his hips. Saint helped him drag them off, and Carmine sat back on his heels between his muscled thighs and whistled, low and reverent.

Saint was sprawled on the bed, chest heaving. His stretchy black boxers had a steadily growing damp patch at the head of his straining erection, and he was gripping the comforter in both hands in an obvious effort to keep still.

"When's the last time someone told you how beautiful you are?" Carmine asked, running a reverent palm over Saint's knee.

Saint blinked, mouth working. "I... don't know."

"Good, then let me." Carmine dropped a kiss on Saint's flat stomach. "You're so beautiful," he said against his skin. "I've thought that for a long time, you know. Remember when you were telling me the rules of your house, all stressed and snippy?"

Saint draped an arm over his eyes, groaning. "*Please* don't remind me. I was such an asshole."

Carmine huffed a laugh and kissed his abdomen again. "I was into it—you—even then. You were so uptight. I wanted to lay you out and kiss you until you forgot your name."

"Is that—ah—still an option?"

Carmine lifted his head, smiling wickedly. "Most definitely. But I have something else in mind right now."

He hooked his thumbs in the elastic of Saint's boxers and peeled them slowly down. Saint's cock was a sight to behold, flushed dark red and leaking steadily in slow, sluggish drops. Carmine licked his lips, staring at it.

"Caz." Saint sounded desperate. "Please *do* something."

"I *am* doing something," Carmine said. "I'm savoring the moment."

Saint groaned again. "I'm gonna die.

You haven't even touched me yet and I'm gonna—" He cut off with a yelp when Carmine wrapped a hand around him, abdomen tightening and hips jerking up sharply.

"Don't do that when my mouth is on you," Carmine warned, stroking slowly. "Bad manners."

"I w-won't," Saint panted. "Please, Caz, please, I need—"

"I've got you," Carmine said, and Saint squeezed his eyes shut and moaned.

Carmine spent a few minutes enjoying the weight and feel of him, the slide of his fist over satiny skin. He traced the flared ridges of the head, rubbing the sensitive spot underneath just to hear Saint swear in a thick, choked voice before stroking him again.

"How am I doing?" he asked conversationally, hand still moving, and Saint cracked an eye open to glare at him.

"You have to—*fuck*—ask?"

"I like to keep the lines of communication open," Carmine said, unperturbed. He twisted his wrist on an upstroke and Saint arched up off the bed with a bitten off shout. "I'll take that as an endorsement," Carmine continued, unable to stop his grin.

Saint collapsed backward, chest heaving. "I can't—I'm not gonna last."

"It's not a race," Carmine said, hand still moving steadily. He smoothed his free hand over Saint's thigh, appreciating the thick muscle. "You can come whenever you want, but if you can hold on just a little longer, I promise I'll make it worth your while."

He waited while Saint fought an internal battle and finally nodded jerkily. Then he bent and blew warm air over the head of Saint's cock.

Saint twitched, jamming a hand against his mouth.

"You don't have to be quiet," Carmine said, not looking up.

"I'm n-not," Saint panted. "I'm trying not to *lose* it, goddammit, *do*—"

Carmine swallowed him down, ready for the helpless buck of Saint's hips and pinning him flat to the bed with both hands before he could choke him.

"I'm sorry, I'm so sorry," Saint gasped. "Oh *fuck*, Caz, I can't—"

Carmine patted his side and set to work. He alternated soft, wet licks around the head with firm suction, one hand steadily jacking what his mouth couldn't easily reach. Saint twisted and writhed beneath him, getting louder and louder until he was begging, something close to tears in his voice.

Carmine had spent years perfecting this

skill, and he was justifiably proud of his ability to drive his partner out of their mind, but he didn't think he'd ever been with someone as responsive as Saint. Every pass of his tongue elicited a shudder. Dropping down and letting the head of Saint's cock nudge the back of his throat produced a string of garbled filth. When he picked up the pace, it was a handful of minutes before Saint was clutching at his shoulders, his hair, hands desperate and shaking.

"I'm gonna—Caz, I can't—"

Carmine took him deep again and Saint curled forward off the bed with a choked cry, filling his mouth with hot, bitter liquid. Carmine swallowed it all, slowing his rhythm as Saint went limp and then finally lifting his head.

Saint's arm was over his eyes again, mouth open as he panted for air. Carmine crawled up his body until he was braced above him.

"Hey," he said gently. "Saint. How are you doing?"

It took Saint a minute to move his arm, and when he did, his eyes were wet. Alarm spiked in Carmine's chest, but Saint smiled, soft and a little shaky.

"That was—" He reached up and pulled Carmine down into an unsteady kiss.

"So… better than fine?" Carmine asked after a few minutes.

Saint's laugh was wobbly. "I've never felt anything like that."

Carmine smiled, tucking his face into the crook of Saint's neck. Saint reached between them, fingers tentative as they wrapped around Carmine's aching shaft.

"Is this okay?" he asked.

Carmine groaned, hips rolling. "Tighter. Can you—yeah, like that." He rolled his hips again, grinding down against Saint's thigh, fucking into his hand. He could feel the orgasm just out of sight, gathering pressure in his chest and the pit of his stomach. "Can I come on you," he gasped, hips stuttering.

"Yeah," Saint said, wrapping his free arm around Carmine's neck. "Please, I want you to."

The bliss broke free and Carmine froze as he came, spilling over Saint's thigh in heavy, erratic spurts. He couldn't breathe, couldn't move, the ecstasy lighting up his nerves like fireworks under his skin until he finally fell forward, limbs suddenly too heavy to move.

Saint grunted but held his weight, hands stroking up and down Carmine's sides in soft, slow motions.

behind, pressing his cheek to Carmine's shoulder blade.

Carmine made a pleased noise, turned off the stove, and shuffled around so they were facing. "Hey," he said quietly.

Saint pushed his face into Carmine's chest. "Hey."

They stood like that for a minute, until Saint finally loosened his grip and stepped away with a reluctant sigh.

"Game day," he said. It was an explanation, of sorts, and somehow Carmine got it. He nodded, a smile creasing his eyes, and turned back to the stove.

Saint made himself coffee, then oatmeal as soon as Carmine stepped aside. They ate sitting across from each other, neither speaking. When Saint was done, he watched Carmine eat for a minute.

"We should talk," he finally said.

Carmine arched an eyebrow, his mouth full.

"Not now," Saint said hurriedly. "And it's not bad, I just—"

Carmine swallowed. "You want to figure out what we're doing." There was no judgment in his voice, but Saint hunched his shoulders anyway. "Hey," Carmine said. He reached across the table and took his hand. "There's nothing wrong with wanting to know where we stand." His hand was solid and warm.

Saint looked at where their fingers were intertwined and finally nodded.

"After the game." Carmine squeezed his hand and let go.

THINGS WENT WRONG ALMOST IMMEDIATELY.

At practice, there was a nick in Saint's skate blade, and someone had borrowed his stick tape. Saint stood in front of his locker and took several deep breaths. *Sharpen your blade*, he told himself, touching the tips of his fingers to his thumbs. *Find your tape, use someone else's, it's just tape, this isn't a big deal.*

David was in an even worse mood than usual, shoving a rookie who got in his way, snapping at Saint, and firing pucks at Felix with far more force than was necessary. After one particularly hard shot, Felix pushed his helmet up and shouted at him in furious French. David flipped him off and skated away.

Saint went after him, motioning for Roddy to talk to Felix as he left the ice.

David was in the locker room, furiously yanking at his skate laces.

"Fuck off," he said before Saint could say anything. "Just—don't."

Saint sat down a few stalls away. There were lines in David's face, carved deep around his face and eyes, and his hands were shaking as he jerked his skates off and dropped them beside him.

"What happened?" Saint asked quietly.

"Women are bitches," David said, standing. "Don't ever trust them."

Saint swallowed the sharp comment. "Do you need to speak to a therapist?"

David scoffed. "Like they could help." He shoved his pants off, dragged his shirt over his head, and stalked for the shower.

Reluctantly, Saint followed him in.

"Are you good to play?"

"I'm fine," David said without looking at him. "Go away."

Saint hesitated a minute longer, but finally left.

Roddy found him in the hall. "What's going on?"

"Breakup, I think. He wouldn't talk to me."

Roddy swore under his breath. "He okay to play?"

"I think so. It's Coach's decision, anyway. Do you know who he was dating?"

Roddy shook his head.

"Ask Sergei. They're friends."

"Not sure anyone's really 'friends' with David, but I'll ask," Roddy said.

Saint nodded abruptly and headed for the exit.

He couldn't sleep during his usual pre-game nap. Lying on his back, staring at the ceiling, he ran through his breathing exercises, touching his thumbs to fingertips, then knuckles, over and over in a vain attempt to get himself back on track. He wanted to go to Carmine, crawl into the bed beside him and be drawn into his warmth. He wanted Carmine's long arms around him, his nose in the hair at the nape of Saint's neck.

But Carmine was trying to sleep too. He wouldn't welcome the intrusion, the disturbance to his own routine.

Saint rolled over and pressed his face into the pillows.

He must have dozed off at some point, because his alarm woke him with a startling jerk. He was halfway upright before awareness came in and he sagged, rubbing his face.

"Game day," he said out loud, and was careful to step forward with his left foot first when he stood.

He couldn't find the tie he'd planned on wearing. After ten minutes of increasingly frantic searching, he was interrupted by a quiet knock on the door.

"Saint? We need to leave soon."

"Just a minute," Saint called. Standing in the wreckage of his closet, he balled his fists. *It's just a piece of fabric*, he thought. *Wearing it won't win you the game.* He was standing on a precipice, teetering on the edge. The slightest push would send him into freefall, and then Carmine would see— he would—

Saint took a deep breath, grabbed a random tie, and slung it around his neck as he headed for the door.

Carmine was waiting on the other side, and his eyes creased with a smile when Saint stepped out. "Hey," he said softly.

Don't. Don't be nice to me. Saint turned away, ostensibly to shut the door but mostly to avoid his eyes.

"You okay?" Carmine said. "David was being an ass this morning."

"Fine," Saint said tersely. "Let's go."

CARMINE'S CAR wouldn't start. Saint sat in the front seat as Carmine looked under the hood, swearing and cajoling in a steady stream, and struggled to stay calm.

It's just Murphy's law. He checked the time—they were going to be late. He called for a car and stepped out.

"I ordered a ride," he said.

"No, it's fine, I just have to—" Carmine's hand slipped and he swore.

"If you hurt yourself before the game, I'll kill you myself and Coach won't have to," Saint snapped. "Go wash your hands, the car will be here in five minutes."

Carmine straightened, eyes thoughtful as he gazed at Saint, but he said nothing. Instead he jogged back into the house. Saint tipped his head back, breathing through his nose, and touched his thumbs to his knuckles over and over.

THEY DIDN'T TALK on the way to the rink. On one hand, Saint was grateful for that, too aware of the driver's eyes on them in the mirror. On the other, it left him alone with his thoughts, a swirling maelstrom of anxiety and fear that was making him nauseous. Everything was going wrong. He couldn't control anything. He was helpless, useless, neurotic and pathetic. Carmine was going to realize exactly what he was like and walk away immediately. Or, maybe worse, he'd try to pretend it didn't bother him, but Saint would *know*. He'd see it in the way Carmine stopped touching him, drew away subtly until Saint was alone again, trapped in his self-destructive ways until he ate himself alive, an ouroboros of guilt and shame.

The car stopped and Carmine stepped out. Saint gathered himself and followed, summoning a smile for the driver. Their walk inside was silent. Saint smiled automatically at the photographers but didn't stop to talk to anyone.

In the locker room, he stopped dead at his stall. His sticks had been *moved*.

"Pat?" he said, keeping his voice even with an effort.

"Yeah, Saint," Pat said, materializing beside him.

"Has someone been messing with my stuff?"

Pat frowned. "No? I know better than to let anyone touch your things."

Kasha, beside Saint's stall, hunched his shoulders. "Saint, I—"

"What happened?"

"Jase—we were fight, yes? Play fight. Wrestle. I lose balance. Trip and fall, into

—" Kasha gestured at Saint's stall and his out of order sticks. "I'm sorry, Saint. I'm try to put back right but I'm not know for sure, think I make it worse." He looked like a puppy waiting to be kicked, and Saint took a deep breath, picking up the stick tape that had been missing that morning, now sitting where it was supposed to be. *Pat's doing, no doubt.*

"It's fine," he said tightly.

"No, I mess up," Kasha protested. "I need to make right—"

"I *said* it's fine, *shut up*," Saint snapped, and Kasha recoiled. Guilt flooded Saint and he gulped air through his mouth. "I just have to—" His fingers cramped around the roll of tape and he spun and hurled it across the room, narrowly missing David, who yelped and swore.

"Kash, I need to talk to you a minute," Carmine said, and caught his elbow, gently pulling him away.

Saint reordered his sticks, making sure they were all neat and straight and none were cracked, and then sat down on his locker. Across the room, Carmine was talking to Kasha, who kept glancing over his shoulder at Saint until Carmine physically turned him so he couldn't.

Good, Saint thought viciously. *Don't look*

thigh and Saint swallowed hard, forcing himself not to listen in.

He had to tell Carmine they couldn't have sex again, that they had to go back to the way they were before. It was for the best —for the team, and for Saint's heart, already so bruised and fragile. Carmine would get tired of the neuroses, the hangups, the constant rituals designed to keep his life on an even keel. Saint was doing him a favor by cutting him loose from all that.

He would tell him that evening, after the game. Carmine would understand. He had to.

THEY LOST BY A HUMILIATING MARGIN, and Saint stood at the half-door to the locker room entrance, watching numbly as each player stepped past him and went down the hall. Somehow, somehow, he got through the media scrum after, forcing down all the feelings threatening to scour him clean from the inside out and focusing on the questions, giving his usual bland non-answers until he was finally free to escape.

Most of the room was gone when he got back from his shower, including Carmine and Kasha. Saint absorbed the pain of that without moving. It was what he deserved, after all.

"Caz took Kasha home," Felix offered. His black hair was wild from his shower, curling damply behind his ears and at his temples, and there was sympathy in his dark eyes.

Because of me. Saint nodded, swallowing more misery. He got dressed as quickly as he could, avoiding eye contact with the room in general, and fled into the night.

23

HIS FIRST INSTINCT was to go straight to his room and hide, but Carmine deserved better than that. He deserved Saint telling him to his face that he needed to move on, that they couldn't be together.

So he went to the living room and sat on the couch, curled up in the corner where he could see the door, and waited.

CARMINE CAME in on quiet feet, shutting the door with a soft click and startling Saint from the light doze he'd slipped into. He padded to the kitchen and Saint unfolded himself and followed. Carmine was digging in the refrigerator, the light over the stove the only illumination in the room.

"How is he?" Saint asked.

Carmine jolted, dropping the sliced turkey, and spun. "Jesus fuck, you scared me. Why aren't you in bed?"

"How is he?" Saint repeated.

Carmine stooped to pick up the turkey. "He's... alright."

"Is he really?" Saint asked, studying his face in the dim room. "Or are you just saying that to make me feel better?"

Carmine set the turkey on the counter and sighed. "His girlfriend broke up with him, Saint. Okay? And then the game, and —" He gestured wordlessly. "He's not great."

"Nadia broke up with him? Fuck, I have to talk to him." Saint turned but Carmine put out a hand.

"Don't."

"I'm the captain," Saint snarled. "I did this, I have to make it right."

"How are you going to make it right?" Carmine tilted his head. "You didn't make Nadia dump him. You can't make them get back together."

"I can a-apologize," Saint said, hating the thickness in his throat. "I can—this is my fault."

"No it's not." Carmine rounded the counter and closed the distance between them.

Saint backed up fast until his shoulders

hit the doorframe, and Carmine stopped dead. Hurt flickered across his face, gone so fast Saint wondered if he'd imagined it, but when he spoke, his voice was steady.

"This isn't something you can fix."

Saint hunched his shoulders. "I have to. I have to try."

Carmine's expression softened. "It was a bad day. A bad game. And it wasn't your fault."

Saint shook his head. "Everything went wrong. *Everything.* Why can't you see?"

"See what? I know things went wrong. Murphy's Law—it happens, okay? Next game will be better. Kasha won't touch your sticks. Everything will be where it should be, work how it's supposed to."

"*No.*" Saint swallowed around the rock in his throat. "You *saw* me, Carmine. You saw how I acted. We can't be together. We can't."

Carmine went so still he didn't seem to be breathing. "Why not?" he asked, lips barely moving.

"*Because.*" Saint clutched his hands to stop their trembling. "Because I'm—" He swallowed again. "I'm too fucked up. I don't know how to... how to have a relationship and be a normal person and keep the team together and *function*, I can't do it. When my routine gets fucked with...." He shook his head. "You saw what happened. Sometimes it's worse than that. Sometimes I break sticks. Scream at people. There's no manual for this, Carmine, I don't know how to fix it when I lose my temper and shout at *you*. You deserve someone stable. Someone who knows how to be a good boyfriend."

Carmine's mouth worked. "Saint, this—the bad day, you melting down—it didn't happen because we had sex. You know that, right?"

Saint blinked at him. "What?"

"Because we had sex and then you had a bad day," Carmine continued. "Did you—do you think this shit day was because we did... what we did?"

"That was yesterday," Saint said, speaking slowly and enunciating every word. "Why would it have anything to do with today?"

Carmine huffed a breath that sounded almost like a laugh. "God, I can't figure you out."

"Which is why you need to promise me that we won't do that again."

"No."

Saint stared. Carmine seemed bigger somehow, looming over him in the dark room, his jaw clenched. "What do you mean, no?"

"I mean no, you idiot." Carmine glared

at him. "No, I won't stop touching you, or kissing you, or figuring out how to be *with* you. Not if you're just trying to break up with me because of some misguided self-sacrificing idiocy."

Saint floundered, the rug pulled out from under him. "But—you saw—" *You saw me having a tantrum. You saw how neurotic and awful I am.*

"I saw," Carmine agreed, voice softening. "I saw a captain with a lot on his mind, careful not to hurt anyone even when he was on the edge of losing it."

"Kasha—"

"You told Kasha to shut up," Carmine interrupted. "His coach in Russia used to beat his thighs with a stick when he fucked up, did you know that? Said it was good for his muscles *and* his character. Trust me, Kash was way more worried about *you* than over what you said."

"I was angry."

"Newsflash, Saint Hockey—people get angry. People say things they don't mean. The ones who matter—your team, your *people*—we get it."

Tears stung Saint's eyes and he clenched his fists. "I don't deserve you," he whispered. "I don't deserve someone as good as you."

"Oh, bullshit," Carmine snapped. "Don't start with the martyr complex, it's

Saint shrugged.

"But you still want—"

"*Yes*," Saint said. "I'm clean, I swear."

"I know," Carmine said, touching their noses together. His breath was warm on Saint's mouth. "I haven't had sex with anyone else in over a year. The question is do you trust me."

"Yes," Saint said instantly.

Carmine kissed him again and Saint arched into it. His cock ached to be touched, but he could ignore it, focused on Carmine's taste and smell, the weight of him as he braced himself above Saint's body.

"Pillow," Carmine said, pulling back and grabbing one at random. "Under your hips —there you go." He leaned across him to pull on the drawer and fished out the lube as Saint ran his hands up and down his ribs, delighting in his presence.

Carmine settled on his heels between Saint's legs, one hand steady and warm on his splayed thigh, and popped the bottle cap.

The lube was cold against Saint's skin but it warmed quickly as Carmine circled his hole, pressing teasingly against his opening and then retreating, over and over.

Saint forced his breathing to slow, relaxing his body inch by inch. Carmine smiled at him, warmth in his eyes.

"I can't believe I get to do this," he said, and slipped in up to the first knuckle.

Saint gasped.

"Have you ever played with yourself?"

"A f-few times," Saint managed. "Been awhile."

"Try to relax," Carmine said, rubbing his thigh, and slid deeper.

"Oh... *God*," Saint said. He rolled his hips, trying desperately to get Carmine in even farther, but instead Carmine pulled out, patting Saint's knee at the protesting noise he made. Then he was back, pushing all the way in and crooking his finger.

Fireworks went off behind Saint's eyes and he bucked, clutching at the bed.

Carmine rubbed his prostate leisurely, watching Saint's face. "You feel so good around my finger," he murmured. "Gonna feel even better on my cock."

There was a roaring in Saint's ears. He couldn't catch his breath, writhing in place. Carmine pulled out and added another finger.

"How are we doing?" he asked, pumping in and out in slow, rhythmic movements.

Saint managed a glare. "Why—fuck—why do you torture me—"

"Can you blame me?" Carmine bent his fingers and rubbed again and Saint thrashed helplessly. His cock was leaking, hot and sticky on his stomach, but he had the sinking feeling that if he touched it, it would be game over immediately.

Then Carmine added a third finger. There was a stretch this time, and Saint stiffened, breathing through it in deep gulps until the burn faded into pleasant warmth and Carmine had picked up his rhythm again, in and out, slow and steady.

"Caz," Saint choked. "I'm not—" He could feel the pressure of his orgasm growing under his skin, threatening to overwhelm him, and he was hanging on by his fingernails.

Carmine shifted position and took hold of his cock, and Saint curled up off the bed in desperation.

"No, *no*, I'm gonna—"

"Come, then," Carmine said, and stroked him rough and relentless until the bliss broke free, overwhelming him as he came helplessly all over his stomach. Carmine eased off, whispering words of encouragement as Saint collapsed back onto the bed, blinking tears from his eyes.

"I didn't want—" He swallowed disappointment.

"Was it not good?" Carmine asked, pulling his fingers free and leaning over him.

"No, it was, I just—" Saint reached for

him, forcing a smile. "I wanted to come with you inside me, I guess."

"Who says that's not still on the menu?" Carmine asked. He kissed the tip of Saint's nose, grinning down at him. "Come on, you're only twenty-three, you can totally go again."

"*Fuck*," Saint said feelingly.

"That's the idea," Carmine said, and kissed him again, lowering himself until he was draped across Saint's body, grinding his erection into the cut of Saint's hip. "God, that feels good," he sighed, and kissed him again.

They made out slowly for several minutes, until Saint's breathing had stabilized. Carmine lifted himself up and ran his hand through the mess on Saint's stomach, holding it up and looking thoughtful.

"Should I feed it to you?"

Saint wrinkled his nose. "Ew."

Carmine laughed and licked his hand. Saint watched, spellbound, and his cock twitched.

"That's more like it," Carmine purred, and scooted down on the bed to take him in his mouth. He took his time, mouthing at the head and along the ridges, letting Saint thicken slowly on his tongue.

Saint reached down and threaded his fingers in Carmine's hair, cupping his skull.

Saint out of his mind. In and out, no hesitation, achingly slow, until Saint was shaking, arching into it and pulling fruitlessly on Carmine's arms in an effort to hurry him up.

"More," he panted. "Faster, come on."

Carmine obeyed, tongue caught between his teeth. Time blurred, fragmenting under the inexorable dragging slide of his cock, and Saint gave himself over to the sensations, aware of nothing but Carmine, in and over and around him.

He wasn't prepared for Carmine to sit back on his heels and pull him upright to straddle his thighs. Saint steadied himself with his hands on Carmine's shoulders, holding still as Carmine got himself in position, and then sinking down in one smooth motion.

Carmine made a guttural noise, hands coming up to grip Saint's hips bruisingly tight. "Let me see," he said, eyes glittering bright. "I wanna see you come on my cock, just like this."

Saint rose and fell, arms looped around Carmine's neck, his cock rubbing against Carmine's perfect abs in a distracting slide. Hockey-honed thighs kept his rhythm steady, gravity plunging Carmine deep inside him. Heat gathered under his skin, radiating along his nerves.

"Caz," he managed.

"Yeah, sweetheart." Carmine's voice was husky, edged with need and something Saint was afraid to look at head-on. "I'm close. I'm really—"

Saint tilted his hips, sitting deep. Carmine swore thickly, fingers tightening, and his head fell back as he came. Saint sobbed and followed him over. He felt like he was being turned inside out, ecstasy lighting up his bones, spilling on Carmine's stomach in helpless jerks.

They sagged sideways and landed on the bed in a sweaty tangle of arms and legs. Saint's face ended up pillowed on Carmine's bicep, Carmine's rapid breath stirring his hair and one of his legs draped over Saint's hips.

It was several minutes before either could move. Finally Carmine moaned and rolled his head to press a kiss to Saint's sweat-dampened hair.

"I'm gonna need a pacemaker if the sex keeps being that good," he mumbled.

Saint didn't try to stop the smile. "Need to shower."

Carmine smacked his hip weakly. "No ruining the afterglow."

Saint lifted his head and kissed him. "The game in Boston," he said when he pulled away.

Carmine's eyebrows went up. "Now? Seriously?"

Saint nodded, determined. "Why were you dogging me so hard? I couldn't get a breath, you were all over me. What did I do to you?"

Carmine sighed and thumbed Saint's dimple. "You didn't do anything to me, sweetheart. You were just... *you*. I had to throw you off any way I could. I'd heard the stories about what would rattle you, what would get to you most, so—" He lifted a shoulder. "That's what I did." A smile warmed his eyes. "You pack a mean right hook, Saint Hockey."

"I hated you," Saint confessed.

Carmine laughed softly. "Means I was doing my job. You don't hate me anymore, right?"

Saint shoved at his shoulder. Carmine barely swayed, smile widening. "No, asshole. I definitely don't hate you anymore."

"Good," Carmine said, and leaned in to kiss him again. "Now that the afterglow is properly ruined, I guess a shower sounds good." He caught Saint's hand as he sat up. "Sleep with me?"

"Well, this bed's disgusting," Saint pointed out. "So yeah."

Carmine laughed and followed him to the bathroom.

24

SAINT WOKE UP EARLY. They'd rolled apart sometime in the night, but Carmine's hand was stretched across the bed, as if he'd reached for Saint in his sleep. Saint slithered silently from the bed and tiptoed out.

He pulled on clothes, called a car, and went down to the gate to wait for it. When it arrived, he sent Carmine a quick text letting him know where he was and then settled back to wait.

Kasha opened the door, hair on end and dark circles like bruises under his eyes. Saint grimaced.

"You look terrible." He held out the coffee and Kasha took it.

"Why you're here so early? I could be sleep."

"But you weren't, were you? Can I come in?"

Kasha stepped aside silently and Saint patted him on the arm as he walked into the apartment. He whistled, looking around at the hardwood floors, the perfectly matching drapes and furniture and the art on the walls.

"This is nice."

"Nadia do it."

Saint winced. "Okay look, there are breakfast burritos in the bag. Sit down and let's talk."

Kasha followed him to the couch, folding his long legs underneath himself and accepting a foil-wrapped burrito.

"I need to apologize," Saint said.

Kasha shook his head.

"No, I do," Saint insisted.

"You have routine. I fuck up. Not your fault."

"No, it's not *your* fault I'm so neurotic." Saint set his own coffee on the table and leaned forward, fixing Kasha with a serious look. "You didn't deserve me snapping at you. I need to be better about my routines getting messed up. I'm sorry I got upset, I'm sorry I was an asshole."

"You're not," Kasha protested. "You're Saint. Saint Hockey. Is okay you be a little bit asshole sometimes."

Saint sighed. "That's really, really not true. If anything, I need to try harder *not* to be. But okay. What happened with Nadia?"

Kasha's face clouded and he hunched his shoulders. "Left. She's not like Portland, wants to be in LA. I told her I can't go, have contract, but she wanted me play for Royals, stay in LA. Not Seabirds, not Portland. Got mad when I said play with you more important."

"Fuck, you said that?"

"Don't want to go to LA," Kasha said. "Want to play with you."

"You're such a good kid," Saint said helplessly.

"Not kid," Kasha pointed out.

"Get your coat, *kid*," Saint told him, grinning when Kasha scowled. "We're going out."

"Out?" Kasha was already moving. "Out where?"

"We're going to explore the city," Saint said.

Kasha perked up, halfway into his coat. "Can Caz come too?"

"Hell yeah he can. We'll go pick him up now."

Kasha was nearly bouncing as he followed him out the door, talking excitedly of the places he wanted to visit. Saint let him babble, affection warming him.

When they got to the house, he brought

Kasha inside and parked him in the kitchen. "He's probably still asleep. I'll go wake him up, you stay here."

Carmine's suite was dark and still when Saint let himself in. He could just make out Carmine's shape in the bed, almost formless under the blankets. Steel whined softly, and Saint slid the patio door open and shooed him outside. When he closed it, Carmine hadn't stirred. Saint crawled onto the bed, holding his breath, and Carmine made a sleepy noise and reached out, catching hold and dragging Saint in close.

"Mmph, Carmine—"

Carmine nuzzled Saint's hair, tightening his grip. He slipped one hand down, over Saint's groin to cup his cock, and Saint bit back a whimper.

"Bad idea," he managed.

"Disagree." Carmine's voice was rough with sleep.

Saint laughed breathlessly and caught Carmine's wrist. "Much as I would love that —and I would, believe me—Kasha's in our kitchen right now."

Carmine lifted his head. "I could have sworn you said Kasha's in our kitchen right now."

"Probably because I did."

Carmine blinked and knuckled his eyes.

"Why's Kasha in our kitchen, Saint? Doesn't he have his own kitchen?"

Saint freed himself and leaned in to kiss him. "Because his girlfriend broke up with him and his captain was an asshole to him yesterday. I can't do anything about the girlfriend, but I can spend the day with him to make him feel better about the rest of it, and he wanted you there too."

Carmine's hair was tousled, falling in his face. He yawned, stretching, and flopped backward onto his back. "Why me?"

"Fuck if I know," Saint said, propping himself on his elbows beside him. "You've got the disposition of a grouchy rhinoceros, can't imagine why anyone would want you around."

Carmine cracked one eye open and glared at him. "You're in a good mood this morning."

Saint grinned. "Well, I had some really excellent sex last night." He pecked Carmine on the lips. "Shake a leg, buddy, before Kasha wonders what's taking so long and comes looking for us." He rolled away when Carmine groped for him, fighting a laugh, and Carmine groaned theatrically and face-planted into the spot he'd vacated.

"I changed my mind," he said, voice muffled. "I don't like you anymore."

"Aw," Saint said, grin widening. "Does

that mean you don't want me to suck your dick after all?"

Carmine jerked upright. "I'm showering now!"

KASHA WAS STILL in the kitchen when Saint came back out. He brightened at the sight of him.

"Is he coming?"

"He's showering but then we'll go," Saint said. "Anywhere in particular you have in mind?"

Kasha fidgeted. "Can we go to zoo?" His eyes were hopeful, and Saint smiled at him.

"You know, it's been ages since I went there. We may have to sign some autographs though."

"Is okay," Kasha said. "I want to see giraffes." He dropped to his knees to greet Steel as he bounded into the kitchen, crooning to him in Russian.

OVERALL, Saint decided, the day was a success. Saint bought Kasha the largest stuffed giraffe the gift shop had on offer and Carmine helped him cram it in the backseat of the car. They went to Saint's favorite restaurant for lunch and talked about their next game while Carmine nudged Saint's knee under the table without looking at him. Saint applied himself to his food and did his best not to think about Carmine's hands and the way they felt on his body. From the way Carmine's lips were quirking as he answered Kasha, he wasn't very successful.

When they dropped Kasha back at his apartment, he waved goodbye to them, almost eclipsed by the giant giraffe, but his beaming smile clearly visible.

"You did good," Carmine said as he drove them home.

"Good would have been not freaking out on him in the first place," Saint said. He leaned back against the seat and watched Carmine's hands, loosely wrapped around the steering wheel.

"Enjoying the view there, champ?" Carmine inquired, a smile tugging at his mouth.

Saint hummed. "Not bad," he said, keeping his tone light.

Carmine snorted and rested one hand on Saint's thigh, thumb stroking along the inseam lightly. "Ever had a road handie?"

"Don't you *dare*," Saint said, bolting upright, and Carmine laughed.

"Relax, I won't." He squeezed Saint's

thigh. "Is that offer of a blowjob still on the table though?"

Saint relaxed, eyeing him warily. "As long as you don't expect it in public, yeah."

Carmine gave him a wicked grin. "No exhibitionist kink, got it. You want me to close the curtains and lock the doors before we get freaky?"

"First of all, don't ever say freaky again," Saint said, glaring at him but unable to suppress the bubble of amusement in his chest. He couldn't help loving the way Carmine teased him, his irreverent disregard for Saint's status as the captain or the face of hockey in the Pacific Northwest. None of it mattered to Carmine. To him, Saint was just another guy, an equal. It made Saint feel *seen*, somehow, and as Carmine rolled up the driveway toward the house, he impulsively unbuckled, slid across the seat, and kissed his cheek.

"Oh," Carmine said, eyebrows going up. "That was nice. Any particular reason?"

Saint sat back, cheeks heating. He shrugged. "Because you're you?"

Carmine smiled, turning the corner and cresting the hill, and then frowned. "Why is there a car in the driveway? Fuck, I'm calling the cops." He fumbled for his phone as Saint turned and then froze, ice flooding his veins.

"Don't," he said through numb lips. "I recognize that car."

"Saint?" Carmine sounded far away.

Saint made a huge effort to summon a smile. "It's my parents," he said, and stepped out.

25

CARMINE SCRAMBLED TO FOLLOW, mind spinning. The car in question was a neat silver sedan, a lanky man rising from the driver's side. He had Saint's brown eyes, but on him they were sharp, judging, assessing, and then dismissing Carmine in a flash before turning to Saint. The smile didn't reach his mouth when he held out his arms.

"Hi Dad," Saint said, matching his smile. The hug was awkward, over quickly, both men stepping apart and Saint turning to greet his mother, a slim woman with gray-streaked brown hair and a sad smile. Saint's smile was more genuine this time and he held on a little longer before letting her go. "What are you guys doing here?"

"Are you going to introduce us?" his father said with a nod in Carmine's direction.

"Right, sorry. Um. Carmine, these are my parents, Victor and Maria. Mom, Dad, this is Carmine. You remember he's staying with me?"

Victor looked Carmine over again. "I remember. I thought he'd have moved out by now."

Carmine held out a hand. "Nice to meet you, Mr. Levesque. Saint's been a great host."

"How long are you staying?" Saint asked before Victor could answer.

Victor's brows drew together. "Is it a problem that we're here?"

"No!" Saint said, stiffening, and Carmine balled his fists at the clear distress in the lines of his body. "No," he said more softly. "I just—you know I like to plan."

"Yeah, you never did like surprises," Victor said. He patted Saint's head, making a wave of fury sweep through Carmine, and popped the trunk of the car. "We were thinking a week at least."

"You're okay with being away from the farm for that long?" Saint asked. He pulled a suitcase from the trunk and Carmine leaned in to grab the other one, brushing against him. Saint's face didn't change, but he took a small step away, waiting for his father's answer.

"We hired Bonnie Masters, you

remember her, to stay for a week. She's home from college, between jobs, and she knows her way around the place." Victor followed Saint up the steps, Maria right behind him and Carmine bringing up the rear. "We always thought you and Bonnie would make a match of it."

Saint's head was down, fumbling with the door key, but the back of his neck was flushed dark red. "I've barely talked to her since I was fifteen, Dad." He pushed the door open and led the way inside, down the hall past the living room and turning left, into the wing of the house they never used.

"Hang on, what happened to our suite?" Victor asked, balking.

"Carmine's in it, Dad," Saint said without looking back at him.

"I want our suite," Victor snapped, mouth set in a stubborn line.

"Honey," Maria murmured, putting a hand on Victor's arm.

Carmine cleared his throat. "I don't mind if—"

"You're staying in here," Saint said loudly, and shoved a door open. He let his parents go through first, meeting Carmine's gaze briefly as they went inside. There was pain in his eyes, misery bubbling to the surface, and Carmine's throat tightened. He wanted desperately to say something, to erase the hurt, but Saint was already turning away, carrying his parents' suitcases into the room.

Carmine followed, setting his load down and taking a step back. "I'll just—go let Steel out."

"Who's Steel?" Victor asked.

"His dog," Saint said quietly.

"You let him bring a dog here? You know your mother's allergic!"

Saint's eyes flashed. "You didn't even let me know you were coming, Dad, and *I'm* not allergic. It's my house, and Steel is welcome here."

"I'm only a little bit allergic," Maria said, sounding almost apologetic, and Victor huffed but didn't say anything else.

Carmine took advantage of the pause and escaped.

STANDING ON THE BACK LAWN, watching Steel dash around and inspect his territory, Carmine called Felix.

"What do I need to know about Saint's parents?" he asked without preamble.

"*Calisse*, Saint's parents are there?" Felix said sharply. "How is he?"

"He's not great," Carmine said. "He's

getting them settled in but he won't look at me."

Felix swore again. "His father—" He broke off, hesitating. "He is not a kind man."

"I already figured that much out. How do I help him while they're here?"

"Victor Levesque cares for one thing and one thing only," Felix said. "And that is Saint winning a Cup. Everything else—*everything else*—is secondary. Saint... he wants his father to love him, Caz, you understand?"

Carmine swallowed, tasting ash in his mouth. "What do I do?"

"Not much you *can* do, *ami*." Felix sighed. "Remind him life outside hockey exists. Keep him grounded. Stay with him as much as he'll let you—his father will curb his tongue somewhat around strangers."

"Shit, then I need to go," Carmine said. He called Steel, who came running, and headed back inside.

He found Saint alone in the kitchen, hands flat on the counter and head bowed.

"Hey," Carmine said, aching to touch him but keeping a safe distance away.

Saint lifted his head. "Sorry," he said.

"For what?"

Saint shrugged a shoulder, not meeting Carmine's eyes. "My dad's... a lot. You don't have to be here if you don't want to be. You can stay in your room, or hell—get a hotel until they're gone."

"You really think I'm going to leave you alone with him?" Carmine demanded, keeping his voice low but not hiding his anger at the thought. Saint's eyes flicked up, surprise in them.

"You don't—it's not your job to protect me," he said.

"Yeah, you've made it clear you don't need to be protected," Carmine said. He rounded the counter and rested his hips against it, leaning back just enough to see Saint's face, downturned again. "Saint," he said softly. "Will you look at me, sweetheart?"

"Dad doesn't know," Saint said, voice low and urgent. He looked up, touching Carmine's wrist. "Please, I can't tell him. He *can't* find out."

"He won't," Carmine promised. It was reckless, maybe, but he'd do a lot to wipe the panic from Saint's brown eyes. "But I'm also not going to hide and leave you on your own."

Saint's lashes swept down and he swayed just briefly into Carmine's space. Then he drew away, sighing. "I should figure out dinner."

"I'll do that," Carmine said. "But you can stay and help me."

DINNER WAS TENSE AT FIRST, Victor seeming irritated that Carmine was there and Maria watching Saint without saying much at all. But Carmine kept a cheerful facade in place, talking to Saint about the team and trading recipe tips with Maria until she softened enough to smile back at him.

Over dessert, Victor cleared his throat. "So, Carmine."

Beside him, Saint tensed.

Carmine took a bite of apple pie and raised a questioning eyebrow.

"You seem to be meshing fairly well with the team," Victor said. "Have you considered anger management courses or anything to help keep you out of the box?"

"*Dad*," Saint hissed, but Victor ignored him.

Carmine couldn't decide whether to laugh or lose his temper. He took a deep breath and did neither. "I think I've got it under control, but thanks for the tip."

Victor didn't look convinced. "Seems like you get in a fight almost every game. That what you consider 'under control'?"

Carmine set his fork on his plate. Beside him, Saint was rigid with fury, and that alone was enough to help Carmine keep his temper in check. "I don't fight for shits and giggles, Mr. Levesque," he said quietly. "I do it to protect my teammates. I fight so they don't have to."

"Very noble of you, I'm sure," Victor said.

"That's enough," Saint snapped, mouth tight. "Carmine is a valued member of the team, Dad. He does a lot more than fight, and you need to back off."

Carmine looked at his plate, swallowing hard and focusing on not grabbing Saint and kissing him in front of his parents. *That'd go over like a lead balloon*, he told himself, but it took everything he had to be still.

HE WENT to bed that night with Steel, achingly aware of the distance between him and Saint. They'd only spent a few nights in the same bed, but Carmine already missed his warm body pressed up against his, the arm Saint would unthinkingly sling over his waist and his little snuffling sighs as he sank into deep sleep.

He pulled his phone out and sent him a

quick message. *Wish we could get freaky :(*

The response was just as quick. *You're an idiot and I'm banning you from using that word.*

Carmine grinned at his phone in the dark. Saint was typing again, so he waited.

Thanks for tonight.

Pay me back by scoring a goal tomorrow night, Carmine sent.

I'll score two for you, Saint responded.

"Oh fuck," Carmine said out loud. Steel whined inquiringly, and Carmine rubbed his ears. "I think I'm in love with him, bud."

Steel thumped his tail on the bed and licked Carmine's chin. Carmine wiped the drool away absently, staring into the dark. It hadn't been that long, he told himself. Maybe it was just a crush.

He did the only thing he could think to do.

"Hello?" Henry said, sounding distracted.

"I'm in love with Saint," Carmine said.

"Hi Henry, how are you? I'm totally calling just to say hi and because I miss you," Henry said, her voice pitched high.

"This is serious," Carmine hissed.

"Oh, of course you're in love with him," Henry said. Glass clinked in the background.

"Am I interrupting something?"

Carmine asked belatedly, and blinked. "Wait. Of course I'm in love with him?"

"I could tell that after watching you two for five minutes," Henry said. "And yes, you're interrupting me seducing a very sweet paralegal with legs for days, so can we hurry this up?"

"But—" Carmine swallowed. "I'm not —how do you know?"

Henry sighed. "Caz, honey. You can't take your eyes off him. You're tuned to him like a fucking radio, and he's just as dialed into you. Anyone with a brain can see it, you're not exactly subtle."

"He's—he tried to break up with me the other day," Carmine said, remembering the hurt that had flared through him when Saint had backed away.

"He—are you *together*?" Henry demanded sharply.

"Oh yeah, did I forget to mention that?"

"Carmine Llewellyn Quinn, explain yourself *right now!*"

Carmine winced at the use of his full name. "He kissed me at the Christmas dinner."

"Oh my God. The paralegal can wait. Tell me *everything*."

"Ugh, no," Carmine said. He rolled onto his back to stare at the ceiling. "The *point* is, I think I'm in love with him."

"And I'm telling you, that's not news. Pretty sure he feels the same way, buddy."

Carmine groaned. "That's impossible."

"Why?"

"Because," Carmine said. "I'm just—I make him feel good. He hasn't had a lot of that. I'm not...."

"If you're about to say something willfully stupid like you're not good enough for him, or he only thinks of you as a fuck-buddy, I swear to God I will fly up there and kick your ass myself," Henry growled.

"You don't understand," Carmine said. "And I'm done talking about this."

"What? No! Don't you dare hang up! Carmine—"

Carmine raised his voice. "Bye, Henry! Love you!" He dropped the phone on the bed and rubbed his face. He couldn't tell Saint. Not with all the pressure already on him, and *especially* not with his parents in town. Maybe once the season was over, or in a few years, when Saint was ready to come out.

What if he doesn't come out until he retires, a tiny voice asked.

"I'll figure that out when we get there," Carmine said aloud. Steel thumped his tail sleepily at the sound of his voice, and Carmine rubbed his head. It was time to sleep.

26

THE GAME WAS GOING to be brutal, Carmine could tell just by walking in the arena. The crowds were raucous, and a sizable contingent of Richmond Raven fans had decided to represent for their team, resulting in a flood of royal blue and black among the teal and silver Seabird fans.

Saint had said nothing on the drive to the rink, touching his thumbs to each knuckle in turn as Carmine drove and watched him. The lines of his body were tense, but the stress from the last game was gone.

He sat now in his stall, looking at the team. Carmine caught his eye from across the room and smiled, and Saint smiled back, eyes softening. Carmine winked and turned away to pick up his shoulder pads, nearly bumping into David.

"Watch it," David snapped, and brushed past.

Saint was talking to Kasha when Carmine glanced back again. Kasha was smiling, nodding as Saint spoke, and he began to bounce on his toes, swinging his arms forward and back to loosen his chest.

Satisfied, Carmine turned his attention to getting the rest of his gear on as Coach cleared his throat and began his usual pre-game speech.

CARMINE waited as Saint sent the other players down the tunnel, then stepped forward. Saint watched him approach, eyes dark in the dimly lit hall, and Carmine reached out and took hold of his jersey, pulling him in. He bumped their helmets together lightly and released him.

"Let's do this."

Saint followed him onto the ice and the crowd's cheers redoubled. The Ravens were warming up on their side of the rink, and Carmine started his own routine, keeping an eye on them. After a few minutes, Saint fetched up beside him.

"There's Fall, down there by their goalie," he said, and bent to stretch.

Carmine glanced in that direction. He'd

never been formally introduced to Simon Fall, but he'd played opposite him a few times. Simon was known for his rough, aggressive style of play, his propensity for dirty hits and willingness to drop his gloves. He was even taller than Carmine with the frame to match and a mop of blond curls that fell over a high forehead and aquiline nose.

"Don't let him bait you," Saint said, still stretching. He looked completely calm, but Carmine could read the nerves simmering under his skin. "He'll try to rile you up, make you angry so you make mistakes."

"I got it," Carmine said. He tapped Saint's skate with his stick and lined up to take shots on Felix, limbering up in his crease.

SAINT SCORED TWICE in quick succession in the first period, slipping under and behind the defense with insulting ease. He met Carmine's eyes after the second goal, and Carmine grinned at him, helpless with love he couldn't express. From the way Saint's eyes softened, though, maybe he'd done a better job than he'd thought.

Carmine kept the others off him as much as he could, screening the Ravens' goalie and watching for Saint's plays. The Ravens couldn't seem to touch him as he floated through traffic and drove for the net, and Carmine could feel their desperation as next Kasha, then Jason scored, and the Ravens' chance of a comeback dwindled with each puck that slotted home.

SIMON'S EYES WERE BRIGHT, laser blue as he focused on Carmine during the faceoff at the beginning of the third period. A smile curved the edges of his mouth, thin and cruel.

"You think you finally found yourself a home, don't you? Think you're more than a brick wall on skates now?"

Saint stiffened but didn't look over.

"You're just like me, you know," Simon said casually, almost conversationally. "You'll never be anything but a goon. Big dumb muscle to be used up and thrown away when they don't need you anymore."

Saint's shoulders were rigid, head down. Carmine watched Saint ready himself for the puck drop, ignoring Simon. Simon's mouth tightened and he jostled Carmine roughly. Carmine steadied himself, shooting him a warning look, as the ref dropped the puck.

The next few minutes were a confusing jumble, with a few discrete moments frozen before Carmine's eyes. Saint winning the faceoff. Simon aiming a hard hit at Saint. Saint ducking under his arm at the last second, grabbing the puck again and racing for the net.

Time sped up again and Carmine hurled himself into the action, driving through the center of the scrum in front of the net and setting up a screen as Saint barreled toward him.

He didn't see the hit that leveled him. One second he was poised and ready in case Saint passed to him, and the next he was on the ice half-inside the net, head ringing and a weight on his chest, a bright throbbing in his shoulder and spine.

Carmine dragged himself to his knees, shaking his head to clear the ringing, but it didn't help. He looked up, struggling to focus, just in time to see Saint drop his gloves and launch himself at Simon.

The fight was quick and brutal. Simon had height, reach, and weight on Saint, but Saint fought like he was possessed, pulling out every trick in his arsenal. He trapped Simon's dominant arm in his jersey so he was forced to punch with his weaker hand, landed three hard blows to his head, and then yanked him forward and twisted, toppling him to the ice and landing on top of him. He got in several more blows before the officials managed to drag him off, shouting something Carmine couldn't make out.

Saint shook the officials off and skated for the box without looking back as a linesman bent over Carmine, a hand on his back.

"How're you doing?"

Carmine pushed himself to his feet, wobbling slightly. His head was still ringing and starbursts of pain went off in his ribs with every breath. "'M okay," he managed, and skated for the bench.

He submitted to being looked over by the team doctor, tipping his head back so she could inspect his pupils, then obediently taking deep breaths when instructed.

"Broken ribs," she said finally. "At least two. I don't think you have a concussion, but you're out of the game, come on."

Carmine followed her down the tunnel reluctantly, turning to look back just once. Saint was watching him from the box, nothing showing on his normally expressive face, and Carmine lifted a hand, trying not to wince.

"Come on," the doctor said impatiently. "We need to get you X-rayed properly and bandaged."

SAINT FOUND him after the game, lying on an examining table in the observation room, ribs bandaged and one arm tucked under his head as he stared at the ceiling.

"Hey," Saint said softly.

Carmine lifted his head. "Hey." Saint looked exhausted, dark smudges under his eyes and a bruise developing on his cheekbone where Simon had landed a hit, hair damp from his shower. "How are you doing?"

Saint closed the door behind him and took a step forward. "I'm supposed to ask you that."

"I'm fine," Carmine said. "Well. Couple of broken ribs. But no concussion. I won't be out too long." He held out a hand and Saint took another step closer. His eyes searched Carmine's form as if trying to determine for himself that there were no other injuries, worry and fear battling in his expression.

"I saw you go down," he began, and stopped, swallowing hard.

"Yeah, what happened?" Carmine asked. "I'm assuming it was Simon?"

"He knocked you into the goal post," Saint said, expression hardening. "It was a dirty fucking hit." He clenched his hands in front of him, swallowing again. "I—"

"Hey," Carmine said. He held out a hand again. "Come here."

"No, I—" Saint glanced at the door.

"No one's coming in," Carmine said. "Come on. Please?"

Saint took a shaky breath and closed the distance between them. He was trembling, Carmine saw, and tenderness swamped him.

"I'm okay, sweetheart," he said, and took his hand.

Saint gripped it hard and bent forward until their foreheads were touching. "I thought—Caz—"

"It's a vicious fucking game we play," Carmine murmured. He reached up with his free hand to cup Saint's cheek, hiding the grimace of pain. Saint turned his face into Carmine's palm, lashes sweeping down.

"I—you went down and—I wanted to kill him," he managed. "Caz, I—"

"Yeah," Carmine said. He slid his hand up to cradle the nape of Saint's neck. "I know, baby. I love you too."

Saint's eyes snapped wide and Carmine breathed a laugh and tugged him down into a kiss. Saint's lips were soft and wet, breath feathering across Carmine's cheek, and he took a ragged breath and then kissed back, hot and desperate.

The door opened and Saint jolted upright.

"Coach wants you," David said.

Carmine looked at Saint, then at David. Had he seen? Nothing showed on his face except faint boredom and irritation. Saint's throat bobbed and he nodded.

"I'll—okay. Felix said he'll give us a ride home. Lacy's here too, remember her from the hospital? I have to say hi to her, but it won't take long. I'll come get you when I'm done."

"Take your time," Carmine said. "I'm not going anywhere."

Saint glanced at him and Carmine winked, hidden from David's view by Saint's body. Saint's lips twitched and then he was gone, following David from the room.

27

FELIX DROVE THEM HOME, careful not to brake or accelerate too hard, and Saint helped Carmine inside.

"I can walk," Carmine said through his teeth. The movement was jostling his ribs and it wasn't helping his mood.

"Sorry," Saint said, but he didn't let go of Carmine's arm. "My room, it's closer."

Carmine resisted briefly. "Your parents—"

"I don't give a shit," Saint snapped. "Now come on."

Carmine made his slow, painful way into Saint's suite and eased himself onto the bed, jaw clenched, as Saint hovered. "Steel needs to go out," he managed once he was as close to comfortable as he could get.

"I'll take care of him," Saint said. "Do you need anything?"

"Pills," Carmine suggested.

"Yeah, of course." Saint hurried to the bathroom and reappeared with a glass of water. Carmine struggled up onto one elbow and gulped the pills down before lowering himself back to the bed with a muffled groan. Saint watched him, a line between his brows.

"I'm okay," Carmine mumbled. The pain and exhaustion had caught up to him and he could feel himself sinking below the waves. "Stay with me."

Saint smoothed his hair off his brow. "Yeah," he murmured. "Let me go take care of your dog. I'll be right back."

CARMINE WAS NEARLY asleep when the bed dipped and Saint curled up against him, careful not to bump him. He rested one hand on Carmine's arm and Carmine hummed. The pills were kicking in and he was feeling distinctly floaty, the pain locked away behind a wall.

"Did you mean it?" Saint whispered.

Even through the haze of drugs and exhaustion, Carmine didn't have to ask what he meant.

"Yeah," he sighed. He half-rolled toward

Saint's body, tucking himself up close. "Meant it. Love you."

"Oh God," Saint managed. "Caz—"

"S'okay," Carmine said. He groped for and found Saint's hand, pulling his arm around him. "Gonna sleep now, 'kay?"

Something soft brushed his temple— Saint's lips.

"I'll be here," Saint murmured.

Carmine smiled and fell asleep.

HE WOKE EARLY the next morning and maneuvered himself slowly out of the bed, breathing through his nose, until he could stand up and wobble into the bathroom.

Saint found him in there, slipping his arms around Carmine's waist as he brushed his teeth and pressing a kiss to his shoulder blade.

"Morning," Carmine said. He turned slowly, ribs protesting, until they were facing. Saint's eyes were sleepy, hair standing on end, and there were sleep-creases in his cheek. Affection swamped Carmine, making his breath short, and he tipped Saint's chin up to kiss him.

Saint sighed and pressed closer, arms going up around Carmine's neck. "How are you feeling?" he asked when he finally broke away.

"A little better," Carmine said. He ran his hands up and down Saint's ribs. "Hungry. And I need to get to my room before your parents see, or they're going to jump to the right conclusion."

Saint scowled but let him go, taking a step back. "I'll bring you breakfast," he said, the jut of his jaw making it clear it wasn't optional.

The house was still and quiet, and Carmine made it to his suite without incident, where he greeted Steel and let him out into the yard before sinking onto his bed. He peeled his shirt up and hissed at the sight of his abdomen and side, stained a violent purple fading toward green around the edges.

Price of the game they played. The bruises would heal, as would his ribs. Of more pressing concern was the fact that he'd told Saint how he felt. He didn't regret saying the words, not really, but the timing —he closed his eyes and groaned. He'd wanted to wait, give Saint room to adjust, not just blurt it out while he was off his head from pain and medication.

The door creaked open and Saint stepped inside, holding a cup of coffee.

"You should scoot up against the

pillows," he said. "I'm gonna try to make eggs for you."

Carmine winced. "I have a better idea— I put some casseroles in the freezer last week. There's a sausage and egg one. Just heat the oven and pop it in."

Saint looked relieved. "That's probably a lot safer." He set the coffee on the table and waited while Carmine dragged himself up the bed until he was propped up against the pillows. Then he handed him the mug and bent to kiss him. "I'll be back soon."

CARMINE fell asleep after breakfast while Saint went to morning skate. When he woke, it was close to lunchtime and he could hear Saint talking to his parents in the living room. He hauled himself off the bed and limped to the bathroom, then out of his suite.

"Hey!" Saint said, hurrying to him with hands outstretched. "You shouldn't be out of bed, what are you doing?"

"Bored," Carmine said, smiling at him. "Can I keep you guys company?"

"Of course," Saint said, and led him to the couch.

"How was skate?" Carmine asked.

"Kasha got a spinorama goal on Felix, it

was gorgeous," Saint said, eyes sparkling. "Felix is pissed, of course, and planning to prank him in revenge."

Carmine settled into the cushions and listened as Saint described Kasha's goal in detail, hands waving. Victor was in the chair opposite, lanky legs crossed, and Maria on the loveseat beside him, a knitting project in her lap.

After a few minutes, the oven beeped in the kitchen and Saint hopped to his feet.

"I'm getting pretty good at casseroles," he said, giving Carmine a private smile. "Be right back."

Alone with Saint's parents, Carmine stretched his feet out and took a slow, experimental breath. It still hurt to exist, but with his ribs wrapped, the pain was slightly blunted.

"So, Carmine," Victor said. "How do you like living here?"

"Here as in Portland or here as in Saint's place?"

"Both," Victor said tightly.

"Portland is lovely," Carmine told him. "Everyone's friendly and welcoming and the weather's great—I'm really enjoying it here."

"And living with my son?"

"Saint's been a great roommate," Carmine said honestly.

Victor scoffed. "Please. I've seen his

hangups in real time, I know exactly how hard he can be to tolerate in close proximity. You're telling me it doesn't bother you to have to deal with that?"

Carmine stiffened. "Your son is a fantastic person," he said, slowly and clearly. "I'm honored to call him my friend."

"Still," Victor said. "Don't you think it's about time you found your own place?"

"*Dad.*" Saint's voice cracked like a whip. He was standing in the doorway, fists at his sides. "That's enough. Carmine is welcome here for as long as he wants to stay."

Victor looked between him and Carmine, eyes narrowed. "Oh, is that how it is?"

Alarm crackled in Carmine's chest and he struggled to push himself upright. "It's not 'like' anything," he said through his teeth. "Saint, I'll go——"

"Stay right there," Saint snapped. His eyes were molten with fury, fixed on his father.

"You need to remember what's important," Victor growled, standing. "Not let yourself get distracted by things, or people, that don't matter. You've always been like this—too easily diverted, flitting from one thing to another. If it weren't for me, you wouldn't even *be* here."

"Oh, you fucking——"

Saint cut off Carmine's explosion with one hand held out, eyes still sharp on his father's form. "So you know," he said softly. "For how long?"

Victor's lip curled. "Since you were a teenager and couldn't take your eyes off Billy Hardin at practice. Why do you think we tried to set you up with girls all the time?"

Carmine couldn't breathe through the rage clogging his lungs. He tried again to stand up, and Saint moved swiftly, gripping his shoulder and pressing him back down. His hand was tight, eyes pleading when he glanced at Carmine briefly before looking back up, and Carmine got the message. This was Saint's battle to fight.

He forced himself to sit back, and Saint's posture eased a fraction before he set his jaw and addressed his father.

"Carmine is a guest in my house and you will not speak to him or me in this manner. If you can't treat us with respect, then it's time for you to go."

Victor's laugh was ugly and jagged. "Respect is *earned*, you ungrateful little shit. After everything I've done for you, and you—"

"Victor." Maria was on her feet, a hand on her husband's forearm. "That's enough."

Carmine blinked. He'd forgotten she

was even in the room. From the way Victor swung to stare at her, so had he.

Maria looked at Saint. "I think you're right. It's time for us to go. Saint, sweetheart, will you help me with the bags? Victor, you go wait with the car."

Victor opened and closed his mouth, looking between her and Saint.

"*Now*, Victor," Maria said, sharp steel in her voice, and to Carmine's amazement, Victor went, casting one last poisonous look at Saint, who lifted his chin and stared back at him.

There was tense, waiting silence for a moment after he left the room, and then Maria covered her mouth with both hands, tears welling.

"Saint," she whispered. "I'm so sorry, I—"

Saint crossed the room and wrapped her in his arms. Carmine couldn't hear what he said, but his eyes were damp when he lifted his head.

Maria wiped her face and turned to Carmine. "I'm sorry," she repeated. "He's—well, he's bitter. He wanted so badly to captain his own team, and he only played in the NHL for three games."

"That's not Saint's fault," Carmine said harshly.

"No," Maria said. She shook her head.

"No, I know it's not. He's just—" She sighed and looked at Saint again. "I should have put my foot down, but I thought you wanted it as badly as he did."

"I did," Saint said, taking her hand. "I *do*, Mom. But I can want more than one thing." He glanced at Carmine, eyes suddenly shy, and Carmine swallowed the lump in his throat and managed an unsteady smile. Saint returned it. "Come on," he said to his mother. "I'll help you pack."

THERE WAS silence after Victor and Maria were gone, echoing through the house. Carmine hadn't watched them leave, opting to stay on the couch while Saint saw them off. He was still there when Saint came back into the living room, hesitating in the doorway.

Carmine held out a hand. "Get over here."

Saint obeyed, crawling onto the couch beside him. He was trembling faintly, and Carmine gathered him close, tucking him in under his arm and letting Saint relax against him.

"You did good," he murmured.

Saint didn't reply, burrowing closer into

Carmine's shoulder. "I love you," he said instead.

Carmine froze. "You—what?"

Saint lifted his head, scowling. "I said I love you. Did you think I didn't?"

"No, I—" Carmine's breath hitched. "I just—I kind of sprang it on you and I didn't mean to trap you or—"

"Oh, shut up," Saint said irritably, pressing closer. "No one's trapping anyone."

Carmine's laugh was wobbly. "As long as we're clear."

Saint pressed a kiss to his throat. "I love you a lot," he admitted, voice muffled. "And I'm not sure why you—no, let me finish—I'm not really sure why you love me, but I'll take it. I'll take anything you give me."

"*God*," Carmine said, and hauled him upright to kiss him. Then winced. "Fuck, ow."

"Shit, your ribs?"

Carmine nodded, flinching.

"I'll get your pills," Saint said, sliding off the couch. "Will you stay in my room with me, now that my parents are gone?"

Carmine took his hands and let Saint pull him to his feet. "Yeah," he said, smiling down at him. "As long as you don't snore."

"Oh God," Saint said suddenly, looking suddenly horrified. "God, I have to tell *Felix*."

"Well, he's your best friend, right?"
Carmine said. "I told Henry literally the
night I realized I was in love with you."

"Yeah but…." Saint shuddered. "Do you
have any idea how much he's going to chirp
me for this?"

"What, for falling for me? Really, who
could blame you?" Carmine preened, and
Saint pushed lightly at his shoulder.

"Shut up and come to bed with me."

28

HE FOUND Carmine in the box before their
next game. Even though he wasn't playing,
he still looked sharp in his game day suit,
cut to flatter his rangy form. The room was
empty except for them, so Saint made no
secret about looking him up and down,
pursing his mouth in appreciation.

Carmine laughed and tugged his sleeves
down. Saint knew him well enough now to
recognize the deprecation in his smile, and
he frowned, stepping closer.

"You know how hot you are, right?"

Carmine rolled his eyes. "Please, of the
two of us, you're definitely winning."

"Sorry, are we in a competition I didn't
know about?" Saint countered. He reached
out, hooking a finger in Carmine's lapel and
pulling him close. "You're gorgeous, bud,
deal with it."

Carmine's laugh was real that time and he bent, tipping Saint's face up to kiss him. "Kick ass out there," he murmured, and ducked his head to press kisses along Saint's throat.

"You—" The door clicked behind Saint and he turned to see it closing. "Did someone just open that?" He took a step away, cold panic dousing his bones. "Did they—did they see us?"

"I didn't see anyone," Carmine said. He looked worried but not afraid, and Saint swallowed hard.

"I should go."

Carmine nodded. "Saint—I'm sure it's nothing. Maybe someone opened the door by mistake and realized they were in the wrong room."

"I should go," Saint repeated. If someone had seen them—

"I love you," Carmine said softly.

Saint swallowed again and edged toward the door. "I—I love you too," he finally managed, but he couldn't meet Carmine's eyes as he slipped out into the empty hallway.

He caught sight of Felix on his way to the locker room and jogged to catch up with him.

"You okay, *cher*?" Felix asked, an

alarmed tilt to his eyebrow. "You look… not okay."

"I was—" Saint gulped for air. "Carmine's in the box."

"Okay…."

"I was in there with him," Saint continued.

Both Felix's eyebrows went up. "Did you get nasty in the box, *cher*?"

Saint mustered a glare. "You and Carmine should never be in the same room. But no, all I did—we just kissed."

"What's the problem then?"

"I don't know," Saint admitted. "I feel… jittery. Like I thought I heard the door close but there was no one there. I don't know. I'm probably just imagining things."

"Probably," Felix agreed, and wrapped an arm around his neck. "Come on, let's go play some two-touch before Coach starts yelling at us."

THE FIRST WARNING Carmine got that things were about to go sideways was a text from Henry that came through in the last few minutes of the third period.

Has David said anything to you?

Below him on the ice, Saint had the

puck, driving for the net hard, and Carmine frowned.

No, he tapped out. *Why?*

Probably no reason, she answered. Saint passed to Kasha, who dropped it to Roddy. *He just doesn't want to believe we're not together. Being a fool about it.*

Carmine tapped the first letter of a reply just as Tye scored and he forgot everything to cheer. When he finally collected himself, the period was over, the Seabirds had won, and he had to get down to the locker room as quickly as possible. He sent Henry a quick text. *I'll let you know if he does anything stupid, but all quiet so far.*

The team was in raucous celebration mode when he arrived, and he was welcomed with delighted shouts of greeting. Most of the media was clustered around Saint, as usual, but a few made their way toward him. Carmine put his media face on, smiling at them.

"Carmine, I don't think we've met," a small, round woman with thick glasses said, holding out a hand. "Victoria Hensley, *Hockey Weekly*. We run a fairly popular blog with insider interviews on the Seabirds and the occasional outside player. So was that photo released with your permission?"

"Sorry, what photo?" Carmine asked,

most of his attention on Saint, sitting in his stall with a tired smile on his face. He was disheveled and clearly exhausted, and Carmine wanted nothing more than to take him home, deposit him in the hot tub, and then maybe give him a foot massage.

"This one," Victoria said, phone out.

Carmine took it and tore his eyes from Saint to focus on the photo. Horror nailed his feet to the floor. He was standing in the box, hands on Saint's shoulders, frozen in the act of lifting his face from kissing Saint's throat. There was a smile on his face, love shining from him. Distantly he noted that there were no distinguishing characteristics about Saint from the pose they were in, nothing that pointed to him and said, "*This is Saint Levesque*".

"Carmine?" Victoria prompted gently. There was something like sympathy in her eyes, and Carmine swallowed hard around the rock in his throat.

"Wh-where did you get this picture?" he rasped.

"Anonymous source," Victoria said, sounding almost regretful. "Can I ask who that is in the photograph with you?"

"No you cannot," Carmine snapped reflexively.

"So you're gay?" Victoria pressed.

Carmine squeezed his eyes shut briefly. He didn't dare look at Saint for fear Victoria and the rest of the journalists would immediately read the truth of the situation in his eyes. "I'm—I need a minute," he finally managed.

Victoria took a step back, but her stance made it clear she wasn't going anywhere. Carmine pressed the heels of his hands to his eyes, struggling to think. Fact: he'd just been outed. Fact: he didn't know by who, but he had a good guess. David was busy undressing on the far side of the room, studiously ignoring the developing situation. Fact: Saint was safe. In the end, that was all that really mattered. Carmine's sexuality had been an open secret for years. While he wished he could have controlled his coming out narrative, the truth was it didn't really matter how it had happened, as long as Saint's identity had been protected.

"Yes," he said aloud, and the journalists immediately crowded around, recording devices at the ready. Carmine took a steadying breath. "I'm gay," he said into silence.

Saint stood abruptly, but Velvet was already making her way across the room, slipping between Carmine and the reporters.

"No questions at this time," she said smoothly.

"But—" Victoria began.

"Sorry," Velvet interrupted. "We'll have an actual press conference about this tomorrow and I promise you'll get to ask your questions then."

"We really just want to know who that is with you," someone at the back of the crowd said.

"That's the business of the people in the photograph, and none of yours," Velvet said, sweetening the sharpness of her words with a smile.

Carmine wanted to throw up. Saint was standing utterly still, watching the spectacle unfold with a blank face.

"Is it Saint?" someone else shouted, and Velvet rounded on them as Saint flinched as if physically struck.

"That's it," Velvet snapped. "You're out. All of you. *Now.*" She began physically herding them toward the door and Carmine finally got his feet unstuck from the floor. He headed, not for Saint, but for Felix, watching with horror on his mobile face.

"I guess Saint was not imagining things, eh?" he managed, but his voice was a pale shade of its usual insouciant tone.

Carmine shook his head mutely. "Do you know who it was?"

"I can guess, *ami*," Felix said, cutting his

eyes toward David. "But I do not know, no."

Saint was heading for the shower, not looking at anyone. His shoulders were rigid and he still hadn't said a word.

"Fuck," Carmine whispered. "He doesn't want—he's not *ready* for this."

"I know," Felix said. "You'll need to talk to him."

But Carmine shook his head again. "Not yet." He crossed the room in several quick steps, fetching up beside David. "Do you want to do this in a conference room or here in front of everyone?" he inquired, just barely keeping his hands from balling into fists.

David lifted a shoulder. "Conference room, but I want a witness in case you decide to jump me."

Carmine sneered but glanced around the room. Felix, Roddy, and Kasha he regretfully dismissed as too biased. "Tye," he said, and Tye jumped, dropping the shirt he was holding, eyes wide. "Need you to come with us, please. All you have to do is bear witness, don't worry."

Tye's throat bobbed but he nodded, bent to retrieve the shirt, and tugged it on as he followed David and Carmine out the door and down the hallway to the nearest conference room.

Inside, Carmine faced him. "It was you, wasn't it."

David yawned. "What was me?"

"Don't," Carmine said sharply. "Don't you *dare* pretend you don't know exactly what just happened. Was it you?"

David narrowed his eyes, studying his face, and then abruptly shrugged. "Yeah, it was."

Nausea swamped Carmine and he swallowed several times. "*Why?*"

"Ask Henry," David snapped. There was fury on his face, but hurt, too, mixing together in a poisonous blend. "Ask her what happens when she refuses to acknowledge what's under her nose."

"And what exactly is that?" Carmine asked.

"I'm in love with her," David spat. "And *she* says there's nothing there, that I need to 'get over her', like it's that fucking easy."

"So—" Carmine held up a hand, struggling for composure. "You outed me—to get at her?"

"Hurting you hurts her," David snarled. "So maybe she can get a taste of what it's like. Maybe she can *feel it.*"

"Jesus Christ," Tye whispered from the corner. Neither man looked at him, fixed on each other.

"You've got a really fucked up definition of love, my friend," Carmine finally said.

David scoffed. "Like I give a shit what you think."

"You realize this isn't going to make her come running back to you, right?" Carmine asked. "That you just torpedoed literally the slightest chance of her *ever* changing her mind?"

"She was never going to change her mind," David said. "So I gave her a taste of her own medicine."

"Did it feel good?" Carmine asked softly, holding back the fury. "Was it worth it?"

"The look on your face?" David said. He almost smiled. "Yeah. It was worth it. And it'll be worth it when she finds out. Serves her right, the heartless bitch."

Carmine took three quick steps away, out of range so he didn't punch him, even as Tye made an involuntary movement away from the wall as if ready to jump between them.

"Don't ever," Carmine said, fighting through the fury blinding him, "*ever* speak of her like that again."

David shrugged again. "I'm never going to speak of her again. Problem solved." He paused, and a smile spread across his face.

"Well, *my* problem is solved. I guess yours is just beginning."

"Get out," Carmine said through numb lips. "*Get out* and don't ever come near me again."

He stood with his back to the door, breathing through his nose in a desperate attempt to keep from hitting something, until David's footsteps receded.

"He's gone," Tye said, his voice low and worried. "Can I—do you need anything?"

Carmine turned. Tye looked miserable, tugging at the hem of his shirt, corners of his mouth turned down. Carmine forced a smile.

"No," he said. "I'm fine. You go on."

Tye hesitated, shifting his weight, but Carmine just sat down in one of the chairs and put his head in his hands. After a while, Tye left, and he was alone.

He pulled out his phone and called Henry.

"What?" she snapped.

"I really don't care if you're seducing another paralegal," Carmine said. "This is serious. David just outed me."

"He *what*?"

Carmine explained as succinctly as he could while Henry listened and occasionally swore in increasingly violent and imaginative ways.

"You can't see Saint's face in the picture," Carmine said. He put the phone on speaker and his head down on the table. He was so *tired*. "But it's *really* obvious I was kissing him, and someone straight up asked if it was him. They suspect. He can't—this isn't—Hen, what do I *do*?"

"You go find him," Henry said. "And you make sure he isn't alone. I'll deal with David."

"No," Carmine protested. "Coach and the GM will handle him. You don't have to do anything."

"This is my fault," Henry interrupted. There was steel in her voice, but Carmine could hear the tears underneath, the guilt she was clearly feeling.

"No," Carmine repeated. "It's not your fault he's a sack of shit. It's not your fault you didn't feel the same way. It's *not your fault* he did this. We'll take care of it. I have to go find Saint."

"Caz," Henry said, and she was definitely crying. "I love you. I'm s-sorry—"

"I love you too," Carmine said, softening his tone. "I'll check in when I can. Don't blame yourself."

He pushed himself upright, wincing at the pain in his ribs, and headed for the door.

Saint was already gone when he got back to the locker room. Felix came to meet him.

"He left before any of us," he said softly. "He would not talk to me, or Roddy."

Carmine touched his shoulder. "I'll take care of him."

"He'll push you away," Felix warned. "Don't let him. He doesn't want you to go, to leave him. He's afraid you *will* leave, so he will try and force the issue."

Carmine regarded him. "You've been through this before."

"Not this exact scenario," Felix said. "But yes. I've known him for nearly ten years. He's my brother, Caz. I know his defense mechanisms, how he protects his heart. Go find him, and don't let him go."

"Yeah," Carmine said, and turned to leave.

It wasn't that easy, though.

Velvet caught him coming out of the locker room and pulled him into a meeting with Flanahan, two publicists Carmine didn't know, and the GM, Kevin Dumont, who'd luckily been in town for the night. Carmine settled at the table facing them and laced his fingers in his lap. He needed to go find Saint, needed to make sure he was alright—but he wasn't leaving this room until he'd reassured the businessmen their investments hadn't been ill-advised.

"How are you feeling?" Dumont asked. He was short, balding, and had the beginnings of a belly, but he'd been a force to reckon with on the ice, back in his day. Carmine had seen his games. He wouldn't make the mistake of underestimating him.

"My ribs hurt," he said honestly. "And I need to go find—" He snapped his mouth shut on Saint's name. "The other person in the picture. He's... upset."

"This won't take long," one of the publicists said. "I'm Mandy, this is Leon." Leon nodded. "We just want to make sure we're on the same page here."

"And what page is that?" Carmine snapped.

Dumont leaned forward. "We're behind you one hundred percent, Carmine. We stand with you. The person who leaked that photo of you will be dealt with, I can promise you that."

Carmine's eyes stung. He took a shaky breath, tightening his grip on his own hands to hide the trembling. "I d-don't—"

"We traded away some good guys to get you," Dumont continued. "And you haven't let us down. You've proven what an asset to this team you are. And even if you *hadn't,* you're still a human being who deserves respect, and so does S—" He caught himself. "The person in the picture with you."

"You know," Carmine said quietly, a sense of fatality settling into his bones. "You know who it is, you know about—" He waved a hand vaguely, hoping that captured his meaning.

"We suspect," Dumont said. His eyes were shrewd and keen, sharp in the dim light, and Carmine wondered what it had been like to face him at puck drop. "We won't confirm or deny anything unless that person chooses to step forward, at which point he will have our full support, just like you do."

Carmine closed his eyes. The relief was like cold water to his face, shocking his system. "I really have to go," he said.

"Say nothing to anyone not on the team," Mandy said. "*Nothing*, do you understand? The most innocuous comment can be spun out of context. You keep your mouth shut, go home, and you 'no comment' until you're blue in the face if anyone says anything, got it?"

"Got it," Carmine said.

"Press conference tomorrow at 9 AM," Leon said. "We'll write something up for you based on what you said in the locker room, but be here early in case you want to edit it."

Carmine nodded. "I will. I—thank you. I didn't expect—"

"What, your family to have your back?" Dumont said. He snorted. "Maybe other teams don't, but we do it differently around here. Go home."

Carmine nodded gratefully and escaped.

29

THE HOUSE WAS quiet when he let himself in, all the lights off. Carmine took his shoes off and padded silently through the empty living room. The kitchen was likewise deserted. So Saint was probably in his suite. Carmine took a moment to let Steel out and change into clothes that didn't chafe the way his suit did, and then he walked back through the house to Saint's suite and knocked on the door.

"Saint?" he called softly.

There was no answer.

Carmine tried the door—it was unlocked. "I'm coming in," he said, a little louder. "Please don't shoot me or anything." He pushed the door open and stepped into the front room, the one where Saint kept his awards. They ringed the walls, cups and

MICHAELA GREY

placquards and trophies all a silent testament to Saint's skill.

Saint was on the floor in the middle of the room, knees drawn to his chest, staring up at the display.

Carmine caught his breath. Saint was in sock feet but otherwise hadn't changed his clothes. He didn't move, gazing at the trophy on the wall.

"Hey," Carmine said gently.

"None of it matters," Saint whispered, almost too low to hear.

Carmine went to his knees beside him. "How can you say that?"

Saint's eyes were shadowed, dark rings below them. He put his cheek on one knee and closed his eyes without answering.

"They don't know it was you," Carmine tried. He wanted desperately to touch him, but he held still. "I haven't confirmed anything, I *won't*. Saint, I won't tell anyone, you have to know I won't. You're safe, baby, no one knows."

Saint opened his eyes. "They asked you if it was me." His voice was empty of emotion. "They know. Or at least they suspect."

"No." Carmine shook his head. "Saint, everything you've done, everything you've fought for—you won't lose it. I don't care *how* many people ask me if it was you. I'll

398

lie. I won't let you lose everything, not for me."

"You should go," Saint said, still sounding empty. He stood, and Carmine scrambled up after him. "People will talk."

Carmine planted his feet. "No."

That made Saint turn to look at him.

"I fucking *live* here, Saint," Carmine said. "If people 'talk' about me going home to *the house I live in*, then they really need a fucking life of their own." He swallowed. "And I'm not leaving you."

Something flickered across Saint's face and he lifted his chin. "I don't want you here."

Despite Felix's warning, the words sliced into Carmine's heart. He took a shaky breath. "I d-don't believe you. I think you're scared, and I get it, baby, I *do*. But you can't push me away and isolate yourself. You need people around you. You need *family* around you."

Saint sneered. "You think you're my family?"

Carmine's resolve faltered. Maybe Felix had been wrong. But then Saint turned his face away and Carmine saw the shine of tear tracks on his cheeks. He set his jaw.

"I *know* I'm your family," he managed, his voice wobbly. "Because I love you. And you love me. And I'd do anything for you. *Saint—*"

Saint's breath caught on a sob and he hurled himself forward, into Carmine's arms. Pain rocketed through Carmine's ribs at the impact but he didn't make a noise, holding on tight.

"I've got you," he said into Saint's hair. "Nothing's going to happen to you. *I've got you.*"

"If I come out," Saint choked, face pressed to Carmine's chest. "If I—Caz, it'll ruin everything, none of it will matter—"

"Hey, breathe," Carmine ordered gently. "Let's get comfortable, okay? Come on." He led him into the bedroom and Saint crawled obediently into bed as Carmine got himself situated beside him, holding his breath to keep from making a noise.

"Your ribs—" Saint began.

"I'm fine," Carmine interrupted, giving him a tiny smile. "Really not even on my radar right now."

When they were side by side facing each other, he ran a hand down Saint's arm. "Tell me what you mean by none of it will matter."

Saint closed his eyes. "If I come out— it'll all... nothing I've ever done will be worth anything. I'll just be 'the gay hockey player'."

Carmine rubbed Saint's arm again. "Adam got nominated for the Selke."

Saint's eyes snapped open. "What?"

"Adam Caron, the openly gay hockey player," Carmine said steadily, watching Saint's face, "just got nominated for the Frank J. Selke award. Because he is a *damn good* openly gay hockey player, and people know it."

"But it's different for me," Saint said, and his voice pled with Carmine to understand. "They say I'm the face of the western league. I can't—I have to be perfect." Carmine flinched but Saint was already reaching for him, apologies falling from his lips. "I didn't mean it that way," he babbled, "I didn't mean you're not perfect, Caz, I swear, I just—"

"You just think being gay is a flaw." Carmine rolled away and sat up. "You think there's something *wrong* with us."

Saint hiccupped and Carmine glanced back to see him with both hands pressed to his mouth, tears rolling down his face.

"I don't know how to do this," Saint managed. "I don't know h-how to be on a pedestal and b-be gay and pl-play every night when I know what other players think, what they'll say."

Frustration and hurt were still tangled in a snarl around Carmine's lungs, making it hard to breathe. He stood, smoothing the wrinkles in his soft pants to give his hands something to do. When he turned, Saint was watching him, tears still leaking from his eyes.

"You have to not care," Carmine said. He shook his head when Saint opened his mouth to speak. "No. You listen to me. What did you do, when parents called you shitty things in Major Juniors? When they hated you for being better than their precious spawn?"

"I cried," Saint said baldly, dropping his hands. "I got in the car after practice and I fucking *cried*, Carmine, is that what you want to hear?"

"And what did you do *after* that?"

"I—" Saint's mouth worked. "I got back on the ice and I made myself even better."

Carmine lifted his eyebrow.

Saint slid out of bed. He stepped in close, until their bodies were pressed together, and his cheek was on Carmine's shoulder.

"Does what I think matter?" Carmine whispered.

Saint nodded silently.

"Felix? Roddy? Kasha?"

"Of course," Saint mumbled.

"Then that's what you hold onto, when people say shitty things. Because they will, sweetheart. They'll say hurtful stuff. Try to throw you off your game. Find reasons why you were never as good as everyone said. So you hold onto us, then. Yeah? You listen to *us*. We'll tell you the truth."

Saint hid his face against Carmine's chest again. "I'm sorry I hurt you." The words came out muffled.

Carmine tightened his grip. "That's what people do. We hurt each other sometimes. But then we fix it."

"God, Caz," Saint said, pulling back suddenly. "You got *outed* tonight. Why aren't you more upset? Why aren't you freaking out?"

Carmine couldn't help the laugh, but it was bitter. "You think I'm not? Trust me, I am. I didn't want this. But—" He lifted a shoulder. "What can I do? It's done. All I can do now is focus on what comes next. And so you know, I spoke to Dumont tonight." He didn't miss the way Saint stiffened. "He's promised his full support at the press conference tomorrow, and going forward. I've got you, and the team. Well, the parts of the team that matter. I'll be okay."

"And... you're okay with me—not coming out?" Saint's eyes were anxious, and Carmine reached out to reel him in.

"Sweetheart, you could stay in the closet

the rest of your career if that's what you needed, and I'd be okay with it. I know you love me. You're with me, in every way that counts."

Saint went up on his tiptoes and kissed him, hard and bruising. "I love you," he panted when he broke away. "God, Caz—"

Carmine tugged him back for another kiss. "Who could blame you?" he murmured, and relished Saint's laugh when it broke free.

30

SAINT INSISTED on going with Carmine to the press conference in the morning, ignoring his protests.

"I'm the captain," he said flatly as Carmine tried to argue yet again. "How would it look if I *weren't* there? Trust me, I'd be there for anyone who was doing this."

"Oh, so I'm *not* special?" Carmine said, folding his arms.

"You should not be so cute when you pout," Saint informed him. He kissed the reluctant smile off Carmine's mouth, smiling back at him. "You know you're the most special, stop sulking." He patted Carmine's ass and turned to choose a tie.

"ARE YOU NERVOUS?" he asked in the car, watching Carmine's hands on the wheel.

Carmine lifted a shoulder. "Ish? I mean yeah. Fucking David—I really didn't want to do this yet. But there's a relief to it, too. I don't have to hide anymore." He slanted a smile at Saint. "It kinda feels good."

IN THE ARENA, Saint led the way to the conference room, which was set up and ready for everyone. Leon handed Carmine three sheets of paper, and Carmine stared at them.

"You know I'm not reading all this, right?" he asked.

"Worth a try," Leon said philosophically. "There's a notepad on your table. Write your own speech, but use what I gave you as the framework."

SAINT SPENT the hour while Carmine worked wandering the arena. He went into the stands, gazing down at the rink from the perspective of a fan and looking up at the Jumbotron, still and dark in the early hours of the morning. Then he went down to the ice and stepped onto it, gingerly in his dress shoes with very little grip.

This—this was home. From the time he'd been tiny, slapping at pucks—and missing, discovering the glee of putting one past the goalie, learning the bone-deep satisfaction of working with a team that understood him—Saint turned in a circle, gazing up into the rafters. He'd never been happier than on this ice. No—he amended that. He'd never been happier than on the ice until he'd been in Carmine's arms. But this was still home. This was where he wanted to be, for the rest of his life.

And it didn't matter, he thought. It didn't matter if the fans or players were shitty to him. It didn't matter, because they couldn't take this away from him. He'd made this place home, he'd carved out a space for himself. He had his friends—his family, the family of his heart—with him. No matter what happened, he wouldn't lose what mattered most. Carmine. Felix. Roddy and Kasha. Hockey.

He could play. He *would* play. And he'd prove to all of them that he deserved to be there, just like he'd always done.

"Thank you," he whispered to no one in particular.

Then he carefully made his way off and back to the conference room, terror and jubilation filling him in equal measure. He thought vaguely he might throw up. Was he doing this? He thought, just maybe, he was.

Carmine was reading over his speech, brow furrowed and lips moving as he worked through phrasing, and Saint wanted desperately to kiss him, to show him how much he meant to him. Carmine glanced up, and from the way his eyes warmed, maybe he'd somehow read Saint's mind. Saint smiled at him and the terror dwindled, shrinking to something manageable. He was doing this.

The first journalist stepped through the door, followed closely by Roddy, then Kasha, then Felix. Right behind him was Tye, who smiled shyly when he caught Saint's gaze. Saint looked at them, his eyes stinging, and then at Carmine, who was hastily wiping his own eyes.

Saint went for Felix and hugged him. "Thank you for coming," he whispered.

"Stupid boy, thinking we wouldn't," Felix said, but his voice was thick and he hugged him back, tight enough Saint couldn't breathe for a minute.

THEY SETTLED AT THE TABLE, Carmine in the middle, Saint immediately to his right, and the rest spread out around them. The journalists filled the room in fits and starts, finding seats, organizing notes, talking amongst themselves and eyeing the line of players with avidly interested eyes.

Saint pretended not to see them, focusing on Carmine solid and steady beside him as he shuffled through his handwritten pages.

"Thank you all for coming," Velvet said, startling Saint back to awareness of the room. "Carmine has a small speech prepared, and then we'll take a few questions. I think one from each, and if any are inappropriate or rude in any way, you will be immediately ejected and black-balled from covering future games. We clear?"

"Velvet," Kevin Dumont said, stepping forward. "One more thing to add." He raised his voice to address the crowd. "David Stahl has been reassigned to the Embers for the foreseeable future and put on waivers. He is not available for comment."

He stepped back and Velvet motioned to Carmine, who cleared his throat.

"Last night, a photograph of me was released without my knowledge or consent. It showed me kissing—someone. Someone who's clearly male." He hesitated, and Saint pressed their knees together in a silent show of support.

"I've known I was gay since I was nine years old," Carmine continued. His voice was steady, but Saint could see the way his free hand trembled in his lap, out of view of the reporters. "It took me a while to come to terms with… everything. But I've been pretty okay with who I am for a while now. The picture being released was—not optimal. I'd like to have chosen my own timing, but life doesn't always play out the way we plan. Truth be told, I'm kind of glad it happened at all. I don't have to hide anymore." He lifted his chin, surveying the room. "I'm gay," he said. "I'm not ashamed of it. It doesn't dictate the quality of my play. This is who I am, like it or not. I guess I'll take questions now."

Hands shot up and Velvet pointed at one.

"Who is it in the photograph with you?" the reporter wanted to know.

Carmine scowled, opening his mouth to answer, and Saint stopped him with a touch to his hand.

"Can I take this one?" he asked, low enough for the microphones to not pick up.

Carmine's eyes went wide and he shook his head. "Saint, no—"

Saint squeezed his hand briefly before leaning forward to the microphone.

"It's me," he said clearly, and Carmine's hand on his tightened to the point of pain. Saint took a deep breath. "Carmine and I are together, and I'm in love with him. Have been for a while. Any *other* questions?"

The room erupted, and Saint snuck a glance at Carmine, who was staring at him, clearly stunned.

"Sorry for stealing your thunder," Saint whispered under the noise of the shouted questions. "I just figured it was time."

Carmine's eyes softened. "You can steal my thunder anytime. I love you so damn much."

Saint grinned. He felt light and airy, like he might float to the ceiling if it weren't for the grip on Carmine's hand.

"I love you too," he said, and turned to face the crowd.

EPILOGUE

FELIX WASN'T USUALLY a heavy sleeper, but it took awhile for the knocking on his door to filter itself into his subconscious. He didn't fully wake up until Jacques meowed plaintively and left his perch on Felix's hips to find somewhere less noisy.

Felix propped himself on one elbow and yawned. The pounding didn't stop. He frowned. He didn't have any deliveries scheduled, and Saint had a key. Everyone else knew to call first.

He swung himself out of bed, scrubbing a hand through his hair as he padded for the door, hitching his threadbare sweats up absently.

It won't be Paul, he thought, jogging down the stairs. *Not after the way we left it yesterday. Not after—what he said.* But a tiny, traitorous part of his heart couldn't help...

413

hoping. Hoping it *was* Paul, his beautiful blue eyes filled with regret and sorrow, asking Felix to give him another chance.

He had his answer half-formed when he swung the door open and a flash bulb went off, briefly blinding him. Felix got a hand up as voices soared with excited questions and someone took a picture of him.

"What—"

The people closest edged nearer.

"Felix, Butterfly, can I have a picture?"

"Can I get an autograph?"

"Butterfly, Butterfly, over here, big fan, *huge* fan, can I get a selfie with you?"

Felix opened and closed his mouth. There were at least twenty people in front of him, all of them with their phones out, more coming up the path. Most appeared to be filming and he didn't recognize any of them.

"Who *are* you?" he asked, fighting the urge to cover his bare chest. "Why are you here?"

"You post your address on Twitter and say you love visits from fans, and this is how you treat us?" one man demanded. He was big and burly, glowering suddenly.

"I didn't—" Felix swallowed hard. *Paul.* Paul, who'd watched him enter his password enough times when they were lying in bed together, who knew he liked to stay active on Twitter and Instagram and interact with his fans.

The big man took a step closer. "Just a few pictures," he said. "Some of us drove a long way to meet you."

His address was posted on the internet, with a literal open invitation for visitors. Felix choked back the panic.

"I'm sorry," he said, clutching the door. "There's been a mistake, yes? I did not—this isn't—I can't—"

He ducked back inside and closed the door, throwing the deadbolts as the pounding resumed, voices lifted in fury now.

Felix ignored them, running up the stairs and skidding into his bedroom. His phone was on the bedside table and he grabbed at it, dropping it twice before he managed to keep it in his shaking hands and pull up Twitter.

There it was, staring back at him.

I'm bored, and there's nothing I love more than visiting with my fans! Come talk to me, maybe we can even play a little street hockey! His address followed, along with a picture of his car in the garage, clearly showing the license plate.

Felix forced back the nausea and deleted the tweet. Thirty seconds later, he'd deleted his Twitter account and was logging into Instagram.

The same message had been posted there, this one with a picture of his house taken from the street.

Felix didn't even bother deleting the message this time. He just deleted his account and then stabbed at the contacts to find Saint's number.

"Fee?" Saint sounded sleepy.

"I'm in trouble, *cher*," Felix whispered. "I'm in so much trouble."

ACKNOWLEDGMENTS

For Aaliya, always. You followed me into the world of gay hockey romance without hesitation, even though you don't give a crap about fighty men on knife-shoes. I couldn't ask for a better friend or beta, even if you refuse to marry me and fulfill my dream of becoming a Canadian citizen. (Unreasonable, honestly.)

For everyone else who read this book and gave me invaluable feedback on its way to becoming what it is today—Sarah, Em, CJ, I thrive on your reactions and grow more powerful with every tear I make you shed. Thank you for helping me bring these characters to life and letting me bounce ideas off you.

And for my readers—I'm here because of you. You keep me writing, keep me hungry to create, ask for more when I think my well's run dry, and never lose faith in me. I'm humbled and so, so grateful you're here.

ABOUT THE AUTHOR

Michaela Grey told stories to put herself to sleep since she was old enough to hold a conversation in her head. When she learned to write, she began putting those stories down on paper. She resides in the Texas Hill Country with her cats, and is perpetually on the hunt for peaceful writing time.

When she's not writing, she's watching hockey or blogging about writing and men on knife shoes chasing a frozen Oreo around the ice while trying to keep her cat off the keyboard.

Tumblr: greymichaela.tumblr.com
Twitter: @GreyMichaela
Facebook: www.facebook.com/Grey-Michaela
E-mail: greymichaela@gmail.com

Want to find out when her next book comes out? Sign up for her newsletter here or follow her on Amazon here

Keep reading for a sneak peek of Felix's
story!

BUTTERFLY

FELIX WAS SITTING in the back of the bar, out of sight of almost everyone and nursing a lukewarm beer when he saw them. The blond one was slim, similar to Felix's build but much shorter, and wrapped around his companion like a clinging vine.

His partner—Felix swallowed hard. His partner was *huge*. Easily six foot five, with dark hair that fell in soft curls into even darker eyes, and muscles to match his height.

And they were both looking at Felix.

Felix saluted them with his beer and an ironic tilt of his head. *Have fun*, it said. *Someone deserves to.*

He wasn't expecting the blond to disentangle himself and slide into the booth beside him. Up close, he had angelic features, hair so pale it was almost white, and piercing green eyes.

"Leo," he said. "I saw you looking at me."

"Who wouldn't?" Felix said, and took another swallow of beer. "You are easy on the eyes, *mon frere.*"

Leo clutched his chest dramatically as the big man slipped into the booth on Felix's other side. "French!" he said, pretending to swoon. "I've always wanted to sleep with a French guy!"

"French *Canadian*," Felix corrected. He eyed the other man. "And you are?"

"Fisher," the man said. "And he's always wanted to sleep with a French Canadian as well."

"It's the accent," Leo sighed. He leaned on Felix's shoulder and batted white-blond lashes at him. "What's your name, gorgeous?"

Felix debated. Neither seemed like hockey fans, but the last one hadn't either, and he still bore the scars.

"Just call me French," he finally said.

"Less of a mouthful than French-Canadian, and I can think of other things I'd rather have in my mouth," Leo said.

Felix snorted. Fisher was so close his thigh was pressed up against Felix's, but instead of feeling crowded or stifled, Felix felt… safe. He looked up through his lashes into Fisher's dark eyes.

"Come here often?"

Leo squeezed closer, running a hand up Felix's bicep. "Not as often as we should, if you're what they have on offer," he said.

"So are you two a couple?" Felix asked.

Leo waggled a hand. "Ish."

"More like no," Fisher said. His voice was so deep it reverberated through Felix's bones. "But we play together sometimes."

Leo propped his chin on his hands. "Do you wanna play with us?"

"It is a tempting prospect," Felix admitted. "What would it entail?"

"You, me, him, and our dicks," Leo chirped. "Anything you want."

"Anything?" Felix swirled the beer in its mug. "That is a dangerous offer, *ami*."

"You don't look like the kind to hurt me," Leo said, shrugging. "And if you *did*, I've got Fisher. Trust me, he will fuck you *up* if you do something I don't want."

Felix arched an eyebrow at Fisher, who also shrugged.

"Someone's gotta look out for him," he drawled. "Since he was born without a self-preservation instinct."

"So?" Leo asked, a hand drifting across Felix's thigh. "You wanna or not?" Slim fingers traced the half-hard outline of Felix's dick, and he twitched.

"Condoms," he managed.

Leo rolled his eyes. "Duh. But first—" He cupped Felix's chin in one hand and leaned in, giving him time to pull away. His lips were soft and tasted like grape chapstick, and he moaned as Felix got a hand free and wrapped it around the back of his neck, pulling him closer.

Distantly, Felix heard Fisher swear softly, but most of his attention was on Leo, currently doing his best to climb into his lap despite the table in his way.

"My turn," Fisher rumbled, and caught Felix's chin, pulling his head around. Their mouths fit perfectly together, Fisher's breath hot and his tongue soft. Felix melted against him, making a helpless noise high in his throat, and Leo cupped his fully hard dick, rubbing it over the stretchy fabric of Felix's pants.

Felix couldn't figure out where to focus —the hand on his dick or Fisher's mouth, so hot and demanding. He tore free with an effort, gratified to see Fisher was breathing as hard as he was.

"Not here," he rasped.

"Aw, no exhibition kink?" Leo pouted.

"I have no wish to be recognized," Felix said, smoothing his hair back.

Leo's eyes widened. "Are you a celebrity? Wait, I know all the local actors and musicians and I don't know you, so who *are* you?"

"Doesn't matter," Fisher interrupted, and Felix glanced at him, grateful. "You know I'm not famous but I don't wanna be recognized either. So let's get out of here."

FELIX FOLLOWED them from the bar, shrugging into his coat against the chilly Portland night. He shouldn't have gone out, should have stayed home and focused on his game, watched tape of the Ravens for tomorrow night, done anything else, but instead here he was, halfway to drunk and about to have sex with two men he didn't know.

"We're calling a car," Fisher said when Felix caught up to him. "And we thought we'd go to my house—it's not far. Do you have anyone you can tell?"

"Yes," Felix said, pulling out his phone. "Sa—" He caught himself before he said Saint's name. "My friend Sinclair will want to know."

"Good," Fisher said. He rattled off the address and waited as Felix texted Saint, who was probably wearing sweatpants, curled up on the couch with Carmine and their dog.

He got an answer back almost immediately. *Play safe and hydrate. Don't stay out too late. Text when you get home.*

Felix glanced up. "How much longer until the car is here?"

"Two minutes, according to the app," Leo said. "We could have some fun while we wait?" He took a step toward him, eyes intent.

"No," Felix said instantly, stepping back, and was startled to see Fisher getting between them at the same time.

"Back of a dimly lit, smoky bar is a little different from making out on the public street," Fisher snapped. "You know that, Leo."

Leo sighed, holding up his hands in a gesture of surrender. "Can't really blame me for trying. I mean *look* at you two."

The car arrived then, saving them from further discussion, and Leo slid into the front seat as Fisher and Felix got in the back. Felix folded his long legs in, watching with amusement as Fisher tried unsuccessfully to do the same beside him.

"Fuck—Leo, scoot your seat forward."

Leo complied, and Fisher sighed in relief. His knees still pressed into the back of the seat and he had to hunch a little, his hair brushing the roof.

Felix stifled a snicker. "We should have gotten the luxury ride, I think."

"God, your accent," Leo sighed as the driver accelerated away from the curb. "Fish, you hear how he drops his H's?"

"Leo," Fisher said warningly, as Felix shifted his weight.

Fisher glanced at him, an apology in his eyes. Felix nodded, twisting his mouth ruefully. He could already tell Leo was going to be a handful.

Sign up for Michaela's newsletter here to find out when Butterfly is available!

ALSO BY MICHAELA GREY

Beloved Scars Series
Broken Halo
Broken Rules
Broken Trust
Broken Promises

Hockey Romances
Blindside Hit
Odd-Man Rush
Roughing
Power Play

Standalones
Copper and Salt

Milton Keynes UK
Ingram Content Group UK Ltd.
UKHW011319110923
428463UK00022B/610